The Alibi

Katharine Johnson

Re-published in 2025 by Bloodhound Books.

www.bloodhoundbooks.com

Print ISBN: 978-1917705387

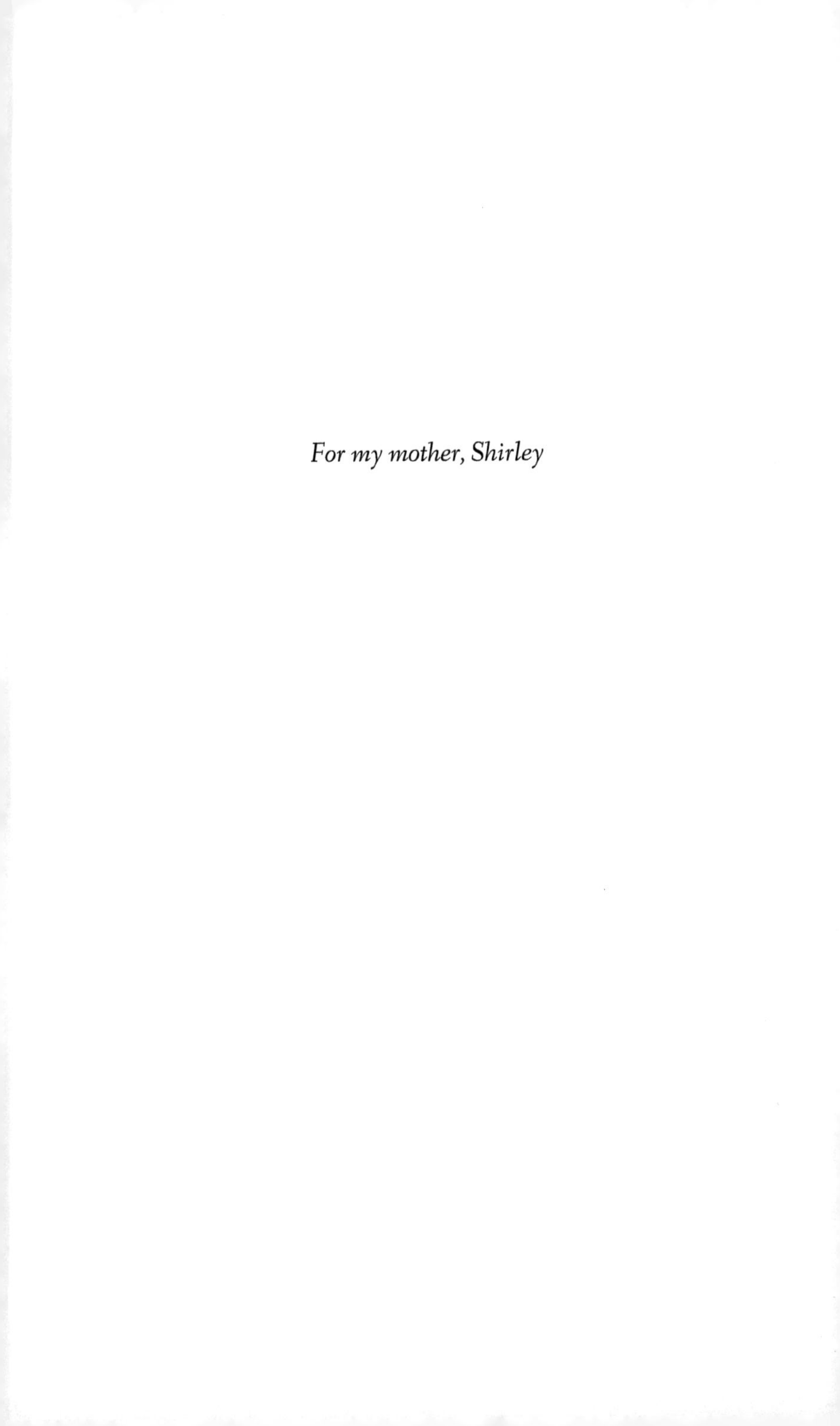

For my mother, Shirley

Chapter One

1950

"Tell me everything."

I rubbed my hand over my face. For weeks I'd had a creeping awareness that someone was on my tail. There had been all the usual signs – the phone going dead when I picked up the receiver, a shadow shifting at the corner of my gaze, footsteps in the street behind me that died when I turned round. So, I should hardly have been surprised he'd caught up with me.

I'd seen him standing in the park, a tall figure shrouded in mist, hands in the pockets of his overcoat, head turned up towards the window where I stood to close the shutters. Watched him cross the road, heard his foot on the stairs even though I'd told my secretary I wasn't to be disturbed. Heard the floorboards creaking outside my door.

Even as he stepped into the room, I'd thought about running – swinging myself out of the window, edging along the parapet to the drainpipe and dropping down into the street. But then what? Where would I go? It would only postpone the inevitable.

I studied the young man's face. Smooth skin, high cheekbones, and bright, curious eyes. He looked too young, to fragile, to be doing this job. It wouldn't surprise me if this was his first day. Had I ever looked so naïve? Perhaps once. Back before everything started.

He cleared his throat. I could refuse to co-operate, but it wouldn't help in the end. Best to get it over with.

"All right. But would you be kind enough to let me get to the end without interrupting?"

He shrugged and nodded as though he could afford to humour me. In a way it was a relief to tell someone after all this time. An end to all the secrets and lies.

1931

If I'd missed the boat-train back to England that morning I'd never have met her, and it would never have happened. On the way to the Gare du Nord a van veered off the road, turning over and sending pedestrians fleeing from its path. My taxi driver braked hard. He managed to turn the cab around and tried an alternative route but the narrow streets were choked with traffic. We reached the station at the time the train was due to leave. I jumped out, and sprinted for the ticket office, praying for some sort of delay.

"The boat train for England. Has it left?"

The man at the ticket office shook his head. "You're in luck. Second class if full but there are a few seats left in first."

The relief dissolved. "Thank you but that's out of the question." As was a hotel for the night. There would be no more trains that day. Not only was my father going to be furious, but I'd also have to spend a cold, uncomfortable night on the streets.

"Enjoy your journey, sir."

Looking down at my hand, I saw he'd given me a first-class ticket instead of the one I'd paid for.

"Thank you. That's very kind."

I couldn't believe my luck as I climbed aboard and settled back in a comfortable seat. The guard blew the whistle and the rooftops and towers of Paris slid away. The girl sat at the other end of the pullman across the aisle from me. Something about her fascinated me. I tried not to stare but couldn't help the occasional glance.

As the train swayed and other passengers moved around, unfurling newspapers and ordering coffee, I glimpsed glints in her tawny hair picked out by the spring sun at the window, a long, elegant forearm holding an ivory cigarette holder, the arched brows, the secretive smile.

She reminded me of a gazelle – long-limbed, alert, and watchful. Her face was still but her eyes held a quiet magic. Clear and honey-coloured, they lifted at intervals from the novel spread out on the table in front of her to the window, flickering back and forth as she focused on passing buildings and the names of stations. What book was she reading? I couldn't make out the title from where I was, even when she sat back and lifted the cover.

The waiter came, and she ordered coffee and a snack in what sounded like fluent French. When she smiled at him, I thought I'd never seen anyone look so lovely.

I guessed she was around my age, perhaps a year or two younger, and wondered why she should be travelling through Europe on her own. She looked alone but not lonely. The sort of person who has a story to tell. She could be a journalist or a private detective or just possibly a secret agent.

I'd always been an observer, inventing a life for faces that caught my attention. But on this occasion I must have made the mistake of looking once too often because she met my eye, raised one of those arched brows almost imperceptibly and gave me a half smile as though wondering if she should recognise me. Feeling my cheeks colour, I shifted my gaze to a travel poster behind her, of a ski resort with jagged mountains piercing the sky.

I didn't usually get caught out so easily. One of the advantages of having an unremarkable appearance is that you can observe others without them noticing you. I'd convinced myself over the years that I could stand in the middle of a crowd anywhere and not look out of place—or at least not as much as I felt. And yet for some reason this girl had noticed me.

Getting off the train at Calais, I spotted the book on the table where she'd been sitting. Had she meant to leave it behind? I picked it up. Couldn't understand a word—it was all in French. *La Joie de Vivre*. I'd have run after her but an elderly woman was struggling out of her seat in front of me. I took the woman's bag and lent her my arm to get down the steps, scanning the platform for the girl, but there was no sign. Ah well. My hand closed around the book. At least I had something of hers to keep.

I joined the throng of well-dressed travellers surging up the ship's gangway, catching snatches of conversation about the weather, the colour of the sea and what sort of crossing they expected. Still no sign of the girl.

The boat juddered beneath us as we watched our luggage being transferred below and the second-class passengers being admitted. As we slipped away from the port and the land receded, the crowd on deck thinned. People were drifting inside for a drink in the bar or a game of cards in the sun lounge. I turned to go but then I saw her.

She was standing with her hands on the rail, face turned up to the weak sun.

"Excuse me. *Mademoiselle?*"

She turned and smiled that half smile again.

"I think this is yours," I said, handing her the book.

She laughed and shook her head. "Oh. Thank you. Yes, it is. I'm hopeless—always leave something behind."

I was about to turn away when she said, "You were in my carriage, weren't you? You were looking at me."

"Ah. I was trying to work out if you were English or French."

She smiled. "And what did you decide?"

"I couldn't tell. I guessed French, based on the book and hearing you speak."

"Thank you. I live in Switzerland. Although, to tell the truth, I'm on the run."

"Who from?"

"Finishing school. Just needed to get away – take some time to myself. What about you? What are you escaping?"

"Oh, I'm on my way home. I just went to France for work." And then I did something I'd never normally have done and asked if I could buy her lunch. After all, the worst that could happen was that she'd say no, and I'd never see her again.

She seemed to be considering it. I thought for a horrible moment she was going to refuse. "Thank you. That would be nice."

If I could have known then where it would all lead, would I still have asked her? It's easy to say no but I think, given the same set of circumstances, I would.

Inside the ship in the warmth of the bar—velvet chairs, potted palms and a man in a white jacket playing the grand piano in the corner—we chatted about the weather, places we'd been in France, things we were looking forward to getting back to in England.

"Champagne, sir?"

I hesitated.

"We're expecting a rough crossing," the waiter said. "Some people find it helps stave off seasickness."

"Oh well, put like that!"

I decided against making a toast because I couldn't think of anything to say that wouldn't sound excruciating, but Giselle raised her glass with a smile and said, "To us!"

I felt other passengers looking at us. It was fun to think they must assume we were travelling together.

"What I was really thinking on the train was how beautiful you are," I told her.

"That's kind."

"It isn't. I mean, it's true. I've never said that to anyone before."

"Never?" she asked with a teasing smile.

She let me light a cigarette for her and told me about her school in the hills above Lake Geneva. Her voice was enchanting, rich with musical notes and perfect vowels. It suggested a privileged upbringing, a life that was mysterious, exciting, a little dangerous. It was a voice that made you lean closer, feel cherished.

"What do you do at finishing school?" I found myself asking.

She laughed. "It's finishing me off, that's for sure. All the things you'd expect. We practise walking across a room with a book on our heads, picking up pins from the floor and getting out of cars with our knees together. But we do plenty of useful things too—French, skiing, typing... And the surroundings are glorious—the chateau and the lake with snow-capped mountains all around. Just like the travel poster you were looking at on the train."

"It sounds idyllic. I can't imagine why you'd want to run away."

She shrugged. "Sometimes it gets too much. I never went to

school – always had a governess – so I'm used to my own company."

As we ate, she told me stories about fellow students—girls called Finty, Minty, Prune and Goose.

"Stop laughing at their names!"

"Sorry."

"You're a photographer?" I noticed the fine freckles on her nose as she eyed my camera.

It was tempting to say I was. It would have given me the perfect excuse for looking at her on the train. In the few seconds while I thought about how to reply, I saw myself as a photographer, living in a Paris attic with a beautiful girl like this, strolling along the Seine, sitting in pavement cafés, visiting galleries and monuments, capturing beauty.

"I – no, I'm afraid not."

I told her about working in my father's furniture shop, how my trip to France had been to visit a factory in Nantes. The manager had invited my father over to see how his furniture was made so he could understand the quality of the craftsmanship. My father, refusing to set foot in France or speak a word of the language, sent me along in his place.

After a while I said, "Sorry, I must be boring you."

"Not at all. But you've only told me about your work. I'd rather hear about you. Tell me something about yourself."

I felt a surge of panic. "What do you want to know?"

She waved her arm. "Anything. The first thing that comes into your head."

I was tempted to make stuff up. My life had hardly been eventful. I'd lived most of it in a terraced house in an industrial northern town where I'd been to the local school. The furthest I'd travelled was a weekend visiting relations in Scarborough until a master at my school persuaded me to try for Cambridge. By some fluke I'd gained a scholarship to study law.

"I thought it would be the big turning point in my life."

"But it didn't work out?" She rested her chin in her hand. She'd been travelling alone since Lausanne so I suppose the truth is, she was just happy to talk to anyone under sixty, but I wanted to hold onto this moment, to being with her, so I talked about anything that came into my head. Things I'd never discussed with anyone before—hopes, doubts, ambitions, and insecurities.

Out it all came—how my father had hidden the letter of acceptance from Cambridge to prevent me from taking up the place and the row we'd had when I found it.

"He had it all worked out—that I'd go into the family business. Thought university was a waste of time, and I was getting ideas above my station."

And how when I arrived at Cambridge I'd been dazzled by the beauty of those honey-stoned buildings, echoing cloisters, dark, panelled rooms, and sunlit gardens. To begin with I'd floundered like a lost soul among my accomplished peers but in the end, I'd got used to the place. It felt like home.

"But then coming back, fitting into my old world again—that was a whole new struggle."

She looked confused. "So why did you go back?"

"What choice did I have? Getting a job wasn't as easy as I hoped. Most firms aren't taking on staff except by the back door. I got a place at a law firm in London but after a few months they had to make cuts."

"So, they let you go?"

"Last in, first out. You know how it is." After all, it was almost the truth.

She nodded with a sympathetic smile. "It's happening all over from what I hear—this beastly economic crisis. Your father must be pleased to have you working for him."

"Oh yes. He's delighted to have been proved right."

I hadn't spoken to anyone about it before. I doubt anyone else would have listened. It was difficult for them to understand. Old school friends viewed me with suspicion since I went down south to do my degree and my student friends had landed jobs in the top firms, helped by their families' connections—if they needed to work at all.

She looked at me while I was talking with her head tilted, making me feel that what I was saying wasn't pointless and I had a right to say it. And yet all the time I was fighting back thoughts: *What are you doing here with me? Can't you see I'm different from you? Can't you see there's something in me, some fatal flaw that always ends up spoiling things?*

"I don't know why I'm telling you all this."

"Because I'm interested. Go on."

It was unusual for me to talk so much but knowing I'd never see her again gave me the freedom to be more honest in that hour than I'd ever been with anyone. That was what made it special; knowing we had such a short time to get to know each other and all we'd be left with was a memory.

"Perhaps you shouldn't go home," she said. "Why don't you take a trip somewhere you've never been and discover something interesting, see where it takes you?"

I laughed. If only I had the money to take off like that. But to pass the time, and keep her with me a bit longer, we talked about places we'd go, things we'd like to see.

"It's funny, isn't it?" she said. "Us being here together. It's not as if someone introduced us or told us to meet. There must be a reason."

It sounded a bit far-fetched but I didn't want to spoil the moment. "What reason could there be?"

She looked out at the sea, a glittering silver sheet broken only by other boats ploughing their way through, carrying different people to different destinations. "I don't know yet," she said with a slight frown. "Perhaps we'll find a way to help each other."

"I hope so. But I don't even know your name. I'm Jack."

"Giselle."

I practised saying it inside my head. "That's a beautiful name. I haven't heard it before."

She pulled a face. "It's because of the ballet, you know."

"Of course." Although I'd never been to a ballet and had no idea which one she meant.

"It's my mother's favourite. Giselle's a peasant girl who dies of a broken heart when she finds her lover's engaged to someone else. She's buried in the forest and joins a group of ghost maidens who all died before their wedding day. They come out of their graves each night and lure young men to their death by dancing with them until they're exhausted."

"Powerful stuff."

"But Giselle can't bring herself to kill her lover, so she defies the sylph queen's order and protects him until dawn."

"I like that. It's a good story."

It would help me to remember her name. I wanted to remember things about her.

"I could tell you liked stories," she said. "Does it ever worry you that no matter how quickly you read you'll never be able to read all the books that have been written?"

I laughed. "I've never thought about it like that but I see what you mean."

The champagne was giving everything a fuzzy-edged unreality. Our surroundings seemed to fade around us as we talked, other diners coming and going like minor characters in our story.

"Tell me about you," I said.

"There's not much to tell."

But she told me she was an only child. Her father was a

baronet ('*only* a baronet' were the words she used). "It hardly means anything—just entitles him to a slightly grander funeral than the rest of us."

She'd grown up in a grand old pile somewhere "up in the wilds" inherited from her great-grandfather who owned a cotton mill. She painted an idyllic picture of Christmas house parties, summer concerts on the lawn, boating on the lake and tennis tournaments with the staff.

"I've been very lucky."

"That's not a crime. No need to apologise."

But despite her privileged upbringing, she seemed restless for something more. Perhaps that was how it was for most people, always believing happiness lay just out of reach. We sat looking out at the waves, asking each other anything that came into our heads. The movement of the ship and the hazy outline of land reminded me that time was running on. I wanted to find out everything about her before it was too late.

"What did you want to be when you were a child?"

"If you could be anyone else, who would you be?"

"If you could live in any period of history, which one would you choose?"

For the first time in my life, I found I was asking questions I wanted to hear the answers to, rather than to be polite.

"Is that land?" People were getting up from the tables and surging towards the doors.

As the white cliffs slid into view, we got up too and followed the crowd out onto the deck.

Giselle placed her hands on the rail and lifted her face towards the sun. People were taking photographs. Checking my camera, I found I had one shot left. I aimed it at the cliffs but at the last moment when I thought she wouldn't notice repositioned it to get Giselle in the frame. Something to hang onto. She looked back at me over her shoulder and smiled.

"You've stolen my soul."

"I'm sorry?"

"That's what some people believe, isn't it—that taking a photograph takes away a part of the person."

I laughed. "I haven't heard that before. Would you like me to send you the picture when I've had it developed?"

But my words were drowned by an announcement telling us we were about to dock. Below us, the umber and white connecting train stood waiting to take us on the last leg of the journey to London. Giselle and I had seats in different carriages. She turned and waved as she climbed aboard hers.

And that's where it could have ended. A perfect memory. We'd have gone back to our different worlds and lived different lives. After all, we had nothing in common. Except perhaps fatal curiosity. One day in the future, I'd have probably found the photograph and asked myself when it was taken and who was the girl, then cast it aside and got back to whatever I was doing.

"Jack!"

In Victoria station I was collecting my case when I heard her voice behind me.

"Glad I caught you. The butler's just tipped me off Granny's awful cousins are staying the weekend—Lord and Lady Ashwell. Do you know them?"

I told her I didn't. It made me smile that she should even think I might, but presumably in her world most people knew each other.

"I wish I'd known. It will ruin the weekend. I can't go home until they've gone."

"Won't your parents be disappointed?"

She shook her head. "They didn't know I was coming. It

was going to be a surprise. Don't know what I'm going to do now."

"Come with me if you like." I made it sound like a joke, but my heart beat a little faster.

"Thank you, but don't you have to get back to work? I can't imagine your father would be pleased to see me."

"Oh, I'm not going straight home. I'm going to wedding in Northumberland tomorrow."

"A wedding? That sounds fun."

I forced a smile. "It won't be. I was engaged to the bride until a few weeks ago."

"Ah. I can see that would be awkward. But why are you going?"

I shrugged, standing back to let passengers surge past. "Pride, I suppose. If I don't, people will think I haven't got over it."

A muffled announcement told people on the other platform their train was delayed.

"And have you? Got over it, I mean."

"Yes. Of course."

All the same, I wasn't looking forward to the occasion. It would be humiliating, arriving on my own, being surrounded by my old student friends boasting about their achievements. What did I have to show for my time since graduating?"

Giselle touched my arm. "I'll go with you. We can pretend we're engaged. Show them you've moved on."

"I can't ask you to do that."

I pictured myself walking into a church with Giselle on my arm, Daphne's eyes on stalks as she swept past us up the aisle, her father's red face bulging, her mother's condescending smile freezing.

"You don't have to ask. I'm offering, aren't I?"

I admired her free spirit. But to take off alone with a

complete stranger? I didn't know whether to be thrilled by her boldness or alarmed by her naivety. Still, who was I to argue? Perhaps I should have thought more but I'd spent my life applying what-ifs to every situation. For once I wanted to do something without thinking.

Whatever the cost.

Chapter Two

We took a taxi to King's Cross where I bought Giselle a ticket to the village in Northumberland, trying not to think about the cost. I called the guesthouse to change the reservation for two rooms. The landlord sounded a bit suspicious so I told him I was travelling with my sister. When the train arrived, we found seats next to each other in a carriage that smelled of soot, cigarettes, and leather luggage. It still didn't seem real.

I was worried we'd run out of things to say to each other on such a long journey, but the time passed smoothly. We played guessing games, looking out at the people in the stations.

"See those two old men on the bench? Secret agents. And the little old lady's a bank robber. That dog on her lap isn't real. It's filled with stolen jewels."

A middle-aged woman sitting opposite eyed us over her knitting.

"What about the nun? She looks like she's torn by a dilemma. Should she go back to the convent or marry the man she loves?"

We asked each other anything that came into our heads. I

was beginning to feel I already knew Giselle better than people I had known for years.

"What's your earliest memory?" she asked.

"Oh, that would be drinking my sister's medicine. I must have been about two years old. My mother had put it up on the shelf where she thought it would be out of reach. I can remember clambering up on the rails of the cot, making a grab for it, taking a gulp. The next moment I was retching, spitting it all down my front."

Giselle laughed. "Lucky it didn't kill you."

"I bawled my head off with disappointment which brought my mother rushing in. When she saw the red liquid all over me, she thought it was blood. Then she smelled the medicine and went into another panic. Still, no harm done. I lived to tell the tale."

As we went north, the sky became darker and denser. Anonymous stations flashed by as the train plunged on through the afternoon.

Are you humouring me? Can you see I'm out of my depth?

"Did you ever have an imaginary friend?" she asked.

"Let me think. I had an imaginary dog. My father wouldn't let me have a real one."

"I had an imaginary sister. The staff used to lay a place at the table for her and she had her own plate of food."

I smiled. "Did she have a name?"

She wrinkled her nose, remembering. "I think she was called Bella."

"Did you miss not having a real sister?"

"A bit. The house was always full of people. Sometimes guests brought children with them but I didn't have friends I could just see whenever I liked."

A spot of rain fell against the window, and then another. We watched them race to the bottom. The drops turned to splashes and then the rain streamed down, turning the flickering fields, trees, and houses into a watery blur.

"What's your house like?" I asked.

"Have you got a pencil? I'll draw it for you." She dug around in her bag for an envelope. I stared in amazement as she sketched a vast gothic building with gables, turrets, and dozens of chimneys. "Then there's the library over here. And this bit's the orangery..."

"This is your home? It's spectacular."

She laughed. "Oh no, I'm making it look nicer than it is. It's a horrible hotch-potch."

"It doesn't look horrible to me."

But her drawing reminded me how immense the gulf was between my world and hers. Just as well we were going to a B&B and not back to my home. What would she make of our redbrick terraced two-up, two-down?

"What is it?" she asked.

"Nothing. I'm just wondering what you're doing here with me."

She laughed and kissed my cheek. "I like being with you. You're not like anyone else I know."

We travelled in silence for a while. Eventually the ordered countryside gave way to wilder moors and hills and then it became too dark to see outside anymore. The rain turned to sleet, landing like stars on the window.

A reflection in the glass made me turn my head. Two men stood in the corridor outside our compartment, peering in.

"It's full," mouthed the gentleman next to me. He wagged his finger and snapped the blind down.

I turned to Giselle to see if she'd noticed this exchange but she shrank down in her seat and twisted towards the window.

"What is it? Do you know those people?"

"No. I thought they were going to tell us we were in their seats. I hate confrontation, don't you?"

After a while, she fell asleep. I studied her reflection in the window, the curve of her forehead, her soft mouth. How long before she realised I was different from her? Boring, common, and inept. But it would be fun while it lasted.

I bundled up my coat and placed it behind her head as a pillow. She smiled sleepily and slumped against my chest. I fell asleep too but jerked awake at intervals as the train stopped at stations.

Each time I woke, blinking in the warm glow of the lamps, the other passengers in the carriage had changed, making it feel as though I were dreaming. A middle-aged couple joined us for a while and a mother with a young boy and later a vicar.

The woman opposite looked up from her knitting every now and then and stared at us with suspicion in her eyes. No doubt she thought I wasn't good enough for Giselle. Perhaps she thought we were eloping. Looking back now though, I wonder if she glimpsed something else in me that I wasn't aware of at the time. Did she have an idea where this might all lead?

Chapter Three

When at last the train clanked to a halt, we jumped down through the cloud of soot and steam into a desolate little station. Trees creaked and snowflakes eddied around us.

"You've brought the alpine weather with you!" I shouted above the elements.

I turned up my mac to make a tent for us and we ran, jumping puddles, to find the car that we had been told would be waiting for us, but the forecourt was empty. We huddled under the Victorian canopy, stamping our feet and blowing on our hands. I could feel Giselle shivering beside me and was tempted to put my arms around her but wasn't sure how she'd react.

"This place doesn't sound very grand," I warned her. I was regretting choosing the cheapest accommodation on the list, the furthest from the wedding venue.

"I'm sure it will be fine. I can sleep anywhere."

"And I hope you don't mind but I told the landlord you were my sister. It just seemed easier, you know, to stop any gossip."

She laughed. "Absolutely. This is going to be fun."

The other passengers gradually dispersed, picked up by

relatives, holding onto their hats and clutching coats to their throats, exclaiming about the weather. I began to think the guesthouse owner had forgotten about us. Perhaps he detected I was lying about us being siblings and disapproved. Eventually, however, a pair of headlamps emerged through the gloom.

I confirmed the name of the guesthouse with the driver. He nodded and opened the doors for us, cigarette dangling from his mouth.

The wipers whipped back and forth and the engine strained as we climbed into the hills. We sat shivering in our wet clothes as he drove for an age through solid darkness, except for occasional glimpses of a shadowy silver lake between skeletons of trees. The driver barely spoke but I felt him studying me through the mirror, which made my scalp prickle.

I began to wonder if he'd lost his way or if he had any intention of taking us to the guesthouse but eventually we reached a shadowy lane between high hedges. Without warning he turned the car and we plunged, tyres skidding, down the long, potholed track. Eventually, we slewed to a halt in front of a slate-roofed farmhouse, the only building I'd seen for miles. It looked abandoned. No pools of golden light at the windows, no sound of dogs barking. That uneasy feeling crashed back in.

"Are you sure this is the right place?" I asked.

"Certain."

It was one of those bastle houses typical of the area, built for defence, with thick stone walls covered in ivy. The window frames were rotten. A broken gutter spouted a torrent of water above the door. The driver beeped the horn and opened the door for us to get out. I looked doubtfully at Giselle as we walked towards the front door. She pulled her coat around herself.

I had half a mind to get back in the taxi and order the driver to take us somewhere else, but he was already pulling away.

After the third tug on the bell a giant, leonine man with a ruddy complexion, came to the door. He stared at us for some moments as though wondering what we were doing there but finally seemed to come to his senses.

"Mr Sanders. You made it! Good heavens, look at the state of you. Come inside before you catch your deaths. I'll just show you up to your rooms and you can change into something dry before dinner."

We followed him down a dark, stone passage. At first I thought we must be the only people staying in the farmhouse but a burst of laughter erupted from one room as we passed. From another, we heard the clink and fizz of an ice cube popping in a glass, the thunk of a billiard ball being pocketed, and a shout of triumph. The voices in a third room stopped as we approached, and the door closed softly.

Giselle's room at the top of the creaking stairs was a reasonable size and had a fireplace but the cornice stopped halfway across the ceiling suggesting it had been divided to create another room. Whoever did it hadn't done a very good job, and the wall felt flimsy.

It was too dark to see much out of the floor-to-ceiling window, and in any case the view was partially blocked by a group of dilapidated buildings across a small courtyard.

Down the far end of the corridor, the owner opened the door to a small room with plain, painted walls, a single bed, and a dank-smelling wardrobe.

"The bathroom's down there," he told me, pointing back the way we'd come. "There's plenty of hot water. Spruce yourselves up and come down to join the others. They're looking forward to seeing you."

I couldn't imagine why but then it struck me they'd all been waiting for us to arrive so they could have dinner. It was almost midnight and I didn't have much appetite. All I wanted was to get dry and apologise to Giselle for bringing her to such a desolate place, but I didn't want to appear rude.

"Thank you. We'll be as quick as we can."

As I hung up my wet clothes and changed into dry ones, I couldn't help wondering what Giselle thought about the place.

A few moments later she knocked on my door wearing a midnight blue chiffon dress which swirled around her legs as she walked. Her hair hung about her shoulders in damp curls.

"You look lovely," I said before I could stop myself.

She looked down at her dress. "Oh, this dress is ancient but at least it's dry."

The owner was waiting for us at the bottom of the stairs. "Ah, there you are."

He pushed open a door to reveal a dimly lit, low-ceilinged dining room. A group of people who had been having an animated conversation fell silent as we entered. A man in his late thirties leaned against the fireplace, smoking. A woman of around the same age sat by him sipping a sherry. A middle-aged man with a white moustache standing by the window checked his watch and in the corner an ancient man snored in a wing chair. Two elderly women who must be twins looked up like birds from their armchairs.

"Our new guests – Mr Sanders and his sister," said the owner.

Did I imagine it or was there a minute pause before the last word? The corners of Giselle's mouth twitched, and she turned her head away.

"At last," one of the sisters cried.

They got up and shuffled towards to the table. It was laid for eight. No wonder these people looked relieved – they'd obviously been waiting for us to arrive so we could eat together. I wished they hadn't – it made me feel awkward.

The owner shovelled some coal onto the smouldering fire

before disappearing down the hall. A cloud of smoke filled the room, making my eyes and throat sting.

"My dear, aren't you cold?" The trouser-wearing twin with cropped hair, eyed Giselle's bare shoulders with disapproval.

"Not at all," she replied, smiling.

"Don't fuss, Delia," snorted the woman's sister. Their faces were eerily similar—beaky with wild, dark brows and staring eyes, but this woman's hair was styled in crisp finger waves like a judge's wig, and she wore a skirt and stout walking shoes.

Eventually, the owner returned with a roast dinner. Dishes were passed with a chinking of porcelain and the young man filled our glasses with red wine.

"Vegetables are overcooked," said the white-moustached man with a sigh.

"Oh, don't get worked up about it, Charles," murmured one of the sisters. "It's hardly surprising given how long we've been waiting."

Presumably to distract him, the crimp-haired twin turned her glare from me to Giselle. "I'd never have believed you were siblings. You don't look a bit alike."

I felt myself colour, but Giselle smiled. "That's what everyone says. If you met our parents you'd see why – they're chalk and cheese."

The woman nodded slowly. Her eyes were disconcertingly pale, different sizes and protruding. I thought when we first arrived, she must be blind, and the staring accidental but now she was clearly appraising us.

"I don't know, there might be something," said the young, dark-haired woman. It was the first time I'd heard her speak. "The cheekbones? Yes, here – around the eyes." She turned to her husband for confirmation but he shrugged irritably. I got the impression the couple had had a row earlier and were as anxious to get away from the place as we were.

"I hope you enjoy your stay," said the crimp-haired twin. "We've travelled all over the world – never miss the opportunity to explore somewhere new – but you can't beat the countryside around here."

She reeled off an impressive list of places they'd been to, waving away interruptions from her sister who quibbled over placenames, dates, and names of dishes. "No, no, that was in March, dear...Oh, good heavens, no. She was his *mother!*"

I could imagine them squabbling their way around these foreign cities.

"I must say it's nice to have new guests," said Delia, the crop-haired twin. "The last couple barely said a word but they kept us up all night. Honeymooners, they said."

"A Mr and Mrs Smith, apparently," murmured her sister. "They could at least have used a bit of imagination."

"I suppose they might really be called Smith," pointed out the younger woman, but her voice was drowned out by a chorus of disparaging remarks.

The man with the white moustache introduced himself as Benson, a doctor from Harrogate. "I noticed you brought your camera," he said. "Wonderful landscape around here. You'll be able to take some great pictures."

He drew up an itinerary of walks for us with things to see, places to eat, hazards to be avoided.

"It sounds wonderful," I told him. "I wish we had more time but I'm afraid we have to leave in the morning. We're going to a wedding."

"A wedding? I do hope you get there all right," said the crimp-haired twin, frowning. "Have you seen the weather? The landlord says snow's on its way."

Benson snorted. "It's already started."

"Well, it's good news for the happy couple, anyway. Snow

on your wedding day's supposed to be lucky, isn't it? A sign of fertility and prosperity."

"Is it? I hadn't heard that before."

"Gosh, I hope it doesn't stick," said Delia, the crop-haired twin. "What if we get snowed in?"

"We'll just have to make the best of it," her sister said. "It might be fun – like being in one of those whodunnits."

"Without the murders, I hope," said Benson.

I managed a smile although surely nothing could be worse than being stuck in that place with those people for any length of time.

"I think it's settling," said the young, dark-haired woman, staring out of the window.

"Right. Let's get out of here," muttered her husband, throwing down his napkin and pushing back his chair.

But she poured herself another glass of wine. "Are you mad? I'm not going out in this."

"It will be worse by morning. If we don't leave now, we'll be stuck here. I can't stand another minute."

While we ate, they quizzed us about our family, asking the same questions in different ways. Were they trying to catch us out? I answered mostly truthfully about my own, as though Giselle was my real sister, Ellen. I was impressed by how easily she picked up on things I said and talked as though we'd grown up together.

"Jack was a terror when he was little. Once he climbed out of his cot and helped himself to my bottle of medicine. He spilled it all down himself and when Mummy came in, she saw all the red liquid and thought he'd been attacked by foxes."

The old people followed her with rapt attention and laughed like an indulgent family watching the youngest child reciting a poem at Christmas. I watched her expressions and asked myself if

I'd have been able to tell she was lying. I didn't think so. It was getting hard to concentrate. I found I couldn't take my eyes off her. She looked lovely in that dress, but I couldn't stop picturing her out of it. I tried furiously to keep my mind on the conversation.

"Will you go to Cambridge like your brother?" the crop-haired, unmarried sister asked Giselle.

"I'm already there," she said. I glanced at her nervously. She was going off script.

"Splendid. Which college?"

"Newnham," she said at the same time as I said, "Girton." I froze but Giselle laughed and rolled her eyes. "Jack's hopeless. He never remembers."

"Newnham," mused Delia. "Then you must know the Brunswick girl. What's her name? Melanie."

"Marjorie," said her sister.

"Oh, Marjorie, yes. I don't know her well but I know who she is."

"And what are you reading?"

I saw a flicker of confusion before she replied, "*Mrs Dalloway*."

Then realising her mistake, she smiled as though of course she'd been joking. "English Literature."

As luck would have it the crimp-haired sister turned out to be a retired teacher. She launched into a list of her most loved and loathed books.

"There's some piffle being produced at the moment. I don't know what publishers are thinking of. Is it too much to ask for a story to have a proper beginning, middle and end?"

"I agree," replied Giselle, her eyes dancing in the candle-light. "But do they necessarily have to be in that order?"

I felt a jolt as her stockinged foot nudged mine under the table. A smile played around her lips as she sipped her wine. I had a vague, uncomfortable feeling that the others were watching us and had somehow spotted this communication, but after all it was none of their business whether or not we were really brother and sister. We'd all be leaving in the morning. We'd never see each other again.

"You *are* cold," said the crimp-haired twin, staring down at the goosebumps on Giselle's arms. "Why don't you move up? That window's terribly draughty."

"Oh no, really, I'm fine."

"No, come on," said Benson, scraping back his chair, "Swap with me."

With a resigned smile Giselle moved into his seat by the fire, furthest away from me. While she kept the ladies entertained with imaginary stories, I faced a barrage of questions from Benson about my time at Cambridge, probably to test whether I'd actually been there. When he realised he couldn't catch me out, he changed tack and interrogated me on why I hadn't put my degree to better use. "I wouldn't bury myself in that shop for too long if I were you or you'll find it's too late."

"Thanks for the advice."

Just as I was beginning to wonder if this gruesome evening would ever end the clock chimed twelve. The old man in the armchair woke with a snort, jumped up and shuffled out of the room. The younger couple, still arguing quietly, declared they must be off too. With any luck, the others would follow them and Giselle and I would at last have a few moments alone.

"Come on. You need a good night's sleep after your long journey."

One of the twins stood holding the door ushering us out as if she owned the place. When we got to the top of the stairs I waited for them to disappear into their rooms but the sisters took Giselle's arms as though she were under arrest and escorted her to her door.

"Our room's next to yours so if you need anything just call

out," Delia told her. "One of us is sure to hear you. We're very light sleepers."

Was it my imagination or did she cast me a look as she spoke? I had the sense I was being warned. At any rate, the doors shut, leaving me in the dark landing with Benson.

"You're down here, I believe," he said, gesturing for me to lead on, "opposite me."

When we reached my room he stood outside waiting for me to go in.

For the love of God, can't you leave us alone?

Once inside, I shut the door, leaned against it, and closed my eyes. For the next half hour or so, I heard the landing creak as feet traipsed up and down, the bathroom door opening and closing, someone going downstairs. Would they never settle? I was desperate to see Giselle, to at least talk to her, if only to assure her we'd be out of there, first thing and would find somewhere else to stay the following night.

When at last, it was quiet, I crossed the floor, skirting the loose board I'd noted earlier and turned the doorknob. I made my way down the corridor in the dark but almost slammed into Delia, the crop-haired twin outside Giselle's room.

She started, bringing her hand up to her chest. "Goodness, whatever are you doing, creeping about?"

"Sorry." *What were you doing?*

"I just brought your sister a glass of water," she said.

"That was kind. I'll just see if she's all right."

"No need." She blocked the door, smiling. "She's fast asleep. All that travelling must have worn her out. Don't worry. If she needs anything, we'll hear her."

"Right. Thank you."

She stood there with a determined smile, making it clear she wasn't going to back down and leaving me no choice but to return to my room. I sat on the bed for hours, torturing myself with thoughts of how things should have been. In a moment of madness I even wondered if the old woman might have slipped something into Giselle's glass of water but why would she do that? Too much talk of whodunnits.

Eventually, I slumped back on the lumpy pillow and slept. In a dream, I watched from the window as the twins led Giselle away across the yard. I shouted and banged on the glass as she climbed into their car, but she didn't hear.

Chapter Four

I woke to find a heaviness in the air, a muffled quality as if I was lying on the seabed. I yanked back the curtain. Outside, everything was white. Snowflakes drifted silently down, covering fields, trees, and the farm track. My surge of childish happiness was followed by a rise of panic. Those people had been right last night about getting snowed in.

I hurried down the corridor and tapped on Giselle's door. She was standing in front of the window, clutching the sheet around her.

"It's beautiful, isn't it?" she said.

"It is, but I'm not sure how we're going to get to the wedding in this."

"I'm sure we'll find a way."

As we came downstairs we found the twins standing in the hall with the landlord.

"No point doing anything until it stops," he was saying. "That track's treacherous at the best of times and even if we clear it Norland says the road up there's impassable. He won't risk bringing the car out in conditions like this. Don't worry. It won't last. You can stay as long as you need."

It was all very well but I was expected at the wedding. I had a job to get back to the next day and a father who would be most unlikely to understand. How long would we have to stay and how much would these extra nights cost? I looked over at Giselle, but she didn't seem concerned. After all, she spent half the year in her finishing school surrounded by snow. It must have seemed ridiculous to her, all this fuss.

The young couple had left before it got light, the landlord told us and taken the old man with them to drop him off at his home in the village. They'd had trouble getting their car up even then and had done some damage to it. The snow had covered their tracks. No sign now that they'd ever been here.

My heart lifted at the thought of being able to spend another day in Giselle's company. If only the remaining three guests would leave us alone.

If the twins were right about snow on your wedding day being lucky, Daphne's marriage looked set to be a roaring success. I pictured her standing proudly at the front of the church with her groom, Douglas Fairley, a big-eared, balding banker who read History in the year above me, the son of a politician. For weeks, I'd dreaded this day but now I realised I didn't hate him anymore. By marrying Daphne, he had saved me from making the biggest mistake of my life.

I didn't blame Daphne either anymore for breaking things off. What infuriated me at the time was that she said it was because Douglas Fairley had better prospects. But the truth was even then, although I'd enjoyed acting the injured party, I couldn't help a sense of relief. I'd already begun to suspect that marriage to Daphne would be pleasant enough but would never feel like an adventure.

"Extraordinary." Daphne's mother's crisp voice on the other end of the telephone was followed by a sharp sniff. "The snow hasn't stopped anyone else getting here. But don't worry, we shan't miss you. I'll pass on your best wishes to the happy couple."

I doubted she had any intention of doing so. I'd long suspected the woman of encouraging Daphne to end our relationship.

The snow fell all day and the next. There was nothing I could do about it. At least it gave me a little while longer with Giselle to store up memories. Watching it fall, transforming the world outside, brought back the same wonderment I'd felt as a child staring out of my bedroom window. The farmhouse and its surroundings, which had looked so bleak the previous night, had become a place of brilliance and beauty. The outhouses across the courtyard had turned into snow palaces with icicles hanging from the roofs.

"Magical, isn't it," I said, gazing out through the window.

"Yes, it's beautiful. But cruel. It lures you and then it kills you."

The sudden change in mood took me aback. "That's a bit morbid, isn't it?"

She shrugged. "It's like the Snow Queen. We can't resist it. It tricks us because we want to be tricked. People get killed by avalanches all the time but that doesn't stop others coming to the Alps. Beauty without danger's not enough."

"That might be true in Switzerland, but there aren't any avalanches here."

I was grateful for the snow. It blanked out everything in our lives that had gone before, erasing everything that separated us.

It gave us a new start, a new set of rules, a place to be who we wanted to be.

"Come on, let's go outside."

That first morning, we crunched through the fields, exploring our new world, pointing out frozen cobwebs that looked like diamond necklaces, frosted trees like candelabras, creating new tracks in the pristine white space, and marvelling at how quickly they filled up again.

"No one would know we'd been here," she said.

We made snowmen, snow women, snow dogs and snow cats, borrowed trays and tobogganed down steep slopes, screaming with exhilaration. Had snowball fights among the trees and made angel shapes lying in the snow, gazing giddily up at the sky, as though we were floating up into space. I found myself falling in love.

"What's the best dream you've ever had?"

"If you died tonight, what would you regret most?"

"If you were allowed to know one thing about your future, what would you want to know?"

It was only gradually that I began to suspect we were being watched. The weather muffled faraway sounds but made noises close to us – snow creaking underfoot, the snapping of twigs, popping of ice in frozen puddles – sounded more acute. At first, I dismissed these as wildlife or the wind moving the branches but once or twice I glimpsed a shadow slipping between trees, saw a flash of colour or fresh prints in the snow. I didn't say anything to Giselle because I didn't know how she'd react. Most likely, I was imagining it anyway.

"What's the best book you've ever read?"

"What's your favourite word?"

"What's the worst thing you've ever tasted?"

I caught her as she tripped over a concealed tree root, brushed the dusting of snow off her frozen cheek and warmed her hands in mine. She tilted her face up until it was close and blurry. My lips felt so stiff with cold I wasn't sure they would work properly but I needn't have worried. We peeled away just long enough to smile in relief, then found each other again.

Something snapped in the trees. A shower of snow fell around us like a snow globe. Giselle stiffened and pulled away.

"What was that?"

I listened. "A bird," I said after a few moments.

But I had that feeling again that someone was watching. It crept up my spine. We set off back towards the farmhouse, trying to keep the conversation light although I kept taking little looks around. I could still feel the imprint of her lips on mine as we walked. It was hard to get out of my head.

During dinner I kept remembering the kiss and the press of her body against mine. I was desperate to kiss her again, but the twins kept us sitting there with tales of their past adventures.

"Do you remember that place in Spain where they jumped over the babies?"

"Good heavens yes. Laid the poor mites out in the street and chaps dressed up as devils leapt over them. Can you imagine if one of them had lost his footing?"

"And the food. Remember the soup?"

"Stone cold!"

Then there was the time they'd set off on a holiday with a suitcase tied to the back of their car.

"When we arrived, the case was empty. We must have left a trail of clothing strewn across the hedges. We had to laugh."

After dinner, the landlord joined the guests for a drink and bashed out some tunes on the piano. He was surprisingly good and had us all singing along. Eventually, when we thought no one would notice, Giselle and I crept out. Outside her door I drew her towards me. Her hair and skin still smelled of the snow and the pine forest. I kissed her again, trying to ignore the worry that one of our inquisitors would come shuffling out into the hall below and spot us.

Reaching behind her, I turned the doorknob, and we fell inside. Moonlight spread across the floor like a silver sheet. Someone had been in and made up the fire while we'd been downstairs. We moved to the rug in front of the fire and made love as though nothing else in the world mattered. Lying there afterwards with my body curled around hers, looking at the dark shapes of our clothes strewn about the room, and the glints in her hair picked out by the moonlight, I felt as though I was living someone else's life.

"Goodnight, dear," said a loud, clear voice in my ear.

I shot upright, heart exploding in my chest, expecting to find one of the twins standing over us. I flung the eiderdown over our bodies, and we clung to each other for some moments in horrified silence. But as my eyes adjusted to the dark, I realised the room was empty. The voice had come from the other side of the wall.

Giselle recovered enough to gasp, "Goodnight."

"Do you need another pillow?"

"Thank you, no, I'm fine."

"Do you think she heard?" Giselle whispered.

"I'm sure she didn't."

But I was sure she had. The old busybody was probably holding a glass to her ear against the wall. If so, she either now knew for certain that we weren't brother and sister as we'd claimed or she must think us very perverted.

It was too much of a risk to creep back across the landing to my own room, so we got into Giselle's bed but I lay awake for hours in the darkness. This would all be so perfect if it wasn't for those people. We had to get away from them.

Chapter Five

I woke on the Sunday expecting to find the snow gone but more had fallen during the night. Looking from my window, I was surprised to see the driver who'd picked us up from the station standing in the yard talking to the owner, Mr Allerton. They were knee-deep in snow, so he must have walked rather than driven. At breakfast, Mr Allerton confirmed that the driver had walked the six miles from the village to bring over a newspaper and a few essentials.

I felt the two sisters and Benson the doctor looking over at us during breakfast as though they knew we'd spent the night together and had been gossiping about it. Last night I'd assumed we'd be leaving today, so they could think what they liked. Now I was starting to doubt the wisdom of lying to them.

"How long do you think this snow will last?" I asked Mr Allerton.

He made a face. "Could be a while. There's more on the way, I reckon. Can't see you leaving here before Tuesday."

Tuesday? Two more days. My father would be furious. I pictured him pacing up and down the shop, asking where I'd got to.

"No snow round here," he said when I rang to warn him. He could barely keep the suspicion out of his voice.

"Well, I can't help that."

As I replaced the receiver, I heard movement behind me. Turning round, I found the elderly twins standing in the hall.

"Now you're here, you may as well make yourself useful," said one. "Mr Allerton needs help around the farm."

I objected to being bossed about, but lending a hand on the farm would at least get me out from under their noses. I helped repair some roofing that had come loose from one of the outhouses and chopped up some logs. In the afternoon Mr Allerton asked if I could help the shepherd rescue some sheep, which had got stuck in the drifts.

The air on the hill bit through my thin coat. At first, I couldn't see any sheep, but the dog sniffed them out under the snow. We dug carefully until we could haul them up. Some of them, especially the lambs, were already dead, which was heart-breaking, but we rescued as many as we could.

Giselle came out to join us. I was surprised by her strength and patience, coaxing the frightened animals out of their frozen prison and holding them firmly. The shepherd, a short, stocky young man with a scrubbed face and lumpy nose, watched her in silent admiration. I caught his eye and he looked away.

We carried logs back for the landlord and put them in the store in the cellar.

"What do you think's in here?" asked Giselle, trying a locked door.

I put my eye to the keyhole, but it was too dark to see inside. "Smells of chemicals. Must be where they keep the cleaning stuff."

We helped ourselves to a few bottles from the rack and drank them in Giselle's room.

"What are you staring at?" she asked.

"I'm drawing you in my head. I want to be able to remember what you look like."

She laughed. "You will. I'm unforgettable."

I traced a small, question mark-shaped scar just above her left hip.

"How did you get this?"

She frowned. "Oh, that. I fell off a horse. I used to dream of running away and joining the circus. Tried to teach myself to ride standing up but it wasn't a great success."

"But why would you want to run away? Your childhood sounds idyllic."

She paused. "Oh, I don't know. Just for the fun of it. I like an adventure."

In the afternoon, we watched the three other guests to see which direction they were going in. Seeing them head off towards the village, we walked in the opposite direction towards the lake.

"I couldn't help overhearing your telephone call with your father," Giselle said. "He doesn't sound like the easiest person to get on with."

"You can say that again." I gathered up fistfuls of snow and packed it into a ball. Giselle heaped another load of snow together and rolled it over and over to make a body. "He's a very unhappy man. I was four when the war broke out, so I had no memory of him. All I had a photograph by my bed. He looked heroic – broad-shouldered, smiling, fit. That's what scares me. Anyone can start off like that and end up like him."

Being with Giselle and answering questions about myself was making me see things I never had before.

"Maybe. But you're not him. It won't happen to you."

I fixed the snowman's head onto the body and searched around for some twigs for the arms. "I wonder sometimes what he'd have been like if the war hadn't happened. All I know is, when he came home, he was nothing like the person I'd imagined. We'd been such a tight family, my mother, my sister, and me. And suddenly there he was, this intruder, too big for the house, always in the way and always in a foul temper."

For a long time, I'd tried to win his approval, running errands, and accompanying him on days out.

"But it always made things worse. He saw it as a sign of weakness. I'd get upset seeing him smash a fish's head in instead of throwing it back or waste all his winnings down at the pub, chatting up young women, letting his hands wander. And he'd catch me looking and explode into a rage and call me a sanctimonious little devil.

"Then he'd take his anger out on my mother, accuse her of bringing me up badly while he was away risking his life for his ungrateful family."

We stood back to admire the snowman. "That looks pretty good," said Giselle. "We can ask Mr Allerton for a carrot and an old hat."

"He was always sneering at me for having my nose in a book. When I told him I wanted to go to university instead of working in his shop he went on and on about snobbery, tradition, and betrayal and not taking responsibility seriously. But you know what I think? He was jealous. I'd found a way to escape whereas he never had."

She nodded. "And now you feel trapped again?"

"Yes. But not here. Not with you. This moment is all I want to think about now."

We climbed up to a ridge. The snow had stopped falling and as the sun pierced the clouds, it spread a kaleidoscope of colours across the lake below.

But I felt Giselle's mood change. She was silent, staring into the space as though she was seeing something different from me.

"Are you all right?"

Her eyes were wide and glassy. I waved a hand in front of them but got no reaction. Suddenly she was backing away, putting her hands to the sides of her head.

"It's such a long way down," she said, sinking to the ground. She was struggling for breath.

"You're afraid of heights? Sorry, I didn't realise."

She took a deep breath, then smiled, waving away my concern. "It's not the height. It's the falling. The suddenness of it. I have dreams about the ground giving way. Earthquakes, sink holes, avalanches..."

"Those things hardly ever happen."

"They do in the Alps," she reminded me. "A girl from finishing school went for a walk and never came back."

I put my arm round her as we walked. "Well, I've learned something about you. I didn't think you were afraid of anything."

"I'm not when I'm with you," she said. "You make me feel safe."

Chapter Six

I thought the snow might last a day or two. Then I began to wonder if it could last a week.

On Tuesday, my father's patience snapped.

"Have you lost the use of your legs?" he boomed down the telephone. "No, well, you can walk to the station, can't you."

"It's twelve miles," I pointed out. "And there are no trains."

On Wednesday, he erupted. "Get back here by tomorrow morning or don't bother coming back at all."

I had no doubt he meant what he said. And much as I hated working with him, I couldn't afford to lose my income from the shop. How else was I going to pay for our extended stay here at the farmhouse? The landlord seemed relaxed about it all and said we could settle up later but I'd have to find some way to pay him. And what about afterwards? I already knew how difficult it was to find another job. If my father refused to have me back home, I'd have to find somewhere else to live, too.

"There's nothing you can do about it, is there?" Giselle reminded me. "Just try and put it out of your mind."

"That's easy for you to say."

But I had to admit she was right. We spent most of our time

in her room, avoiding the other guests, making love, smoking, talking. Hours and days began to lose their meaning as though time had frozen.

Whenever we emerged, the others viewed us with suspicion. They seemed determined to catch us out together. Once or twice, we caught Mr Benson, the doctor with the white moustache, watching us from a window or spotted the twins in the distance deep in conversation with the owner. Their heads turned towards us and then quickly away.

"They don't believe we're brother and sister," I said. "I wish I'd never told them we were. Why can't they mind their own business?"

"Let them gossip. What's it got to do with them?"

"I don't see how you can find it funny. It's driving me mad, the way they follow us about."

I tried to see the funny side too, but it unnerved me. Why couldn't they leave us alone? But she was right – there was nothing we could do.

At night with our bodies curled around each other, looking out over the white fields bathed in a spectral light, we listened to the owls in the wood and watched the snow tumble like stars. This new world created just for us made the real one seem far away and unimportant, erasing all the things and people that had bothered me in my life before.

"Do you believe in God?" I asked her over a game of chess by the fire in the snug.

She stuck out her chin. "I refuse to."

I laughed. "I'm not sure it works like that."

"Well, if there's such a thing as hell, I'm not going to waste this life worrying about it."

"Well, I very much doubt you're going to hell. What makes you think you might? What have you done that's so awful?"

She shrugged and laughed.

"So, if you don't believe in God," I asked, "what do you believe in?"

She moved her knight, checkmating me. "Love."

Something sparkled on her hand as she moved the piece. I hadn't noticed the ring before. The pink solitaire must be worth a fortune.

"Who gave you this?" I asked, trying to ignore the jealous knot forming in my stomach.

She looked as though she had forgotten it was there. "It's not an engagement ring if that's what you're thinking. I've had it since I was a child."

Relief washed through me. "It's very pretty. Is it a ruby?"

"No, a diamond."

"I didn't realise you could get pink diamonds."

"They come in lots of colours. The pink's something to do with volcanic activity reacting with the rock."

The ring I'd bought Daphne with its tiny little stone had taken all my savings but compared to this one, it seemed tawdry. I felt less bad now about hurling it into the Cam when Daphne returned it to me the night we broke up. Afterwards, I'd regretted being so impulsive but now it felt the right thing to have done. I didn't want anything from my old life back.

I kept praying that the snow would last one more day so I could have one more day with Giselle. Over the next few days, despite their annoying habits, we were getting used to our little group. The sisters seemed less sinister, and some of their stories did make me laugh. I started to fool myself that this could end well.

But as we relaxed, we became forgetful. Coming out of Giselle's room in the middle of the night I met Mr Benson, on the landing. I stood back to let him pass but he fixed me with a filthy stare.

"A word if I may."

I tried to get past but he blocked my way.

"It hasn't escaped our attention, the things you and your sister get up to. And I have to say I find it disgusting. Apart from it being unnatural, have you any idea of the medical consequences?"

His moustache twitched as he spoke. "Makes me sick to think about it."

I could have taken the opportunity to come clean about the siblings lie. I wished I'd never made it up in the first place. He'd still have disapproved of a young unmarried couple travelling together but being unmarried was nowhere near as bad as being related. But it was none of his business and I'd had enough of being judged by everyone.

"Then I suggest you don't think about it."

He drew himself up. I thought for a moment he was going to hit me. Eventually, however, he walked off saying, "You should be locked away."

"What was all that about?" Giselle asked as I got back into bed.

"Nothing."

But I was already regretting speaking to him in the way I had. The last thing we needed was for someone to complain about us to the landlord. I tried to put it out of my mind, but it kept me awake.

The next morning as we crunched through the fields Giselle asked, "If you could have one special gift what would you choose?"

I dug my hands into my pockets. "It would be fun to travel through time. Be a Roman or meet Shakespeare. What about you?"

"I'd like to be able to turn invisible whenever I wanted," she said. "My mother had a pot marked vanishing cream on her dressing table. I covered my face in it once hoping it would make me disappear. When I'd look in the mirror and saw it hadn't worked, I was so disappointed."

I laughed but in the distance I was aware of shapes moving through the snow. Traffic on the larger roads. Time was running out, but I didn't want to acknowledge it. I wanted to hang onto everything while I still could.

"What's your biggest fear?" she asked.

"I'm not sure I want to tell you."

Her eyes lit up. "Oh, now I have to know."

"All right then. It's fear of myself, what I might do. That one day I'll make a terrible mistake and do something I'll never be able to get back from."

She frowned. "What sort of thing?"

"I don't know. Cause an accident. Run over a child..."

"There's probably a name for that type of fear. But why worry about something that hasn't even happened?"

"Well, that's just it. I feel if I stop looking out for it, that's when it will happen. No, you're right. It does sound ridiculous."

I had no choice but to laugh along with her. There were things I wanted to know about her, too, before it was too late. Why was she afraid of the dark? Why could she remember so little of her earliest years? And why had those men on the train upset her so much?

There were times when I suspected she was keeping back

the truth and times when I wondered if I really knew her any better than I had at the start, but I managed to convince myself she was honest about the things that mattered.

"Once I pretended to my sister the wind had changed when I was pulling a face, and I was stuck looking like this for ever." She rolled her eyes and stuck out her tongue. "I kept it up for about a whole morning."

I laughed. "Wait a minute. You don't have a sister."

"I used to."

"No, you didn't. Or only an imaginary one. You definitely said-"

She stopped. Was it the cold air making her cheeks flush? "I had a sister. She died, all right? That's why I don't talk about her."

"Oh, I'm sorry. It's just, you didn't tell me before."

It was as if the temperature around us plummeted. "I don't have to tell you everything. Why do you keep trying to catch me out?"

"I'm not, I just didn't realise, that's all."

I reached out but she walked off, wrapping her arms around herself. Before I had the chance to go after her, one of the twins, Delia, came up behind me.

"I'd like to talk to you, young man."

Another lecture. "I'm sorry. Can we talk about it later?"

"No. I'm afraid this can't wait. It's about the young lady you're travelling with. She's not your sister, is she?"

I felt myself bristle. "I don't think it's any of your business, is it?"

A note of steel entered her voice. "I think you should know-"

"Thank you but if you'll excuse me..."

"You're making a mistake," she shouted after me.

I pretended not to hear.

Why couldn't they all stay out of our lives?

Later, back in the bedroom, Giselle seemed to have forgotten our row and talked animatedly about her home.

"I'd like to meet your parents," I said.

I felt her body tense. She sat up and twisted away.

"Why? What's it got to do with them?"

"Nothing. I'm just curious. I want to see if they're the way I've imagined them."

I could picture her mother, an older version of Giselle, still pretty but more measured, and her father, tall, quiet, and dignified, indulgent to his only remaining daughter.

She was silent.

"What is it? Why don't you want me to meet them? Are you ashamed of me?"

She hugged her knees. "I thought you were interested in me, not my family."

"I am. You know I am. Look, it doesn't matter."

It crashed in on me again, that feeling that she was hiding something. Somehow I managed to change the subject and a few moments later we were laughing again but now it had been planted, that small doubt continued to nag.

Chapter Seven

The scream. It sliced through me. I shot upright in the darkness.

"What is it?"

Her eyes were open, but she wasn't seeing me. I reached for her but she pushed me away. Her body was rigid, unnaturally strong.

"It's all right," I told her. "You're dreaming."

She gripped her head in her hands, taking shallow, jagged breaths. I tried to hold her but she recoiled. She was whispering but I couldn't make out the words. It was obvious she couldn't hear me. Someone told me once you shouldn't wake a sleep-walker and this seemed to be a similar state so I moved potential obstacles away and put pillows along the wall to make sure she didn't injure herself.

It seemed to go on for ages. I felt helpless, listening to her terror but unable to do anything about it. I wondered if I should go and get help but she stopped as suddenly as she'd started. Gradually her breathing returned to normal. I stroked her face and found it soaked with tears.

"What was the dream about?" I asked at breakfast. "It sounded terrifying."

"What dream?" she asked, pouring coffee.

"The one you had last night. Surely you remember?"

She looked puzzled, then smiled and shook her head. "I never remember my dreams."

I noticed the sisters exchange glances. Mr Allerton looked at me strangely as he set down the toast. I wondered if Mr Benson or the twins had complained about us after all. He must have heard the screams or heard about them. God knows what he thought.

As the days passed, I became less bothered about the other guests. It became a bit of a joke between us, seeing how desperate they were to catch us out and discover the truth about our relationship. But something about the landlord disturbed me. Several times, I looked up during a conversation and found him staring at us for no obvious reason. Sometimes when we were coming back through the snow, I saw a shape at the window as though he were watching us. Once or twice, I saw him locked in conversation with the twins or Burris the shepherd or Norland the driver who walked over from the village most days, bringing cigarettes and other supplies.

But one afternoon it all became clear. We'd been making love in front of the fireplace in Giselle's room. I wandered over to the window to see if there had been any fresh snow. Something caught my attention. The barn door was open. As I stood looking something glinted in the window. It struck me as strange because there was no sun on the glass.

I drew back. Must be mistaken. No, there it was again in the hayloft window, and behind it, a dark shape.

"What's the matter?" Giselle said sleepily. "Come back to bed."

My stomach twisted. I pulled the curtains closed.

She frowned, propping herself up on her elbows. "What can you see?"

"Nothing."

"Tell me." Panic rose in her voice. "Is someone out there?"

I closed my eyes. I thought about not telling her, but it didn't seem fair. "Mr Allerton. He's in the storage barn."

"Do you think he saw us?"

"I think he's watching us."

She drew the sheet around herself. "Are you sure? Are you sure it's him?"

"Quite sure. I saw him go in there earlier. I'm sorry. I didn't think. Why are you laughing? I don't see what's funny about it."

"He's only looking," she said.

"Are you serious? We told him we were brother and sister."

She settled back against the pillow and lit a cigarette. "So? What can he do about it—send us to hell?"

"He could throw us out. He could tell the police."

She blew a column of smoke upwards. "He can't. Not without telling them how he knows. And even if he does, we'll tell them the truth—that we're not related. That will be easy to prove. He'll be left looking stupid."

But running over in my head all the things we'd been doing, I felt sick at the pit of my stomach.

At dinner Mr Allerton showed no sign of embarrassment. I kept looking at him and wondering if I could have made a mistake. He returned my gaze with a friendly smile. I felt myself colour. I should say something, challenge him, beat him to a pulp but now that I thought about it, I couldn't be absolutely sure it was him in that building or that he had been watching us.

The thaw started on Saturday, a week after the bad weather had begun. The hills were still white but the snow in the yard was contracting and developing holes like dirty lace. Soggy lumps slid off trees and rooftops. As colours started to re-emerge in the landscape, I had to remind myself this life was temporary. I couldn't hold onto it. Time was almost up.

I tried to imagine what the last moments would feel like. We'd be leaving soon and would never see each other again. I was powerless to stop it. But Giselle didn't seem to share my anxiety. She kept asking her questions.

"What colour is Wednesday?" – "What's your favourite piece of music?" – "If you weren't English, where would you like to have been born?"

"Doesn't it bother you?" I asked. "That it's nearly over? In a week or two you'll have forgotten me."

"That's nonsense." She was looking up at me, her eyes bright with possibility. "It doesn't have to end here just because the snow's melting. We can go somewhere else. Up to Scotland. Down to Rome..."

"I can't. You know I can't. You don't seem to understand. I must get back to work. That's if my father hasn't given the job to someone else. It's different for you. You live in a world where people can take off for weeks on end. Where money isn't an issue."

Any day now, it would be over. We'd go back to being the people we used to be, leading the lives we always had. I'd return to my grimy town and stand in our stifling shop, being polite to rude customers while my father fussed away, repositioning furniture I'd arranged and tidying fabric books I hadn't had a chance to put away.

And Giselle would go back to her finishing school and attend glamorous parties with wealthy people. I could hardly complain – it had been the deal all along. And yet in those last couple of days I felt desperate to make every second count. I felt haunted by ghosts of men she'd meet in the future who would mean more to her than I did because they came from the same background and had more money. As the minutes ran out, I felt the future I'd glimpsed falling away.

"Why did you come here with me? Why don't you want your parents to meet me? Are you bored of me? Has this meant anything at all to you?"

Fists banging on the other side of the wall where one of the sisters slept brought me to my senses. "Is everything all right?"

"Fine," I shouted. "I'm sorry."

Giselle was very still in the darkness.

"I'm sorry," I said at last. "It's being here in this blank void, knowing I'll lose you. I don't recognise myself. This isn't me."

"Perhaps it is. Perhaps it's more 'you' than you realise," she said, dropping her chin onto her drawn-up knees.

"What's that supposed to mean?"

A shaft of moonlight slanted in through the window, illuminating her pale skin. I couldn't see her face because it was curtained by her hair.

"Love and jealousy are sometimes hard to tell apart."

"All right, so I'm jealous. It isn't fun, you know. It's painful – it feels like being poisoned. And it's a horrible thing to admit to. But the truth is I can't imagine my life without you."

Her voice was low and quiet.

"Stop. Forget you met me. Go back to how you were."

"How I was?" I laughed. "You really don't understand, do you?"

She was still for a long time. When she spoke again her voice sounded distant. "There are things you don't know about me, Jack. Things it would be better not to know."

Chapter Eight

"What things?"

She shook her head.

"What things?"

She didn't answer, just sat there on the bed, biting her lip. Tears leaked from her closed eyes. I pulled her towards me. She was stiff at first, trying to control her emotion but finally she buried her head in my chest and clung to me like a child.

"When you first met me, and I told you I was running away, that was true."

"What are you talking about?"

"I should never have come back to England. I don't know what I was thinking of."

She pulled the eiderdown around her shoulders. "I had no intention of going home. I meant to stay with a friend in London but when I rang from the station her parents told me she was away. I didn't know what to do. Then I saw you and you invited me to the wedding."

"And it seemed convenient."

She gave that half smile. I nodded. It was what I'd suspected all along. I'd never been the real attraction.

"It's my father," she said at last. "I can never go back. I'll never be safe."

"What are you saying? I don't understand."

Explanations raced through my head—that her father would be furious with her for taking off with a man she hardly knew. That she'd stolen some money or damaged something precious. That the finishing school had thrown her out and he'd found out about it... But none of those things were believable.

"It's because of what I saw."

"What do you mean? What did you see?"

"Everyone thinks it was an accident," she whispered. "But he killed her. And he knows I saw."

"Killed? Sorry, who killed who?"

"My mother. He killed her and he'll kill me too if he gets the chance."

Silence crackled between us. "What are you talking about? None of this makes any sense. Your mother's fine, isn't she?" Only yesterday, Giselle had been telling me one of her funny stories and I'd laughed along.

"No, Jack. She's dead."

"But you didn't say any of this before. Your family sounded so nice."

Even as I said the words I realised how stupid they were. No family's perfect, no childhood is as idyllic as the picture Giselle had painted.

She looked up at me, anguished. "That's because I wanted everything to be normal again. I wanted to forget."

When I thought back to all the things she'd said about her father, the picture I'd formed of a genial man who'd fought bravely in the war and despite debilitating injuries had always been kind and gentle... Now she was telling me he was a brute who'd killed his wife and would kill his own daughter if he got the chance.

I had no idea what to say. In all the time we'd spent together there'd been no hint. Or had there? Had Giselle's dream meant something after all? Was that why she was so scared of those men we saw on the train? Did it explain her reaction to finding that the person spying on us in the farmhouse was only the landlord? Or was she making this up? Did she even know what was true anymore?

All I could think of to say was, "He won't find you. I won't let him. Come back with me. You'll be safe, I promise. We'll go to the police together and get it all sorted out."

She shook her head. "You don't understand. The police won't believe us. Or if they do, they won't help us. He's a powerful man. He has people out looking for me. You aren't safe either while you're with me."

"I don't care about that. Come back with me. He'll never find you. I won't let him."

It all sounded so far-fetched. I wasn't sure I believed it. But I couldn't help also feeling relieved that she didn't want to leave. I checked myself. What sort of person was I becoming? She'd just told me her father wanted to kill her.

And it had made me happy.

It was the suddenness of the end that shocked me. We fell asleep to the sound of rain streaming on the window and woke up to the sound of shovels in the yard. When I opened the window and looked out, the snow had gone from the trees and rooftops. The cold air stung my face but the sky was a serene blue. Down in the yard, Mr Allerton and the driver were clearing the track.

The bed was empty. I had a moment of panic wondering if Giselle had already left but after a few moments I saw her crossing the yard below and talking to Norland, the driver. They seemed to be having a disagreement about something. In the end, he shrugged and walked off.

The conversation from last night kept going through my head. Did I dream it? No, it was real. Giselle was coming back with me. I had no idea how or where we were going to live but we'd somehow find a way forward together. I had to find a way of keeping her safe.

I went down to the yard and gave the landlord a hand clearing the remains of the snow. With every scrape of the shovel, I knew I was bringing our time at the farmhouse closer to the end but now that Giselle would be coming with me it no longer mattered. I could hear the twins trying to get their car started with the surgeon's help. The engine groaned and coughed but finally came to life.

"What were you talking to Norland about?" I asked Giselle when the track was finally clear.

"He says it's havoc at the station. All the trains are delayed."

"We'd better get going then."

Neither of us mentioned our conversation during the night, but she seemed so much happier and more relaxed. As the car heaved its way up the track I took one last look at the farmhouse. It had returned to its dour state, stripped of magic. The sky was heavy with rain, which when unleashed would wash away the rest of the snow.

The driver seemed in a better mood than he had been when he picked us up. He was quite chatty, asking if we'd enjoyed our stay, where we were heading and wishing us luck with our journey. "You're in good time for the train," he said as he helped us out with our bags and pointed out the ticket office. "All the best."

Sitting on the train, watching the station retreat into the distance, the conversation of the previous night kept creeping back. I was desperate to ask Giselle about it but with other people sitting so close I'd have to wait. She seemed back to her usual playful self, asking questions and making observations about other passengers. I even wondered if I'd misunderstood in some way.

Around twenty minutes into the journey the train shuddered to a halt. The couple sitting opposite us got out at the bleak little station. A young man came running down the steps of the bridge opposite and shouted to the guard. The door slammed further up the train, but we didn't move.

I put my head out of the window. Nothing was happening. After another ten minutes, wondering what the reason for the delay could be and worrying we'd miss our connecting train, I went in search of the guard. I eventually found him near the front.

"Nothing to worry about. Go back to your seat. We'll be moving again soon." His explanation was drowned by another train huffing into the station on the opposite platform in a cloud of steam and screech of brakes, but he gestured that everything was fine.

I opened the door, then stopped in confusion. Had I got the wrong compartment? It was empty except for a man doing a crossword puzzle and an elderly woman opposite him who looked asleep. No sign of Giselle. I sat down, sure she'd turn up again at any minute. But as doors slammed up and down the train and the engine started to rumble, anxiety crept through me.

I tapped the sleeping woman gently on the shoulder. She sprang back, as though she thought I was trying to rob her or worse.

"I'm sorry, the young lady who was sitting in here—did she say where she was going?"

The woman blinked in confusion. "I've no idea who you mean."

I appealed to the man. He looked up from his crossword with an irritable grunt. "Can't say I noticed."

I went out into the corridor where a couple stood looking out of the window. They hadn't seen Giselle either, but had only just got on, they told me. And no, they hadn't noticed her on the platform.

I jumped out, asking the guard if he could wait a moment and pushed through the passengers on the platform. She must have got off the train for a reason, possibly to ask someone about the delay. Or another passenger had left something behind as they got off and she'd run after them to hand it back.

"Excuse me, a young lady, green coat. I think she just got off that train. Did you see her?"

They all denied it. Some didn't even bother to stop. I ran up to the end of the platform but there was no sign of her there. I crossed the bridge to where the other train had passed through and stood there like an idiot, staring in one direction and then another at the gleaming, empty rails stretching for miles into nothingness. There had to be an explanation.

I ran back down the platform and opened the door of the ticket office. A line of people turned and stared at me with blank expressions.

"Are you sure she didn't get on the other train, the one that's just left?" someone asked.

I tried to keep my patience. "No, she wouldn't have done that. We were on the right train, travelling together."

He shrugged. "Perhaps she realised she'd forgotten something and went back home for it."

The whistle blew and the guard stood with his flag raised,

looking at me expectantly. Something wasn't right. Something must have happened to her. Perhaps she'd fallen or been taken ill. I tried the door to the ladies' lavatory, ignoring the squawk from a woman applying her face powder in the mirror but it was empty.

"Are you getting back on or not?" shouted the guard.

I walked slowly towards the train. Where would I be most likely to find her, at the station or on the train? I'd already checked the train once but then I'd checked the station too. The train started to move. I jogged alongside it as it huffed, still not sure what to do.

"Make your mind up!" bellowed the guard.

Heads popped out of windows. Other passengers were shouting to me now. At the last moment I swung up onto the train. I walked up to the front and checked every carriage. How could she just disappear? I felt people's suspicious glances and was reminded of the two men we'd seen on our journey up peering into our compartment and how frightened Giselle had been.

It began to dawn on me that this wasn't just a simple misunderstanding. I hadn't paid enough attention to what she'd told me about her father. Why had I left her on her own? I searched the train again from end to end. It felt like a dream, looking frantically for something that was always just out of reach. I had to steel myself before each door. Remembering her words about her father sending people to look for her, I had nightmarish visions of finding her mutilated body slumped in an empty compartment.

At the next station, I jumped off and took the train back up to the original one where the driver had left us. The place was deserted. I tried the ticket office but it was closed. The whole place looked shut up, as if no one had been there for years. I ran everywhere looking for her and even went out to the front to see if by any chance the driver was there again picking up a new set of guests for Mr Allerton, but he wasn't. I tried calling the B&B in case Giselle had for some reason rung and left a message but there was no reply. The whole episode seemed unreal.

What had she said to me on the boat about chance encounters and how we'd been meant to meet so we could help each other? What if this was the way I was supposed to help her? If so, I'd failed. I had to put this right. Had to find her.

Chapter Nine

Someone gave me directions to the police station. I went along full of hope they'd point out something obvious that I'd overlooked. I'd end up feeling a fool and apologising for wasting their time but at least Giselle would be safe.

But the pot-bellied sergeant eyed me suspiciously as though I had nothing better to do than waste his time.

"Are you sure it wasn't just a misunderstanding?" he said.

"No, it's more serious than that."

I explained what she'd told me about her father. He sat back in his chair and scratched his moustache.

"You don't think she might have been pulling your leg?"

"I know she wasn't. If you'd seen her, you'd understand. She was terrified."

He shrugged. "We've had no reports of an accident in the area or a crime so I'm afraid there isn't much we can do."

"You're going to wait until something happens?"

He sighed, obviously deciding to humour me. "Let's take some details anyway. What's her name?"

"Giselle."

His pencil hovered over the paper. "Giselle...?"

"I don't know."

His eyebrows shot up. "You don't know her second name?"

I felt myself colour. I dropped my head, ran my hands though my hair. "Look, the point is she could be in danger."

"She's probably just gone home. Where does she live?"

"I don't know."

I suddenly realised how little I knew about her. I told him she was at a finishing school near Lake Geneva, but I had no idea which one.

He laid the pencil down and rubbed his eyes. "You don't know the name of the school? And you can't tell me her second name. It's going to be rather difficult."

I was losing patience. "The point is, she told me her life was in danger. And then she disappeared. Doesn't that sound suspicious to you?"

He shrugged, stifling a yawn. "Possibly. Although, it's just as likely she changed her mind and went back to school."

I closed my eyes. "Will you please listen to me? I think someone took her. I promised I wouldn't let her out of my sight and then I did."

He wrote down my details with a sigh and slapped his pen down on the notepad. "People have a right to disappear. We can't do any more at the moment. Go home. If we find anything we'll call you."

I couldn't accept she'd vanished. Why would she have agreed to come with me and then gone off in the opposite direction? Had she changed her mind? I couldn't leave, not while there was a chance she might still be there. I had a moment when I thought I might have dreamed the whole thing, taken something inadvertently and the whole two weeks had been part of some bizarre hallucination.

I took a taxi to the guesthouse just in case Giselle had gone back there for something she'd forgotten. Mr Allerton looked startled seeing me at the door.

"I didn't expect to see you again," he said, giving me one of his disconcerting stares. "What's happened?"

I explained the situation and he ushered me inside.

"Dear me, this is very worrying. Tell me what happened from the beginning."

At last, someone who had a little sympathy. It made me feel bad for suspecting him of snooping on us. It seemed obvious now that there must be another explanation. It also occurred to me that if I had got it wrong, my jealousy and paranoia could have put Giselle in danger, persuading her that the snoop was Mr Allerton when it had been one of her father's men.

He looked shocked and was all for ringing the police but I told him I'd already done so. "She's not been back but have a good look to put your mind at rest."

He let me check everywhere, even in her bedroom although it had been cleaned since we left. I opened the door full of blind hope she might have slipped back there. I sat on the bed trying to recapture her fresh scent, the sweetness of her breath, the silky touch of her skin, the silhouette of her body in the moonlight, the weight of it against mine as she'd cried before we left.

Nothing. The wardrobe was empty, the floor clear, the sheets changed. As though she'd never been here. But staring at the floor with my head in my hands, I became aware of something glinting. I slid off the bed, and knelt on the floor, putting my eye to the gap between the boards and there it was. Her ring. It must have fallen from the bedside cabinet during the night when she was so agitated. It took ages to get it out, but I had to have it. I tried first with a pen and then my comb, scrabbling like a grave robber. Several times I gave up and sat back on the bed but eventually I held it up to the light, then folded my hand around it.

"I'll let you know if I hear anything, of course," said Mr Allerton. "You'll stay tonight, will you? It's too late to get a train now, I'm afraid."

He offered me a drink and it seemed rude to refuse. We sat for hours talking. I went over and over what had happened until the alcohol fogged my brain too much to think any more. I must have fallen asleep at some point because I woke stiff and cold on the sofa with a blanket over me. I dreamed Giselle was sliding into bed beside me, stroking and kissing me and telling me everything was fine but each time I woke the room was dark and empty.

In the morning, I tapped on the kitchen door but there was no reply from Mr Allerton and no sign of breakfast being prepared. I had a quick look around outside, but he must have been up on the hill checking on the sheep. I thought about waiting for him but he'd probably be away for hours. Besides, I'd had enough of the place, so I picked up my bag and left.

Chapter Ten

A small part of me clung to the hope that Giselle might have somehow found her way to my house anyway but that thought died as soon as I let myself in at the kitchen door. My parents stared at me as though I'd returned from the dead.

"Jack," said my mother. "We've been worried sick about you."

The house seemed half the size I remembered even though I'd only been away a few days. The kitchen was full of steam and smelled of paraffin from the heater. An assortment of washing hung from the gantry above the table and the windows were clouded with condensation.

My father was sitting at the table with a newspaper spread out in front of him. "Where've you been?" he asked without looking up.

"What do you mean where have I been?"

"You heard."

"You know where. I told you I was going to Daphne's wedding—"

"Oh, the wedding! You should have been the one getting

married, not sitting there like the spectre at the feast. But that was nearly two weeks ago."

"I told you, I was snowed in."

"Snowed in? We haven't had a single flake here."

For a moment I felt relieved that Giselle wasn't with me in this claustrophobic space and didn't have to witness the row that was sure to erupt at any moment but then I remembered how serious her disappearance might be. I should be out there looking for her, not having this pointless conversation.

"How was the wedding anyway?" my mother asked.

"I don't know. I didn't go."

My father exploded. "You didn't even go?"

"I told you, I was snowed in."

"I don't understand why you wanted to go in the first place. To put a spanner in the works?"

"Of course not."

He gave a disbelieving snort. "Yes, well while you've been enjoying your little holiday, I've had to run the business without you. I hope you're not expecting to be paid for it. Did you even go to France?"

"Of course I went to France." I started telling him about the furniture factory.

"You don't know how lucky you are." He got up and paced round the room, stopping at intervals, and digging his knuckles into the table. "Most youngsters round here would kill for a job like the one I offered you instead of working down the pit or in the factories, but it wasn't good enough for you, was it?"

"I never said that."

"You didn't have to. It was written all over your face."

My mother busied herself putting on the kettle and sorting out the ironing.

"You always thought you were above everyone else, didn't you? I told you going to university was a waste of time, but you knew best. That degree was bloody useless. Didn't help you find a job—or not one you could hold on to. Five minutes with that London firm and you get yourself sacked..."

"I'd hardly put it that way. I was made redundant. It's happening everywhere at the moment. You must know that."

He put his face close to mine and said with a sneer, "Not to good workers. They don't get made redundant. When you got yourself kicked out, you came crawling back to me. I gave you the job you'd turned your nose up at and what happens? You go gallivanting off to god-knows-where leaving me high and dry."

The kettle whistled. My mother poured the tea and put it in front of us with a plate of biscuits as though we were having a convivial afternoon.

"That girl was no fool." He pointed his mug at me. "She's better off, married to someone who's prepared to make a go of things. So, that's another opportunity you wasted."

He sat down, removed his glasses, spat on a handkerchief, and rubbed them, then shovelled three spoons of sugar into his mug and slurped his tea. He thrust the Garibaldis at me and took offence when I declined.

Sitting there in that dismal room was bringing back memories of being a child, bending over this same table to receive a beating. He'd seemed so big and intimidating back then. Now he was much smaller than I was. One smack would send him flying.

Indignant rage swept through me as he ranted on. I told him I'd long ago given up trying to please him because I'd realised that I never could. He'd never tried to see things from my point of view, never accepted that I was different from him, interested in different things. He'd dismissed any ideas I had and made fun of any ambition.

He shouted back, his red face inches from mine, finger jabbing my chest, that he'd have gladly encouraged me in any sensible pursuit but how could he when I'd been useless at everything and could barely string two words together?

"Always liked to stir things up, didn't you? Made it clear you didn't want me around and upset your mam, making up spiteful stories instead of minding your own business."

I laughed at that. "Don't blame me for your marital problems. Any fool can see-"

"Stop! Just stop!" My mother crashed the iron down on the board, filling the room with a hissing cloud of steam. She tore off her apron and left the house, slamming the back door.

"Well done," he said quietly as he always did in these situations. "I hope you're proud of yourself."

We sat in silence in that dim room with the light flickering and the rain hissing outside, not looking at each other. Then he cleared his throat and said he'd never thought of himself as domineering. To him my reserve had seemed like arrogance or at best indifference and he'd only said things to provoke some sort of reaction. "All of them nights I spent in the trenches, I were desperate to get home. But when I got back, it was all different. I tried to connect with you but you rebuffed me every time. I felt redundant."

We had the longest conversation we'd ever managed and eventually agreed to try and see things from each other's point of view in future which was as close as either of us would get to an apology. He gave me my job back on condition I started looking for something else, which I fully intended to do anyway.

Besides, I wanted to concentrate on finding Giselle.

The uneasy truce lasted a couple of weeks. Sleeping in my old room that I'd shared with my sister Ellen for so many years, I felt lonely and claustrophobic. It still held reminders of different stages of our childhoods—my old adventure books and tin soldiers on the shelves, Ellen's swimming certificates on the wall and a drawer full of cigarette cards with pictures of famous cricketers.

I was desperate to find Giselle but the more I thought about it the more hopeless it seemed. I had so little to go on. I didn't know anything for sure about her. It was beginning to seem like a fantasy.

I saw her everywhere over the next few weeks—in cafés, parks, streets. Just glimpses, broken images, shadows, reflections, the sound of her voice, her laughter. But it was never really her. I called the police several times to check if they had any more information.

"No, sir. Please rest assured, we'll call you if we have any news."

I put an advertisement in *The Times*, planning to do the same each year on the anniversary of the day we met.

Giselle wherever you are, I will never stop loving you. Please get in touch if only to let me know you're all right. Jack

I took my camera film to be developed. When the pictures were ready to collect, I stood in the shop flicking through the shots of furniture and a few from the top of the cathedral in Nantes, holding my breath, not letting myself skip to the end, almost expecting the final picture to be missing or overexposed or to show someone else entirely.

So, it was a shock to see Giselle exactly as I remembered her, standing against the rail of the boat in her green coat. I stood and looked at it for ages. It brought back other things like the tilt of her head, the timbre of her voice, the sound of her laugh. It was the first confirmation that I wasn't going mad and hadn't invented the whole episode as the police seemed to think. It had happened. She looked so lovely, so laughingly alive, so unquestionably real.

As soon as I could afford the fare, I took the train back up to the station where she'd disappeared. I walked up and down the track, along the footpath and surrounding area. Every now and then I'd think I glimpsed her. My heart would jolt with hope but when I got closer, I asked myself how I could have made that mistake.

I showed her picture to people at the station, in pubs, and the street. Most of them didn't even bother looking properly. Some put their greasy fingers on the print, and I had to ask them to be more careful. They all denied seeing her. It was as though they all knew something, were part of a conspiracy to pretend she'd never existed.

I rang the B&B to ask Mr Allerton if he'd heard anything from her but there was no reply. I thought about visiting him but concluded it would be a wasted journey and in any case, after everything that had happened, I was reluctant to return to that place.

Back home, I wrote her a letter, the first of hundreds I'd write over those next few months. I couldn't send them because I had no address, but it made me feel a connection with her. One day, I'd be able to show them to her to prove I had been looking. I had still cared.

April 1931

... I have your ring. If nothing else, I'd like to return it to you. I wish you'd get in touch. I've tried everything but no one seems to be taking this seriously. The police have done nothing to help. I'm so angry and frustrated. I want you to know that I will never give up. I will find you. All I want is to know what happened to you and if you are safe.

Jack

The following weekend I went down to London to see an old college friend. I can't pretend I liked him much, but I had to give it a try because if anyone could nose out the truth about someone Harry Winterton could.

He breezed down the steps of his newspaper office in a three-piece striped suit, looking like he was born into the role. His hair gleamed gold and his moustache was clipped into two slick lines.

"Well, well, Sanders, good to see you," he said, clapping me on the back. I let him talk as we walked down the busy street about the day he was having, the news stories he was working on and the useless people he had to work with.

I'd always known Harry would be a good journalist. He enjoyed the power of knowing more about other people than they knew about him. At college, I'd discovered a set of files he kept on fellow students, including me, and was shocked by the level of detail although he insisted it was an entirely innocent *aide memoir*.

He took me to a private club down an alley near his office, an ancient building full of shadowy nooks where I could imagine secrets being sold and reputations ruined over a few drinks.

"We missed you at Daph's wedding," he shouted above the chatter as we stood at the bar. "Awful bore about the snow although we ended up having quite a house party. Could you really not make it, or did you have second thoughts about seeing her marry Douglas so soon after she ditched you?"

"Not at all," I said. "I'm very pleased for Daphne."

I could tell from his superior smile he didn't believe me. We collected our drinks and moved through a curtain of smoke to some tub chairs in a quiet corner.

"So, what's this business you wanted to discuss?" He spread his arm over the back of the chair. "Not in any trouble, are you?"

"No. But I'm afraid someone else might be."

He raised his eyebrows, and his eyes glinted with hope of a scandal. I told him about Giselle, what she'd told me about her father and how she'd disappeared.

"Lovely girl," he said, looking at the photograph.

"Yes, she is."

I caught him staring at me in that bemused way he had.

"What?"

He smiled and shook his head. "You haven't changed, have you? Always after the unattainable. If you set your sights a little lower, you might have more luck."

He had always thought it his role to advise me, perhaps because I was the only person he felt superior to at Cambridge. The truth was, he didn't belong there any more than I did, he was just better at hiding it.

You always knew when he'd caught you out passing the port to the right or cutting the nose off a cheese—not by anything he said but by a snide little look he gave. He'd hold your gaze just long enough to let you know he'd spotted it, and his lips would twitch into that mirthless smile. Much later he might bring it up in a chummy anecdote and watch you squirm.

"So, we're looking for a girl whose surname you don't know and whose first name may well not be her real one?" he said, sticking a cigarette in the corner of his mouth and lighting it. "You don't make things easy, do you? But look, she can't have vanished into thin air. Either she doesn't want to be found, or she isn't able to get in touch. I know you won't want to hear this, old boy, but my hunch is the former. She gave you the slip. Best to forget about it."

"I can't."

He narrowed his eyes. "Look, it's not that unusual is all I'm saying. She's probably just moved on to have fun with someone else."

"Perhaps. But I need to know. I need to be sure she's safe."

He sighed in a long-suffering way. "You must have at some stage asked where this grand house of hers was?"

I had of course but she'd given vague answers like "in the sticks" or "the back of beyond" and the talk had passed on. It was how all our conversations had been—a race to reveal things and find answers to things and even then, you were often left afterwards with a heap of questions you didn't know the answers to.

"Are you sure she didn't take anything from you?" he asked.

"Of course not."

"And you didn't lend her any money?"

"No."

"Didn't it occur to you to look inside her passport to see if she was who she said she was?"

I tried to conceal my irritation. "Why would I have done that?"

He shook his head and sucked his teeth. "Well, if you had you wouldn't be having this conversation, would we? Without a second name it's hopeless." He downturned his mouth, considering. "Well, almost hopeless. If her father's really a baronet, he'll be in *Burke's Peerage* with his offspring—at least the legitimate ones. You'll have to go through the whole thing looking for one who has a daughter called Griselda."

"Giselle, for god's sake."

He shrugged. "At least it's an unusual name. That might help. People will remember it."

He waved at someone across the room, sat back and crossed his legs.

"Then there's the school. There are dozens of them around Lake Geneva. Your best bet is to write to each one, but you'll have to be careful how you word it. They're very protective of their young ladies. They won't give information out to just anyone."

"Of course not. Can you get me a list of the schools?"

He flicked the cigarette and ran his hand through his hair. "Shouldn't be too difficult. But if you're not even sure of her name..."

"Yes, but surely if a girl has gone missing from one of the schools...?"

He threw his head back and blew a column of smoke up to the ceiling. "If she had we'd have heard about it, wouldn't we? There'd have been an outcry. It would be all over the newspapers, especially ours. Quite frankly we'd love a story about a beautiful society girl disappearing. Bit of intrigue amid all the economic woe. Are you sure you don't want me to run it?"

I shouldn't have been surprised by his lack of tact, but it still angered me. "I've told you her life might be in danger. It's the last thing she needs."

"All right. But if it turns out she isn't missing from any of the finishing schools you can be reasonably sure she either lied about being there in the first place or she's back there now using her real name, perfecting her vowels and creating pretty table settings or whatever it is they do."

I pulled out the tobacco tin holding Giselle's ring. "She left this behind."

His eyes widened. "May I?" He held it up to the light and sucked his teeth. "Good god, it must be worth a fortune. If she knows you have it there's a good chance, she'll come back. Not many girls would walk away from a gem like this. But I hate to point it out, old man, doesn't it look as though she's already engaged to someone else?"

I shook my head. "She said she'd had it since childhood."

He handed it back with some reluctance saying, "For god's

sake care of it. Look, if she's really top-drawer someone will know her, even if she did give you a made-up name. Everyone knows everyone in those circles. Can you get me a print of this photograph? I can make some discreet enquiries."

I hated the idea of Harry bandying Giselle's picture around and saying to people I used to know, "Remember poor old Sanders? He's way out of his depth." But it might just work. I had to let him try.

"What are you doing in June?" he asked as I was leaving. "A few of us are renting a castle in Amalfi. Fancy coming along?"

"Thank you. It sounds nice but I doubt I'll be able to make it."

"Too busy in the shop?" He gave a knowing wink.

Chapter Eleven

June 1931

Did I do something wrong? Did I drive you away? I feel ashamed looking back and remembering some of the things I said. I didn't know the right words for what I was feeling. I know we hardly knew each other. I didn't expect it to last, but I'd like to have at least had the chance to say goodbye.

What I really want to say is that I love you and miss you. Thank you for every moment we spent together. If you ever need me, even if it's many years from now, I will be here for you.

Jack

I saw them moving through the shop. They weren't ordinary customers. That was obvious from the way my father was standing, straight-backed, taut-eyed. He ran his thumb and finger down his moustache and looked back at me across the shop and then away again. Then he jerked his head, signalling for me to follow as he led them through to his office. I excused myself from a couple who wanted to buy a bed, inviting them to look round on their own for a few minutes.

"I'm sure Jack will help you in any way he can," I heard him say as I stepped into the office.

I detected a tremor in his voice as he shut the door behind me and sat down heavily. Typical of him to think I must be in trouble. The policemen looked at my father and then at me to check if I minded him staying. I saw no reason why he shouldn't.

"Have you found her?" I asked.

The inspector looked puzzled. "Found who? I think we're at cross purposes."

I sat down next to the window overlooking the street. A boy was chaining a bicycle up to a post outside the butchers and a queue of people was forming at the bus stop.

My father sighed. He opened the door a crack and signalled to one of the girls to bring some tea. The office felt smaller than usual with so many people in it. Through the glass I could see customers milling around the furniture, sale opportunities being lost, but my father seemed not to notice.

The inspector opened a briefcase, removed a photograph, and slid it across the desk to me.

"Did you know this person, sir?"

Instinct told me to brace myself but even so, I jumped at the sight. It took a few moments to understand what I was looking at. The face was a ghastly mess. The head was oddly misshapen, the eyes were dark, bloody hollows, and the mouth stretched into an agonised grimace. My first response was that the face wasn't familiar. Relief washed through me in because I wasn't looking at Giselle, as I was expecting.

But gradually as I adjusted my gaze to see beyond the bruises and swelling and caked blood, I realised who I was looking at. Bile shot up.

"Well?" he said. "Have you seen him before?"

I could feel my father's eyes on me and hear him breathing through his mouth. *Speak up, son.* Beyond the glass a few customers were eyeing up sofas and coffee tables or flicking through wallpaper books, looking around for help, getting impatient.

I nodded slowly, still struggling to accept this was real. "I think so, yes." I pressed my thumb between my eyes. "His name's Allerton. Gerald Allerton."

"And how did you know him?"

"I didn't know him well. He ran a guesthouse in Northumberland."

"He did indeed." He consulted his notebook and gave the name of the village. "I believe you stayed there from the third to the thirteenth of April this year?"

I nodded, my heart thumping. The inspector's finger hovered above the photograph, drawing my attention to the injuries and how they appeared to have been sustained. I didn't want to look but found it impossible not to. It kept drawing me back.

The poor man had endured a prolonged, ferocious attack. There was significant bruising to the body and some tissue under his fingernails suggesting he'd put up a strong defence. But in the end his assailant had overpowered him, and his head had been staved in with a blunt instrument. At some point—there seemed to be some question over whether this occurred before or after death—a corrosive substance had been thrown at or poured onto the victim's face, causing burns to the eyes and surrounding skin.

The inspector leaned back in his chair, watching me. He lit his pipe, shook out the match and took a long draw and several puffs. My sternum felt crushed as though I'd been shot in the chest.

"You look pale," he said.

I'd never seen a dead body—at least not anyone I'd known, or who'd met such a brutal end. I kept trying to associate the mild-mannered farmer with this grotesque image in front of me.

"How...who...?"

But it was already sinking in, the purpose of this interview.

There was a gentle tap on the door and we heard the rattle of the tea tray. My father sprang up, opened the door a crack and tried to send the girl away but the inspector looked disappointed. "I quite fancy a cuppa, don't you?" he said to his sergeant.

He turned the photograph over and we waited in silence while the girl poured the tea and handed the cups round, eyes down. Whether she had any idea what was going on I didn't know. The police waited for her to leave the room before resuming.

"What was your reason for staying at the farm?"

I told him about the wedding and the snow.

He frowned. "So, you invited someone you'd never met before to accompany you to this wedding which you didn't go to in the end, and you then spent another ten days together at the guesthouse?"

"We were snowed in. We didn't have a choice. The driver couldn't get the car out to us and the trains weren't running."

The policemen looked at each other. "Our enquiries show that the trains were running again from the sixth," said the sergeant.

I saw my father's body tense.

"You see, from the information we've been given you were the last person to see Mr Allerton alive."

"What? No, that's ridiculous. He was fine when I left."

Sweat broke out on my forehead.

"What time did you leave on the twelfth?"

"I can't remember. Quarter-past nine? The train went at ten or just before."

"And you caught that train, did you?"

"Yes."

He looked confused. "But your father's just confirmed you didn't come home until the following day. According to a witness you returned to the guesthouse on your own. Would you care to explain why?"

I had to think straight. "Yes, I did. In the afternoon, around four or five. To look for someone. The girl I'd been staying with. She disappeared. I explained all this to the police up there."

I told them about Giselle, what she'd said about her life being in danger and how she'd vanished from the train and how I'd gone to the police for help but received none. Perhaps today's misunderstanding would turn out to be a good thing because it would alert a more active set of police to Giselle's disappearance.

"And did you find her?"

"No."

"You went all the way back in person. Couldn't you have used a telephone?"

"I wanted to look for myself."

"You didn't trust Mr Allerton?"

"I didn't say that."

"And you used the same driver?"

"No, I rang a number from an advertisement at the station. I thought it would be quicker to use someone local."

I could feel my father's eyes burning into me. He must have been wondering why this was the first he'd heard of Giselle and her disappearance.

"Whoever did this to Mr Allerton was probably after Giselle," I told them. "I'm very worried about her."

The inspector raised his eyebrows. "Really? Because rather

than go out looking for her you then spent the night with Mr Allerton, didn't you? Had a few drinks?"

I started to answer but he cut in. "Let me tell you what I think. That you made a show of leaving on the twelfth, then returned when you thought the other guests would have left..."

"No, that is not what happened."

"Then I suggest you enlighten me," he said quietly. He drew on his pipe and sat back in his chair, waiting.

I fumbled for a cigarette in my jacket pocket but had difficulty disguising the shaking in my hands as I lit it. "I had to stay another night because there weren't any more trains that day."

I saw them exchange glances.

The sergeant looked back through his notebook. "There was a later train you could have caught. The five forty-five."

I shrugged helplessly. I hadn't checked but then why wouldn't I have taken Mr Allerton at his word? I kept looking back at the photograph and remembering what Giselle had said about me not being safe while I was with her. This could have been me lying there.

Had her father sent someone to the farmhouse to look for her, found Gerald Allerton and tortured him to find out where she was? My stomach curdled as another thought struck.

What had he told them before he died?

I looked across at my father, sitting hunched in his chair. I pictured my mother doing the ironing, alone in the house. Had I put my family in danger by coming home?

"This Giselle... There's no mention of her in the booking record."

"I don't know why that is. I suppose Mr Allerton didn't get round to changing it."

They asked for her details, expressing surprise that I could tell them so little.

"You were together for ten days. And yet you don't know much about her, do you?"

It was hopeless. I couldn't make them understand even if I wanted to that we hadn't wanted to know too much about each other. It was never about the world outside. Those things didn't matter. At least they'd seemed not to.

"How was the landlord when you went back to the guest-house?" asked the sergeant.

"Alive and well."

"Don't shout at me. He was pleased to see you, was he?"

I shrugged. "Probably not, but at least he was polite. More helpful than anyone else has been."

"What's your opinion of him?"

I spread my hands. "I really didn't know him that well. Considering none of us had intended to stay that long he was a good host."

"Did you fall out for any reason?" the inspector asked. He eyed me shrewdly, puffing at his pipe.

I looked straight at him. "I know what you're suggesting. Do you really think I'd have stayed the night there if I'd killed him?"

His dark eyes bored into mine. "I'm not suggesting anything. I'm asking. And you haven't answered my question."

My father said quietly, "Answer it, Jack." He was slumped like a mechanical toy that had wound down.

"No. Of course I didn't."

My father cleared his throat. "All right. I'm sure Jack's told you all he knows. Now if..."

As though he hadn't heard him, the inspector continued, "What I'm having difficulty understanding is that none of the other people we've spoken to remembers seeing Mr Allerton after you left. And a witness saw you leaving the farm in a hurry at around eight o'clock the following morning. Why the rush? You had plenty of time for the train."

I pressed my head against the window. Down below in the street the butcher's van had pulled up and pig carcasses were being unloaded.

"Are you going to answer me?"

I explained that I left early because I hadn't wanted to spend any more time in that wretched place when I could be looking for Giselle.

He raised his eyebrows. "And you're telling me you didn't see Mr Allerton to say goodbye?"

"No. I've told you. Look, this is ridiculous!"

"Do you always have such difficulty controlling your temper? I'm afraid I'm going to have to ask you to answer some more questions down at the station."

"What? No. This is absurd."

"It would be best to come quietly," said the sergeant.

The last thing I remember is my father sitting with his head in his hands, too ashamed to look at me as I was escorted through the shop floor and out into the car.

I'd seen inside cells during my degree course and had even played at imagining what it must be like to spend time in one, but I'd never seriously considered being on the wrong side of the law. They took my fingerprints and made me turn out my pockets and hand over my wallet and cigarettes. I sat on the low bunk looking around me at the tiled walls and the locked door, going over and over it all in my head. I'd never felt so abandoned.

I thought about sleeping but noises from the neighbouring cells jolted me awake.

A drunkard was screaming obscenities and throwing himself against the door of his cell. An aristocratic voice shouted,

"You're making a huge mistake. Just you wait till my lawyer gets here!"

I found myself permanently on edge. The hardest part was not knowing when they'd be coming back, what they'd ask, what piece of evidence they'd produce, whether they'd try the soft approach next time or scream threats at me or beat me into confessing to some appalling deed. I knew my rights but did any of these people care about rights?

Mr Allerton's face haunted me, the way it had looked in that photograph. I kept thinking about those injuries, trying to imagine what it must have felt like to be on the receiving end of that brutal attack.

I lost all sense of time. I must sleep, or I wouldn't be able to keep a clear head and would trip myself up and say things I didn't mean but I was afraid to drop my guard in case they wrenched me out of that sleep.

I kept running through everything. It did look bad. I had no convincing reason for having returned to the guesthouse and no one to back up my story about Giselle.

I couldn't stop wondering what the landlord's last moments must have been like. That of course led to me thinking of Giselle in the same state. Where was she? Why hadn't she got in touch? Had whoever killed the owner got to her?

The police asked about the other guests and the staff, what they'd looked like, what they'd said. Trying to remember details was exhausting and frustrating. As my anger subsided, the full extent of the trouble I was in began to dawn on me. If I couldn't persuade them that I hadn't killed the landlord, I would hang for it. Of course, theoretically I was innocent until proven guilty, but my studies had taught me the police weren't above corruption and that you could prove almost anything you wanted, given the right set of circumstances. There seemed no way out.

Chapter Twelve

I made things worse for myself due to fear, hunger, and lack of sleep.

"Why aren't you listening to me? Whoever killed that poor man is still out there. Why aren't you looking for him instead of trying to trip me up with stupid questions? I'm trying to tell you about a girl who has quite possibly met the same fate."

"You haven't given us a plausible explanation of why you made it look like you were leaving but then you came back when you knew everyone else had gone."

"I keep telling you! How many times do I have to say it?"

Stay calm, I kept telling myself, but I couldn't stop shaking. I was making a mess of this. I wanted to scrub everything out and start again but I knew that wasn't possible. I had to persuade them about Giselle's disappearance. It had never been more important.

"Has your temper got you into trouble before?"

"No."

He frowned. "Hmm. Mrs Daphne Fairley says she was frightened of you on occasion."

"That's nonsense. You've been talking to Daphne? Why?"

"To find out what sort of person you are. She says you attacked her husband at *The Eagle* pub in Cambridge a few months back."

I put my head in my hands. "I hit him once. I found out he'd been sleeping with my fiancée. I'd had a few drinks and so had he. Is that so surprising?"

"Do you normally hit people when you're angry?"

"No. I honestly can't remember another time."

What else had Daphne told them and who else had they been talking to? I could imagine my old friends discussing the grisly business between themselves.

There was always something about him.

But it was Daphne who disappointed me most. It was completely unfair of her. After all, Douglas had got his own back. His father had a word with my employers, and I'd been dismissed the following day.

I tried to appeal to their logic. "If I'd killed Mr Allerton, why would I walk into a police station to report Giselle's disappearance, and tell them where I'd been staying, knowing they'd find the body?"

He raised his brows as though it was for me to give the answer.

"And why would I want to kill him? What could I have had against him?"

They exchanged looks.

"Hmm, these for a start."

I felt myself tense as the inspector spread some photographs on the desk in front of me. I had to look closely to convince myself this was really happening. There were dozens of pictures of me. Most were innocuous shots of me walking, sitting, standing in the snow.

But some had been taken at the most intimate moments. I

felt the hairs on my neck stand up as I recognised the eaves window of Giselle's room.

I thought about the space in front of the fire where we'd made love and the window where we'd stood naked, watching the snow believing no one could see us. And the footprints in the snow outside the barn opposite. I remembered the wink of light and realised now it had been a camera lens. I'd been right all along. Mr Allerton had been watching us making love. Giselle had been cut out of some of the pictures and in those that were left she was too indistinct and shadowy to be recognisable. But it was finally sinking in that it had never been her the landlord was watching. It was me.

There were even pictures that must have been taken that last night when the drink—or whatever substance he'd added to it—had knocked me unconscious. So that was what he got up to in the locked room in the cellar that smelled of chemicals – developing pictures.

"You don't remember these being taken?"

I felt my face burn and brought my hands up to my head. "No. Never."

"You're saying this isn't you?"

"Yes. No. I'm saying I knew nothing about it."

The inspector sighed. "You see, it's making me wonder if this tale about a young lady who nobody else remembers seeing is really a cover story for a different kind of relationship. One with Mr Allerton. One perhaps that you had second thoughts about, knowing it was not only immoral but illegal. Perhaps you felt ashamed."

"No. That's not true."

Silence hung between us.

"May I have a glass of water?"

"No."

"Why don't you ask the other guests...the twins. Mr Benson. The young couple we met on the first night..."

He shook his head. "There's no record of any of those people staying at the guesthouse. If you can produce them, I'll happily talk to them."

"They were there!"

"So, you keep saying. What are you suggesting? That a group of septuagenarians set on Mr Allerton and killed him?"

"No, of course not."

What was the point? Remembering how they'd whispered about us and the way I'd spoken to them, I doubted the other guests would be interested in helping me now. They might even make things worse.

My lawyer took a defeatist attitude from the start. He had the air of someone who'd seen it all before.

"The best thing would be to plead guilty to manslaughter and then we'll see what we can do about getting the sentence down."

"I'm not doing that. I didn't do anything."

He continued as though he hadn't heard. "We need to appeal to the jury's sympathy. It was a crime of passion. Tragic to see a young man's life ruined for the sake of one awful but momentary loss of control. You have no previous convictions, whole life ahead of you. Strong morals, quick reactions. You didn't welcome his advances. Tried to rebuff him. Just saw red, did you? We'll see about arranging bail while the defence case is prepared."

"But that isn't what happened. You're not allowed to tell me what to say. I tell you, there's a girl out there who could confirm everything if only someone would make an effort to look for her."

He sucked his teeth. "Let's leave the girl out of things for now. Best get this business out of the way. You can resume your enquiries about her later if you find you still want to. Most importantly, try and stay calm. It won't do you any good to get worked up about things.

"That's easy for you to say. You're not the one accused of murder. Don't you see, she could back up my story? She can explain everything."

"Hmm, I'm not so sure. Because it doesn't alter the fact you were seen coming back on your own. You could have been in cahoots and done the crime together. Or if we do convince the court she was with you but are then unable to produce her as a witness people are bound to start wondering what happened to her as well, aren't they?"

"Are they? If I'd harmed her, why would I have spent these last weeks trying to track her down?" What hope was there if I couldn't even convince my own lawyer? This useless man was all that stood between me and the gallows,

My chances of coming out of this alive looked slim.

They played games. Sometimes the inspector would seem apologetic, asking questions as a matter of routine. At others he'd shout in my face, hit me, or slam my head against the wall, accusing me of the worst brutality.

I began to see myself through their eyes: worthless. I even bizarrely began to see them as my only real friends, my only chance of survival, although I knew they had the power to send me to my death. And I supposed my behaviour alternated as well. At times I was meek, co-operative, eager to please, at others, belligerent, foolhardy, my own worst enemy. None of it mattered anyway. I wasn't in control of my destiny.

In my weakest moments, I even began to question if I could have done it. If I could have killed the landlord and even Giselle as they suggested and suppressed the memory. I knew from my studies that such things were possible. I saw it all play out in my head, awaking from a trance and seeing her mutilated body lying there in front of me. But I continued to deny it.

None of it seemed to get through. They took whatever I said and twisted it. In the end, they charged me with murder. My lawyer told me he'd done what he could, but bail was out of the question for such a violent crime.

"I'm afraid your fingerprints were found on the shovel that was used to smash the victim's skull."

"The shovel? Well, of course my prints are on it. I used it to clear the snow."

He nodded thoughtfully.

"There must be other prints too," I told him.

"There may well be," he said, although he didn't seem hopeful. "It's the ethanoic acid poured into the man's eyes that's particularly hard to explain. Such a calculated act."

"For god's sake, I don't even know what that is."

A month passed and then another. Alone in the dark I revisited some of the questions Giselle had asked as we watched the snow pile up against the window, blocking out the world.

"Would you prefer to live forever or die a hero?"

"Would you choose to go to Heaven or live on Earth forever?"

I kept writing to her. They took the letters off me, said they might be needed in the future, but it didn't really matter because in writing them down I was writing them into my memory. Everything that happened there has stayed with me. Even so, I reproduced the letters when I had the chance because

I was still hoping that one day I'd be able to show her the story from start to finish.

It's killing me not knowing where you are, what you're thinking or whether you'll ever see this letter. I hate myself for letting you go. And yet if you're safe, I don't understand why you haven't you come to help me.

I don't know how I deserve this. Did I misunderstand everything? Perhaps it was different for you – a bit of fun between moments that mattered in your life whereas for me it was everything.

Remember you said to me once "Tell me who you are"? Well, you tell me. Who are you? Because I don't care anymore. If you'll tell the police what really happened, you're welcome to get on with the rest of your life.

Please help.

Jack

"You've got a visitor. A young lady."

My heart leapt. She'd come at last. Now everything could be sorted out. I held my breath.

"Hello, you."

I felt my smile freeze as my sister Ellen walked into the visiting room. Her own smile faltered.

"You don't look very pleased to see me. Were you expecting someone else?"

"Sorry. I'm delighted to see you. It's just—"

"Are we allowed to hug?"

The officer pointed to the rules on the wall. "Once now, once at the end. No touching in between."

Ellen's warmth and gentleness and the softness of her hair made tears prick my eyes.

"You poor thing, you look such a mess," she whispered.

I managed a smile. "Thank you for that."

She cleared her throat. "I brought you some books and your favourite lemon cake. I had to leave them with the staff." She bit her lip. "Dad doesn't know I'm here. He's banned us all from seeing you, but I promised Mum I'd find out how you were."

"Well, as you can see, not brilliant. Look, I didn't—"

"I know you didn't. And it will all get sorted out. I know it's hard to imagine now but, in the future, we'll look back at all this and laugh. It will be a story to entertain people at dinner. I just wish there was something I could do to help."

I thought about it. "Maybe there is. Could you find someone for me? A girl called Giselle."

I told her as much as I could in the time we had. "So, you see I blame myself. If I'd paid more attention to what she told me, if I hadn't left her alone on that train—"

"But how will I find her?" she asked helplessly.

"I don't know. There must be a way."

I gave her instructions for where in my room to find the photograph I'd taken of Giselle.

"You know I'll do whatever I can," she said.

"You look so well," I told her and as she got up, I saw why.

"Yes. I'm having a baby. So, you must come out soon because we want you to be godfather."

I smiled. "Dad's not going to like that."

"It's not up to him."

"Well, thank you, I'm honoured."

But I almost choked on the words because I couldn't see how it would happen. It was getting harder to imagine being part of the outside world again where people did normal things like attend christenings. Would I even live long enough to see the baby?

"You mustn't worry," she said as she left. "We'll get you out of here."

I so wanted to believe her, but it was getting harder to imagine how.

At my lowest moments it even crossed my mind Giselle might have killed the landlord. It was just conceivable she'd returned to the B&B after I'd left. Perhaps because she realised she'd lost the ring. It was far too valuable to leave behind. If she'd asked Allerton, he might have denied seeing it. She might think he'd stolen it. He'd be affronted. They'd have a row. He could have lost his temper and struck her, and she could have killed him in self-defence. But to pour acid into someone's eyes... That wasn't self-defence. That was a whole new level of horror that required cold-blooded planning. Could she have done that? How could anyone do that?

Her screams tore through my head when I was alone in the cell, reminding me of her nightmare. What had she been through in the past? What had really happened with her parents? Who was she?

I wasn't going to put the idea to the police that she might be to blame although it might be the only way of ensuring someone actually started looking for her. I didn't really expect her to put her own life in danger by coming forward and confessing to the crime, alerting her father to her presence. But I'd have given anything just to know where she was. Each day that passed left me feeling more desperate and alone.

. . .

Help me. At least write! Say something. I'm so scared, so lonely. I will hang for this. Is that what you want? Was it your plan all along?

But as the days merged with each other and my situation became more hopeless I felt abandoned and grew more certain Giselle had left of her own accord.

I know you'll never see this letter so I can say what I want. So, why me? Was I an easy target? Was it all a game to you? Did you despise me that much? What did you ever want?

Jack

Chapter Thirteen

It ended as suddenly as it began. When the officer told me they were dropping the charges I sat there wondering if it was a joke.

"Why? What's happened?"

He rolled his eyes. "Just be grateful and be on your way. You'll find out in good time if you keep an eye on the papers."

They gave me back my things, but the clothes no longer felt like mine. Stepping back into the world, I experienced none of the euphoria I'd envisaged, only numbness. I was a changed person, suspicious of everyone, frightened of what their intentions might be. It had all happened so quickly. One minute I'd been on the right side of the law, the next heading for the gallows. If it had happened once, it could happen again at any time.

My father refused to have me back in the house so I walked down road after road with no real idea of where I was going, thinking all the buildings looked flimsy, as though they were made of cardboard and would collapse at the slightest kick. I didn't know what to do or where to go. Everything around me seemed chaotic. The traffic was moving so quickly. I was getting in everyone's way. A bus swung round the corner, and I thought maybe it will hit me, maybe it won't.

I went into a dismal bar and drank one whisky after another, watching people laughing and clapping each other on the back. I caught sight of myself in the mirrored wall behind the bar and was shocked by my pallor and the dark shadows beneath my eyes. Around me people were singing and shouting and someone kept responding to bad jokes with a silly, high-pitched giggle. A group of young men tried to outdo each other with crude comments about the barmaid, which she returned with mock admonishments instead of giving them the response they deserved.

I must have said something. Probably a lot of things. My main recollection is of being picked up and dragged outside. I woke up in the gutter in the early hours of the morning, face pressed into the dank cobbles and the smell of blood and vomit in my nostrils. Perhaps I fell asleep again or perhaps it happened straight away, but I heard a voice in my ear.

"Stop looking for her. Keep out of things you don't understand."

I struggled to my feet, peering into the dawning light but the street was deserted.

I imposed on a series of old friends, staying as long as their patience could stand which was usually no more than a week. The time passed in an alcoholic blur. I drank too much, got into fights, threw up in the street, gambled money I didn't have and found myself waking up in strange places with women I didn't know or care about. I knew I was losing control, and I was frightened I would get to a place where I couldn't get back up again but I didn't know how to stop.

In a short telephone conversation with my mother, I learned several things had changed in the time I'd been away, one of these being that Ellen's husband had found a new teaching post in a place called Tonbridge, so they were moving down south. It was a blow because there was nobody else who understood me so well, or to whom I could talk about Giselle.

I wouldn't have gone back to my father's shop even if he'd agreed to have me back, but I had to find something. I was desperate for money, chiefly to fund my drinking. There was so little work about I couldn't afford to be fussy. Having to explain away the gap in employment while I'd been in custody made it even harder. I'd have to take whatever I could get.

Eventually I found a job at a building firm. After the slum clearance, new houses were shooting up – decent homes with two or three bedrooms, an indoor bathroom, and a good-sized garden. The work was tedious, I found myself taking orders from people who had been dunces at school, and my body ached all over in the evenings after all the lifting but there was plenty of overtime, so I'd eventually be able to pay for a room of my own.

During the monotonous work I tried to chase away thoughts of the landlord's murder but scenarios still flashed through my mind. I scoured the papers for news of the killer. Whoever it was must have cheered when they learned I'd been arrested, thinking they'd got away with it. They probably sent the police after me in the first place. Anger simmered inside me. I had to find out who they were.

Day after day, I checked the personal columns for any word from Giselle but there was nothing. Desperation sometimes tricked me into seeing encrypted messages inside innocuous birth and anniversary announcements, but I held onto just enough sanity to stop myself believing these.

Eventually, I found digs in a townhouse by the bus station.

It was a chilly, dismal room and I was kept awake by people shouting, running, and slamming doors inside the building, and the buses pulling in and out.

I wrote letters to Giselle although my fingers were often too numb to write clearly. I resorted to wrapping my feet in my scarf. After a few weeks I bought a typewriter off a man in a pub and bashed out my thoughts, trying to ignore the hubbub of voices in the other rooms and the fights in the street below.

Would you have let me hang? That's what I need to know. I don't know what to think about you anymore. Whether I should feel heartbroken, guilty, or full of hate. Mostly what I feel is jealous because I'm not with you and someone else is...

Jack

I met Ellen in a park one evening after work. She was heavily pregnant and out of breath as she came through the trees to where I stood leaning on the railings by the duck pond.

"I was afraid I'd never see you again," she said, clinging to me.

I managed a smile. "You don't get rid of me that easily. You're the one who's going away."

She stood back, examining me. "But look what it's done to you. You're so thin. You're not looking after yourself."

"I'm fine. A lot better than when I last saw you."

I knew I wasn't fooling her.

"What happened?" she asked. "Why did they let you go?"

"I don't know. I suppose they found the real killer. Which is great of course. But it leaves me with questions that can never be answered. I've no way of knowing what happened to Giselle—if she left of her own accord or if she was taken. Whether by leaving her on her own for a few minutes I gave someone the opportunity to harm her. You see, I've always had this fear that one day I'd make some careless mistake that could turn out to be really serious and someone could die because of it."

Ellen looked away across the water to where some children were sailing boats. "Stop blaming yourself, Jack. I think the simple truth is, she left."

"What do you mean?"

She took a breath. "I promised you I'd find out what I could. I went up to the station where you lost her and showed people that photograph you took."

"And?"

"And it took a long time but eventually I met a woman who said she recognised her."

"What woman? Why didn't you tell me this before?"

"Because I didn't think it would help. The woman remembered catching the train the same day you did. She was visiting her mother for her birthday. She remembered someone who looked like Giselle sitting in the carriage with two elderly women who looked like sisters.

"Elderly sisters? What did they look like? Did she hear any names?"

My heart froze as I thought back to the strange little group at the farmhouse and the dream, I'd had in which I'd seen them escorting her away. But why would those sisters be on the train? They had a car. And why would Giselle have gone anywhere with them? We had spent most of our time trying to avoid them. Or had she known them better than I thought? Had it all been prearranged?

Ellen shrugged apologetically. "That's all she said. Except that she thought Giselle looked upset. Something about a man bothering her. And the two ladies were reassuring her."

"Who is this woman? I need to speak to her."

"I asked her name, but she became suspicious and took off. She must have thought I was a journalist or a detective. I went after her, but I can't move fast in this state. I'm sorry, Jack. I'm not much good at this sort of thing."

"No, you did well. Thank you."

I was still reeling from the news that Giselle – if it had really been her – had boarded another train in those moments I was away. And with those people. Why would she have chosen them over me?

"It doesn't make sense," I said at last. "Why tell me her father was out to kill her and agree to come back with me if she was already planning to go with the others?"

Ellen shrugged. "Perhaps she had second thoughts?" She looked away. "You don't think it's strange her disappearance coincided with that man's death?"

"I've thought about it," I said, "but she had no reason to harm Mr Allerton. She liked him. And even if she'd wanted to, I don't see how she could have overpowered him. She was quite strong for her size, but he was a big man."

Ellen laid a hand on my arm. "But if what the woman at the station said is true it's good in a way, isn't it? If Giselle left of her own accord, she's probably alive and well. I know it's disappointing but at least you have nothing to feel guilty about."

I gripped the rail, watching one duck chase away another. "Unless she suspected the sisters would come after her? And that's why she asked to travel with me."

"It didn't sound like she was travelling with them against her will," Ellen pointed out gently. "And if she'd wanted to get in touch, she's had plenty of opportunity, hasn't she?"

She handed me back the photograph of Giselle. I ran my fingers over it before returning it to my jacket pocket. I didn't know what to think anymore.

"I'll miss you," I said as I walked Ellen to her bus stop.

"It's not that far. And we'll have a telephone. Come and stay after the baby's born."

I said I would, although I knew it wasn't likely. I couldn't afford the train fare. Waving Ellen off as the bus trundled down the road, I'd never felt more alone. My head filled with visions of Giselle sitting on the train with the strange twins, laughing. No, it had to be a mistake. It couldn't have happened like that. I went into the first pub I saw and downed more whiskies than I could count until the pictures stopped crowding my head.

It's been so long I'm starting to wonder if you'd recognise me now. The truth is I hardly recognise myself. That time in the prison changed me. I lost a part of myself I'll never get back. Old friends avoid me, and I don't want to make new ones. The other workers treat me with suspicion. I don't know how much they know or have guessed about the Allerton murder. I drink too much. I sleep with people I don't even like. I'm a mess. But as much as I disgust myself, it's you I blame. I wish I'd never met you.

Jack

I don't know why the police brought me back to my parents' house after they found me unconscious in the street that night. Perhaps I'd given them the address, or they'd found it on me or perhaps one of them recognised me. But my mother screamed when she saw me. That sobered me up, at least for a moment.

There was a lot of blood, and I could see from her face she was frightened.

"This has to stop," she said, patching up my cuts. "Why are you doing this to yourself?"

I managed a smile despite the pain, then vomited down the front of my shirt.

I woke up the next morning in my old bed in my old room. My head felt like it had been split by an axe and my face was swollen and bruised. I lay there staring at the familiar cracks on the ceiling waiting until I heard my father leave for work.

I answered a tap on the door, barely aware that I hadn't shaved or combed my hair, and my braces were still hanging down at my sides. My mother came in with a cup of tea, clutching some letters.

"These came for you while you were away. All from abroad. We didn't think you'd want us to bring them to you in there."

"No. Thank you." I started tearing them open but they all said much the same thing – thanking me for my interest in their esteemed establishment, regretting they were unable to divulge details or enter into any correspondence regarding their students but words to the effect that I had absolutely no reason to be concerned as none of them had gone missing.

There was one from Lord Ashwell, saying he'd love to be able to help but although he knew several baronets none of them, as far as he knew, had a daughter called Giselle. Besides, he'd been away during the dates I mentioned, skiing in a place called Val d'Isere so it seemed I'd mistaken him for somebody else.

"I'd better go," I said at last.

"Your father's at work. As long as you're gone by the time he comes back, he won't know you were here."

She sat on the bed and studied me for a long time. Her eyes looked paler than I remembered, and the crease between them deeper. Climbing the stairs had made her breathless.

"It's been an awful shock for both of us," she said at last. "It's made your father ill. You've no idea what it did to him, the police coming into the shop and arresting you in front of his customers. He's lost business, you know."

"Yes, well, it hasn't been fun for me either."

She sighed. "He cares a lot more about you than you realise, he's just no good at showing it. We're both so worried about you. That awful murder. Of course, we never believed for a second you killed the poor man. But if you had anything to do with it..."

I felt a flush of indignant rage. "What are you talking about?"

She coloured at my tone and shifted uncomfortably. "I know you'd never deliberately harm anyone but..."

"I didn't batter him to death and burn his eyes out by accident, if that's what you're suggesting."

She winced. "All I'm saying is, the police must have some reason to suspect you."

My voice shook as I told her, "I barely knew the man. I stayed at his guesthouse, that's all." I was beginning to feel like I was back in the police cell. Would there ever come a time when I didn't have to justify my actions during those few days?

She shook her head. "It's just been such a shock. The last thing we knew, you were on your way to a wedding. And then suddenly all this happens. You end up staying in a place we'd never heard of with people we've never heard of and you're writing these mysterious letters..."

I felt myself colour. "What letters?"

"I found a couple under the desk when I was cleaning. Who is this Giselle? Why does she have such a hold on you?"

She broke off in a coughing fit and for a moment I thought I was saved. I had no idea what she'd learned about Gerald Allerton's murder. It made me wonder how far the story had spread. I felt a wave of nausea and opened the window to get some air. A group of children were playing a skipping rope game in the street below, chanting the months of the year.

"I'll get you some water," I said but she shook her head.

"Stay where you are. It's just a cough. Bloody nuisance. Now tell me, who is Giselle?"

She pronounced the G like the J in Jemima.

I fumbled for my cigarettes in my jacket on the back of a chair. I told her as much as I thought she'd want to hear. Everything from seeing Giselle on the boat-train to her telling me her father had killed her mother. So much time had passed and so much had happened, it felt strange describing Giselle, as if I were inventing her. I could see my mother thinking the same thing.

"Your father said the police don't believe she exists," she said, watching me carefully. "He says she isn't real."

"Of course she's real!"

I hadn't meant to raise my voice. Seeing her shrink back made me feel ashamed. I gripped the frame to control my trembling. Two young women pushing prams along the pavement, looked up.

"All I know is that no girl is worth getting this upset over," my mother said quietly. "Concentrate on what you have. You're young, handsome, intelligent... Someone else will come along."

I lit a cigarette. "Perhaps. But I don't want someone else."

Her body tensed. "Oh, for goodness' sake, pull yourself together. You're not the only person around here with problems. Everyone else has them but they don't end up getting mixed up in a murder. Your father's had to see the bank manager again. If they don't lend him the money he'll have to close his business. The Boyces down the road have been evicted because they can't keep up with the rent and next door's baby was born with a horrible deformity. But you've ended up like this over someone you hardly know. I don't care if she's real or unreal, but you must stop this nonsense."

Silence filled the space between us.

"It's not that simple. I'm worried Giselle's in danger. Or even dead."

She grabbed me by the shoulders. "The girl lied to you! You don't even know her real name. Leave it now, Jack. Whatever happened, it's over. Don't let it dictate the rest of your life."

She was overtaken by another bout of coughing, hunching her shoulders, and leaning against the wall for support.

"Are you sure you're all right?" I asked.

She waved me away. "It's getting better, the doctor's given me something for it. Now please stop trying to change the subject. Promise me you'll put all this behind you."

"I'll try."

I felt exhausted by the whole thing. And yet I couldn't give up – I was no closer to finding out what happened to Giselle than I had been on the day she vanished.

Chapter Fourteen

I was becoming desperate. I looked into hiring a private detective, but their fees were exorbitant, and I had no way of knowing they'd find her in the end. I tried a hypnotist to see if I could unlock any secrets I'd hidden from myself, but these sessions produced no answers. I even started going to spiritualist meetings after seeing a poster outside a local hall. I'd heard a lot about spiritualists and always dismissed them as charlatans so couldn't quite believe I was setting myself up for their tricks, but anything was worth a try.

I didn't tell anyone I was going and didn't speak to anyone, slipping in quietly and sitting at the back, giving no information to anyone. I hoped so much to be persuaded but after watching vulnerable people being exploited, I left in disgust.

Private psychic readings were another option but each clairvoyant I turned to gave different answers. Giselle was dead. She was not yet in the spirit world. She was in danger. She was happy. I was in danger. She wanted me to know it wasn't my fault...I felt cheated by everyone.

During one of my work breaks, I opened the paper and found a familiar face staring back. The name Clive Norland meant nothing to me at first. But the article said he was to stand trial for the murder of Gerald Allerton. He was thirty-eight, according to the article, and unmarried.

The clue came further down when it said he lived in the neighbouring village to Mr Allerton's farmhouse and was employed as a driver. I thought back to the driver who had taken us to and from the station. I remembered the way he'd turned up several times during that week without a car and stayed for a drink. I'd seen him walking away from the farmhouse early in the morning on more than one occasion. I remembered him talking to the twins and having what looked like a heated discussion with Giselle on that last morning although she denied it. I studied the picture. Was this the face of a murderer? I felt sick as I imagined him dropping us off and, believing everyone had left, returning the next day to kill the landlord.

A sense of betrayal seized me. We'd entrusted ourselves to this man and he'd done this. He'd been happy to let me stand trial for the murder he committed. Yes, I was free, but Norland had destroyed the man I used to be.

And yet I couldn't think why he should want Mr Allerton dead. From the very limited contact we had with him, he never struck me as a malevolent person and there had been no sign of animosity between him and the landlord. I couldn't help wondering if the police had made a mistake arresting Norland just as they had with me. But I hoped they were right. I wanted it all finished. My case hadn't gone to trial so if they started to doubt Norland's guilt after all they could come back for me, and I would have to go through it all again.

A few weeks later my father turned up at the building site office in the evening just as I was about to leave. We'd had no contact since my arrest. He always hung up when I rang and I was sure he'd instructed my mother not to talk to me either. She always sounded nervous and kept the conversation short, as though afraid he might be listening.

I hurried towards him thinking he might have news about Giselle or Clive Norland's trial but he said, "It's your mother."

"What's happened?"

He was having trouble controlling his speech. "She's not well. She's been asking for you."

My stomach dropped. "What's wrong with her?"

"A growth. She was due to have an operation yesterday, but they didn't do it. Turned out to be more complicated than they thought. I can take you there now if you like."

"How long have you known?" I asked him as we drove to the hospital.

"She wouldn't let me say anything. Didn't want to make a fuss. You were away when it all started and there was that business with the police."

I felt frozen in fear. I thought back to the cough my mother had when she visited me and I'm ashamed to say it but all the time it was going through my head *why did it have to be her rather than him?*

When we got to the hospital, the doctor asked to speak to my father, so I walked down the ward alone. She was in the last bed, looking much smaller than I remembered.

"Jack, this is a nice surprise."

I tried to help her sit up but she insisted on doing it herself, grimacing with the effort. Her face was grey and glistening as she tilted it to kiss me.

"Why didn't you tell me? You said it wasn't serious."

She smiled apologetically. "I didn't want to give you anything else to worry about. I hoped the operation would sort it out. Then you wouldn't have needed to know. I feel all right, just tired. The nurses are very kind."

Beside her bed were flowers and cards from some neighbours, some people from church and an old school friend.

"Can I get you anything?" I asked.

She gave me a reproachful smile and clutched my hand with surprising force. "You can make me a promise. Stop drinking."

"All right."

"Promise me. And mean it this time."

"I promise."

"And abandon the silly search. You're still looking for that girl, aren't you?"

"I just wanted to know what happened to her but I've reached a dead-end." I told her about the hypnotist and the clairvoyants.

"Really, Jack." She shook her head in exasperation. "Put that awful business behind you. Have a second go at life. It's not too late for you."

We talked about the nurses and the people in the beds around her and things she had heard on the wireless until her eyes started closing. I adjusted the pillow for her and sat watching her until she fell asleep.

My father dropped me off at my lodgings but wouldn't come in, saying he had things to sort out at home.

"I'll visit again tomorrow,' I said. "Will you be all right?"

He nodded, and looked for a moment as though he might cry but instead he clapped me on the shoulder.

Back in my room, I realised my mother was right. I had to get things in proportion, move on with my life and not spend any more of it looking for Giselle.

. . .

This is my last letter. It's not doing me any good, continuing this relationship in my head. For a long time, I wouldn't allow myself to move on. I couldn't bear the thought that you might come back and find me gone but it's clear now that's never going to happen.

I've done everything I can to find you. You're more likely to be alive than dead, or I'd have read about it, which probably means you don't want to be found. I'm not even sure who you are anymore.

I'm finding it harder to distinguish the person you are from the person in my head, but I know they are different. I can't keep lying to myself.

So, that's it. I've said all I wanted to say. I wish it could have ended differently.

Jack

Chapter Fifteen

I did my best to move on. My mother died a month after that first hospital visit. I was sober at the funeral although I wanted a drink more badly than ever. I knew she was right. I had to sort out my life. I'd done everything possible to find Giselle. Although I would always feel guilty about her disappearance and not doing more to keep her safe, I had to accept she was now part of my past.

The following month I went to my godson's christening down in Kent and made a silent promise to him that I would get my life back on track and be a better person.

In the spring I began seeing someone although I wasn't looking for love at that stage, just a distraction, a way to block out my thoughts about Giselle, and Gerald Allerton's murder. Janet couldn't have been more different from Giselle, but she was everything I needed at the time. She offered change, someone to take charge and turn me around, rescue me from myself. Someone who would take me over so completely there would be no space in my thoughts for the mess I had made of everything in my life.

It didn't happen straight away. All I thought when I first saw her on a cold, bright afternoon was that she was refreshingly different from the girls I'd been seeing who mostly worked in the factories.

We met over a game of tennis. Trevor, a friend from work, had asked me along to make up numbers.

The first thing she said to me was, "Your collar's not straight."

During the match she told me I should come up to the net more often, shorten my backswing and throw the ball higher during serves. I could see Trevor growing irritated and given that my shots had more success than hers I should have been annoyed too but I found myself laughing.

I liked the way her nose tilted, and her dark, shiny, bobbed hair bounced as she ran about the court, her face pink from exertion. Her features were large with a smattering of freckles and dark eyes, full of mischief.

She refused to take a second serve when the bumpy grass surface knocked her ball off course and insisted on calling one of ours in when her friend was convinced it was out. When she got excited, her cheeks flushed even brighter, and her voice got squeaky.

We had tea in the pavilion tearooms after the match and she asked us in turn if we were married, what we did for a living, how much we earned, which political party we voted for, where we lived and how we spent our evenings. Her friend blushed and winced.

"You really are too much," she said a few times and assured us we didn't have to answer.

"Am I being too nosey?" Janet asked, looking surprised.

"You do ask a lot of questions," I told her.

"I suppose I do. But that's only because I like to know where I am with people."

The questions she asked were very different from the ones

Giselle had posed. Janet struck me as someone who liked to be armed with facts rather than have surprises sprung on her.

"You should be a journalist," I told her.

"Perhaps I should. I'd like that."

But both girls were doing a clerical course at the local college.

"I'd love to manage an office," said Janet. "I know I'd be good at it if only I could persuade someone to give me a job. The problem is I have my opinions and don't find it easy to keep them to myself."

I smiled. "I had noticed. But at least you have opinions."

She volunteered a lot of information about herself. Her mother was English and her father German. The family had moved to England from a village near Hamburg after the Great War. She remembered riding on an elephant at the zoo and swimming in a lake before breakfast and disappearing for hours each day on her bicycle through the forests to little fairytale villages.

"It sounds idyllic," I said.

"It was. Well, it seemed like that to me. I had no idea about history or politics or how poor people were."

"Do you think you'll move back one day?"

"Good heavens no. I've been here since I was ten. I don't even speak the language anymore."

I asked what she liked doing and she told me she loved music and played the violin. It was hard to imagine her having the patience to play an instrument, but she was clearly determined. I could imagine her going over and over a piece until she was satisfied.

"I sing too. What would you like me to sing?"

"Oh, not here. Please don't," begged her friend.

But Janet had already launched into *Something to Remember You By*, oblivious to the stares from waitresses and other diners. Her voice took me completely by surprise, rich and sonorous on the low notes and effortless on the high ones. I felt the hairs on my neck lift. When she finished, the place was silent for a few moments and then someone broke into applause and gradually others started joining in.

"Who knows this one?" she asked.

We all groaned. It was one of those songs that drives you mad but worms its way into your head and won't go away. But as she sang, I found myself joining in *Everybody Loves My Baby* and before I knew it half the tearoom was shouting out the words, miming the instruments, dancing their hands on the table.

Others looked on in disapproving silence and one or two customers slipped out.

"Does she make a habit of this?" I asked Janet's friend.

"Oh yes. She sometimes has people up dancing."

The friend and Trevor moved away to a different table. Later, when the girls had left, he warned me off her. "She's too much."

I noticed her down at the courts a few times after that and she asked me to a concert in an old theatre where she was to play a violin solo. I told I her I knew nothing about classical music and the experience would be wasted on me, but she batted away all my excuses. I went along expecting to be bored but her playing had me transfixed.

From soft, melancholic notes the piece built to a sweeping climax that brought tears to my eyes. I couldn't believe someone so clumsy and excitable as Janet could also be capable of such control.

"Well?" she asked afterwards, seizing my arm so hard that I spilled my drink.

"Spectacular," I said, mopping myself down.

"Thank you. Although I suppose it's not such a compliment coming from you. You told me you were tone deaf."

"Ah, I should have said tone dumb," I assured her. "I hear notes perfectly well. I just can't always reproduce them."

"You weren't too bad in the tearoom the other day."

"Yes, well the trouble is, I can never be sure what's going to come out. Do you know, if I could choose a gift that would be it: to be able to hit any note. What about you?"

She looked confused. "I could play better if I practised more."

"But if you could have anything at all. Like be able to read minds or change your appearance whenever you wanted?"

She stared at me as though I'd gone mad. "What's the point of wondering about things like that? They're never going to happen."

"Well, don't you ever wonder about pointless things?"

I was relieved when she said she didn't. I was starting to see that Janet's strength and realism, were what I needed. She didn't give a damn what colour the number eleven was, what animal she'd choose to be turned into or whether we were really alive or just characters in someone's novel.

Over that past year, I'd lost sense of who I was. The drinking and the womanising were no more a part of me than the brightness and glamour of my student days, or the stultifying claustrophobia of my school days. The only time I'd really felt I was myself was during those ten days in a farmhouse with Giselle but even I had to admit now that had been an illusion.

But just as I was congratulating myself for having moved on, a letter arrived.

I'm writing to you because you are the only person who knows how it feels to be in my position. I didn't kill Gerald Allerton. I loved him. I was tricked into confessing, but nobody will believe my story.

I must talk to you. Please come. If you help me prove my innocence, I will tell you what I know about the girl you were with. I know her real name and what she was running away from. I also know where she is now.

Clive Norland

I was drunk when I read it. I had to go over it again in the morning several times to convince myself it was real. The thought of being back in that prison where I'd been on remand made me shudder. I couldn't help thinking it might be a trick to lure me back inside and then lock me up for good. Even if Norland was telling the truth, the experience of being back there might send me back down that destructive spiral I'd struggled so hard to climb out of.

I wrote a short letter back.

I'm sorry to hear of your situation but I'm afraid I'm unable to help.

Sealing the envelope, I felt sick with guilt, but getting involved in the Allerton murder again could be disastrous. Much as I felt sorry for Norland, I had to put as much distance between me and the death as possible.

Chapter Sixteen

"What are your plans for Saturday?" Janet asked.

"Nothing at the moment."

"Good. Then you can come to the races. Daddy's got tickets but he's too busy to go."

"In that case, it would be a shame to waste them. Although, I must warn you, I know even less about horses than about music."

By some fluke, however, a smoke-coloured horse called Earl Grey I'd picked purely for his looks came in first.

Celebrating our win over cocktails in the racecourse bar we talked about places we'd been, books we'd read, things that amused and annoyed us.

"One thing that drives me mad is insincerity," she said. "It would save so much time if everyone said what they meant. People who lie and people who don't want to hear the truth are as bad as each other. Both cowards."

"I can see I'll have to be careful what I say."

"Oh no, I know I can trust you."

A little disconcerted, I tried to warn her I wasn't the right person for her to get involved with, but she said, "Isn't that for me to decide?"

She broke off to intervene in a discussion on a neighbouring table. "I'm sorry," she said, turning back to me. "You probably think I'm speaking out of turn."

"Not at all. I admire you for saying what you think. It's refreshing."

She sipped her wine. "Why waste time worrying about what other people think of you? It's not as if you can control their opinion."

"That's true. Although I suspect most people find it hard not to care."

She shrugged. "If someone doesn't like me, it's their loss."

I laughed. "I believe you're right."

I saw her a few times after that and then we began to meet up regularly. The things she said seemed to make such good sense. Being with her was what I needed.

Over the next few weeks, we went to the pictures, dance-halls and had meals out. I began to wonder how I'd functioned on my own for so long. After a while, I was invited to tea with her parents and then Sunday lunch and before I knew it, I'd slotted into their family.

I found myself having lengthy conversations with her parents while Janet careered around the place looking for a shoe or a hairpin. I helped her mother, Marian, with crossword clues and explained the rules of cricket to her in a way she said finally made sense.

Janet's father, Bernardt, asked my opinion on news stories and enlisted my support in disagreements. "Come on, Jack, give us your honest opinion. Is it healthy for a dog to be this fat?" The clipped way he spoke made him sound like an upper-crust English gentleman which made me sometimes forget he was German.

At the back of my mind was always the worry that Janet's family might come across an old newspaper, or a neighbour might whisper in their ear that the man stepping out with their daughter had been a suspect in a murder case. But as the weeks slipped past, I started to relax.

She asked about previous relationships. I told her about Daphne and mentioned one or two of the women I'd been with recently but I'd known so little about them there wasn't a lot to say.

"It's all right – they don't bother me. I'm not interested in your past. If any of those girls meant anything to you, you'd be with them now."

She'd had one or two suitors, she told me. One of them had almost proposed. "I stopped him because I wouldn't have said yes so it wouldn't have been fair."

I never told her about Giselle. She wouldn't have understood. That whole episode seemed less real even to me by then and was becoming harder to recall.

My relationship with Janet was much less complicated which seemed healthier. Her reaction to abstract questions was always the same. 'What on earth does it matter?' or 'If that situation ever arises, I'll think about it then.'

Over the next few months, I felt she was rebuilding me. I drank less because I was on my own less and felt ashamed of the empty existence I'd been leading. There was no reason for Janet to know about it. When I was with her, I felt anchored and my worries about Giselle disappeared.

Until another letter arrived.

Each time I thought I'd left the past where it belonged, Norland reminded me it wasn't over. His tone was becoming increasingly desperate.

Please help me. Tell them what you remember.

Just looking at the envelopes brought back some of that awful angst I'd felt in prison. Unable to open the last few that arrived, I threw them into the fire and watched the flames swallow them.

Janet and I were coming out of the pictures a few days later after seeing *The Ghost Train* when a face jumped out at me from the newspaper stand. I ushered her past as quickly as I could but slipped the man some change and stuffed the paper under my arm. Norland's trial had begun.

The crime was outlined in more detail than most decent people would think necessary. There was a picture of the landlord, Gerald Allerton, looking much as I remembered him from my brief stay in the farmhouse. I had difficulty these days recalling him like that. Whenever I thought about him, the image changed into the mutilated face in the photographs the police had shown me. Although I'd cursed the way he behaved towards me and the wrong conclusions the police had drawn from his behaviour, he in no way deserved what happened to him.

The article had some salacious details about Norland's sexual preferences and past relationships. A villager confirmed Norland had been in a turbulent relationship with Gerald Allerton and there had been a number of rows. A witness testified to seeing Norland driving to the farmhouse on the morning of the landlord's death.

A sense of unease settled in me I knew why Clive Norland went to the farmhouse that morning—to take me to my train as arranged the previous night. But tired of waiting and anxious to get away from the place, I'd left early on foot and caught a bus from the village. Had his car been at the house when I left? I couldn't remember. But in any case, he could have called for me later and finding nobody there gone away again, unaware that Gerald's body was lying in the kitchen.

However hard I tried to think otherwise the possibility gnawed away at me that this man might be innocent. He'd asked me for help, and I'd refused.

Janet was appalled by the state of my room and couldn't resist "straightening things out a little" when she came round even though I asked her not to.

"It might look a mess to you, but I know where everything is."

That evening after seeing *The Ghost Train* she was rummaging about on my desk and suddenly went quiet. I looked up and saw her agonised expression. She tried to hide something.

"What is it?"

"I'm sorry, Jack, I've spoiled your surprise, haven't I?"

To my horror I saw in her outstretched hand Giselle's ring. "At least, I assume it's for me?" Her face was pink with excitement, her eyes bright.

I tried to snatch it out of her hand, but she held it up to the light between thumb and forefinger, gazing in wonderment.

I could have told her the truth. At least told her it belonged to somebody else. But if I did, things might get complicated. I might lose her forever. And it wasn't as if Giselle was ever coming back.

"But it's too soon," I said. "We haven't known each other all that long. I was waiting for the right moment."

"Oh. I see." Reluctantly, she handed it back. "Well, you let me know when it is the right moment. Because it feels right to me now."

Perhaps if I hadn't just read the news about Clive Norland, I wouldn't have done it. But getting engaged suddenly seemed the solution I needed to move my life forward, away from the past.

"If you don't like the ring, I can change it. Perhaps you'd rather choose one yourself," I said hopefully.

She gave me a crushing hug. "Don't be ridiculous. It's beautiful." She tilted her hand this way and that, watching the diamond sparkle in the light. "How much did it cost?"

"You know I can't tell you that."

"You must have spent a fortune." She thumped my shoulder so hard I staggered backwards. "How could you afford it?"

I mumbled something about selling a few things I no longer needed. It did strike me that if someone who knew Giselle ever saw her ring on Janet's finger, I'd have some explaining to do but at the time I couldn't think what else to do.

"I can't believe we're going to be married," she kept saying. "I can't wait to tell everyone." Suddenly she became serious. "A marriage can only work if there is absolute trust. No secrets between us."

"Of course."

"You won't ever lie to me, will you? It's the worst thing people can do to each other. It shows contempt."

"I won't. Of course I won't."

It was an easy promise to make because I meant it. I had no idea how things were about to change.

Chapter Seventeen

"We thought you'd never ask!" Bernardt said when I broached the subject of marrying his daughter. Marian cooked a special dinner and he uncorked a bottle of champagne. Shortly after, he introduced me to a friend who was a solicitor and offered me a job in his law firm so I could complete my legal training. It was hard to think how life could get much better.

Over the next few months Janet and her mother threw themselves into organising the wedding. There were endless discussions about venues and food and the guest list. How many bridesmaids should we have, what colours did we want for the flowers, what size should the buttonholes be, what music did we want at various stages?

"Who do you want to ask, Jack?"

We'd just finished lunch in Janet's parents' garden. The grass was freshly cut and the lavender was full of bees. I mentioned my sister and Trevor and one or two others. But thinking about the guest list, I felt a stab of anxiety. Was it such a good idea, bringing together lots of people who would be aware of the trial of Clive Norland?

"Do we have to have all this fuss?" I asked. "Why don't we just keep it small?"

She looked disappointed. "What's the matter? Are you having second thoughts?"

"No, of course not."

But I knew the police had spoken to Daphne and Douglas. How many others had they interviewed? Inviting anyone who had known me in the past was a risk. The last thing I wanted was for my old friends to be comparing notes. And what if one of them said something to Janet or her family? A wedding suddenly seemed a terrible idea. The problem was, I couldn't think of a good reason to back out.

Worrying wrecked my sleep. And then the dreams started. The first time I had the dream I was standing with Janet at the altar saying our vows. When the vicar invited me to kiss the bride I lifted her veil. But it wasn't Janet under there, it was Giselle, looking exactly as she had when I first saw her on the boat train. I woke feeling hopelessly confused.

The second time I dreamed it, I lifted the veil and the whole church gasped in horror. She looked awful, her face bloody and mutilated. But it was her reproachful look that made me wake with tears on my face.

I didn't feel right all the next day. I couldn't stop thinking, how would I react if I saw Giselle again? Would I be able to resist her? If not, what was I thinking of, getting married to Janet? But I had to remind myself that whatever had happened to Giselle it didn't alter the way I felt about Janet, and I couldn't let it dictate the rest of my life.

Fortunately, on the morning of the wedding there was so much going on all thoughts of the dream were banished. The bride who joined me in front of the altar was veiled but her short, curvy form and clear voice were unmistakably Janet's.

We spent our honeymoon in London, as Janet had never been. On the second day, we were in the National Gallery of British Art when a familiar voice made me swing round.

"Sanders, good lord it's you!"

"Harry." My heart sank as my old Cambridge roommate sauntered towards me with a young blonde woman. "What are you doing here?"

"Meriel dragged me along to see the artwork," he said with a grin. "This is my fiancée." Turning to her, he said, "Jack's an old friend from Cambridge."

I held out my hand. "How do you do."

"So good to meet you," she lisped.

Harry's eyebrows shot up when I introduced Janet as my new wife. "Congratulations. How splendid. You always were a dark horse, Sanders. Glad to see you're still in the land of the living – no one's heard from you in ages. We hoped you might have joined us in Amalfi."

I told him it hadn't been easy to get away.

He couldn't help a smirk. "Impossible I should say, given your circumstances at the time."

"What circumstances?" asked Janet.

I glared at him and caught a triumphant spark in his eye. He'd clocked that she knew nothing about the case.

"We were very busy at work," I said.

"What a shame. It sounds fun."

"Still selling chairs in the back of beyond are we?" Harry kept talking, allowing the conversation to dance back towards the Gerald Allerton case on several occasions and then away again, watching my face with delight. "Heard from Daphne?"

"No."

"She's got twin boys. Fabulous little things."

"Good, she must be thrilled."

"Have you seen the Turner paintings?" he asked Janet. "They're quite extraordinary." Turning to Meriel, he whispered, "Why don't you show her, darling?"

We watched the two women wander off round the corner to see the paintings.

"Well, well," said Harry, "you don't hang about. Glad to see you've made a sensible choice this time. And I'm very relieved you've managed to put that unpleasant business behind you. Absurd, the police arresting you. It was me who put them right, you know."

"Really?"

"Yes. As soon as the story broke, I did some digging into the victim's background. Came up with Norland. And surprise, surprise, his fingerprints were all over the shovel."

I wasn't sure whether to believe him but thanked him anyway.

"Don't mention it. You know they were lovers, Norland and the landlord? Only it seems the landlord had someone else on the go and Norland found out about it. Hell hath no fury, eh?"

Sweat broke out as the thought struck me that if the police hadn't tired of trying to pin the crime on me and turned their spotlight on Norland instead people would have been conjecturing like this about me. I didn't tell him about my communication with Clive Norland or Norland's plea for me to visit him.

Harry leaned forward to examine a bronze. "What happened to the girl? Ever hear from her again?"

"No," I said, recovering my composure. "I don't suppose I'll ever know what happened."

"Just as well, perhaps. But it's a bit odd when you think about it, how she took off at the same time as that poor fellow was murdered."

"I don't see how those things need be connected."

He made his mouth into a downward horseshoe. "I'm not saying she was involved in the murder. But she might have seen something. I asked around for you. Showed everyone that photograph you gave me. Nobody knew who she was. Funny thing is, I saw a girl who looked very like her a few weeks back."

My heart thundered. "What do you mean? When?"

A victorious spark leapt into his eyes. "In a club. I... Oh, hello, they're back. What did you think, ladies?"

"Wonderful," said Janet. "It was worth coming to London just for this."

"We should all meet up before you go back," Harry said.

I could think of nothing more dreadful, but Janet was already saying how lovely and Meriel had whipped out an engagement diary and was writing down the name of our hotel.

"What a lovely man," said Janet as we watched them leave.

"He's not. He's awful."

She thumped me. "Why do you always have to think the worst of everyone?"

The following evening, the four of us spent an excruciating evening in a restaurant in Covent Garden. Meriel was clearly affronted by Janet's directness (she'd told Meriel within minutes she needed to eat more iron and that her hair would look much better pinned back from her face) and Janet was hardly able to conceal her irritation at Meriel's simpering.

Harry was the only one who was enjoying himself. He laughed uproariously at things Janet said and she seemed to enjoy his teasing, but I wasn't sure if he was laughing with her or at her, or whether by doing so he was trying to annoy Meriel, or me, or both.

"Now, that's a ring and a half," he said, catching hold of Janet's hand as she picked up her glass.

I felt my face freeze. Had I told Harry about finding Giselle's ring? Yes, I'd shown it to him. It took all my strength not to look at him.

"Is it a ruby?" asked Meriel.

"No, it's a pink diamond," Janet told her.

Harry whistled. "What's your secret, Jack? Did you rob a bank?"

"Beneath it all he's a real romantic," she said, tickling the back of my neck.

I managed to change the subject but caught him looking at the ring several times during the evening, his head on one side, upper lip pulled back into a slight smile.

When Janet and Meriel went to the bathroom he said, "You know they're talking about us, don't you? Women do that."

"What did you mean about seeing Giselle?" I asked him.

He threw back his head and laughed. "Steady on, I didn't say I'd seen her. Only a girl who looked like the one in your photograph. She was a dancer in one of the clubs. Very exotic.

He lit a cigarette and shook the match. "To tell the truth I spent a night with her. Don't look at me like that – it was all in the name of research. I tried to get her to tell me her real name, but she refused. Mind you, she was very obliging in other ways."

I thought about hitting him, but he wasn't worth it. I knew he was lying, trying to get a reaction from me.

"Relax. It wasn't her. I checked with the manager, and the girl was working there during the time you were staying at the farmhouse. But it got me thinking. I went back through our archives and eventually found this."

He dug in his wallet for a photograph cut out of a newspaper. It was a close-up of a girl's face.

I stared at it in disbelief. "This is her! How did you find it?"

"Are you sure?" He pulled a face. "Slight snag is this girl died a few weeks before Daph's wedding. Tragic skiing accident. So, unless you were making love to a ghost..."

I stared uncomprehendingly at the picture. It looked so like Giselle.

"What I'm saying is, she had one of those faces. There are lots of pretty girls like her about. That's why you haven't found her. So don't be too hard on yourself."

Reluctantly I had to concede he had a point. I was also starting to realise that after so much time my memory of Giselle wasn't as clear as it had been. The Giselle I knew existed only in my head.

A few weeks later as I opened a newspaper, a chill swept up my spine. Clive Norland had been found guilty of the murder of Gerald Allerton. My stomach dropped as I read the piece. It could have been me standing there in the dock facing the death penalty. I felt sick, remembering the letters Norland had sent and I had ignored. What if he were innocent and there was a way I could help him?

And yet if it all went wrong... I dreaded jeopardising what I had with Janet. Some people will always believe there's no smoke without fire. How would Bernardt react if he found out his son-in-law had once been arrested for murder or that he was in communication with a violent killer? And could I really help Norland anyway? For all I knew he had killed the landlord. Best not to interfere, I decided, although I hated myself for it.

Chapter Eighteen

The first few years of my marriage to Janet were happy. Had we been luckier, it might have lasted. With a reference from my boss for the mortgage and help from Janet's parents we were able to buy one of the new semi-detached houses with a garden that were springing up everywhere.

Our neighbours were mostly young couples and families, and we made some good friends. When I wasn't working, we'd play tennis, walk, or go to the pictures. As each month passed, my fears about the past intruding into this new, simple life faded. Janet was impatient to start a family. She talked constantly about names and clothes and how the children should be brought up.

"How many shall we have?" she asked one day as we sat down to lunch in the garden.

I smiled. "One would be fine, wouldn't it?"

"One? Jack, that's selfish."

"All right, two. Three? Ten! As many as you want. I don't mind as long as you're happy."

She hit me with a cushion. "Now you're being ridiculous.

I'd like a boy first and then a girl. And then perhaps another girl. Or a boy."

"We just have to take what comes, don't we? Why don't we wait a bit, save up some money and just enjoy being with each other?"

"If we wait for a perfect time, it will never happen."

Unfortunately, her keenness to become a mother didn't match her enthusiasm for making love and she approached the whole thing with an off-putting stoicism.

"Do you enjoy it?" I asked once.

"It's fine."

"But I don't want you to feel fine. I want you to feel amazing. Perhaps if you'd let me..."

"I'd rather we just got on with it."

For me it took away the enjoyment and made the whole business feel like a chore, but I was hopeful that side of things would improve. It was a relief when she didn't become pregnant in the first few months. I'd seen friends' lives turned upside down by their babies, delightful as they were, and wasn't sure I was ready for all that.

Janet accepted the situation or at least she talked less about it, throwing herself into her hobbies instead, making clothes and cushions with the sewing machine in the evenings while I read or finished off paperwork. So, it was a shock to find her crying in the kitchen when I came in from work one day.

"What is it?"

She wiped away tears from her hot face. "I thought I was going to be able to give you some good news but I was wrong. Again."

"There's no rush, is there?"

"Do you think something's wrong? It's been nearly a year."

"I'm no expert but I doubt this counts as very long."

But it was clear she'd been building up hope each month

and those hopes had been dashed. On a couple of occasions, we thought it was happening, but it always ended the same way with Janet a little more heartbroken. She distracted herself by knitting little jackets and bootees "for the future" which added to the pressure I felt but still nothing happened.

The verdict on Clive Norland nagged away at the back of my mind. The thought of an innocent man being sentenced to hang reminded me how close I'd come to the same fate. I preferred to think the verdict was just and he was guilty but what if he wasn't?

In one of those letters, he'd said he knew what had happened to Giselle. Was he bluffing? Or was it simply a ruse to get me to come and see him? Although I'd promised myself I'd abandon the search and didn't want anything to come between me and Janet, my curiosity about Giselle's disappearance wouldn't be satisfied until I found out what had happened after she vanished and whether she was safe.

When another letter arrived, along the same lines but even more desperate in tone, I decided I couldn't ignore the man any longer.

"I've going down to see my sister for the day. She's not been well."

Janet was all for coming too but it would mean missing a concert and I managed to dissuade her. "Why don't you come next time when Ellen's better and we can all enjoy it."

She waved me off at the station but instead of going south to Kent, I took the train back up to Northumbria.

I felt a frisson of fear as I approached the prison gates but also a mounting excitement. At last, I would get some answers.

"I've come to see Clive Norland," I told the officer.

He sucked his teeth. "Not possible, I'm afraid."

"What do you mean, not possible?"

"You're too late."

For a moment I thought he meant Norland had been released.

"He was hanged this morning."

I couldn't believe it had happened so quickly. I walked away in a daze, went into a pub, and drank far more than I should, missed the train back and had to ring Janet with a lie about my sister taking a turn for the worse. There was no reply from our telephone at home, so I tried her parents. Bernardt told me she'd gone out with her mother. "Any message?"

I heard the suspicion in his voice when I told him I wouldn't be back until the next day, but he wished Ellen a speedy recovery.

Chapter Nineteen

To take my mind off Norland's fate, I threw myself into my job but was only partially successful. One evening in spring Janet threw herself at me, as I came in from work, knocking me over.

"It's happening. You're going to be a father."

"Are you sure?"

She laughed. "It's all confirmed. The doctor says it will be a summer baby. July."

"That's wonderful news." Despite my earlier reservations, I was relieved and caught up in the excitement.

The next few weeks were filled with preparations for the new arrival. I decorated the box room and neighbours gave us their old cot and pram. We had endless discussions about names.

"Belinda?"

"I don't know. Reminds me of my history teacher."

"Is that so bad?"

"Warts, *pince-nez*, bald patch..."

"Say no more. Grace?"

"Hmm, you'd be under such pressure to live up to a name like that. The Grace in my class was very clumsy..."

We finally settled on Michael for a boy, Ruby for a girl. Janet didn't get any sickness or cravings but suffered from heartburn towards the end and couldn't get comfortable in bed, which left her tired and bad-tempered during the day.

"Put your hand here," she said one day. "Can you feel it?"

Something jumped under my fingers. The feeling was magical. I was looking forward to us being a family and determined to be a better father than mine had been.

But a few weeks before the expected arrival date I found the back door open when I got in from work. My gaze fell on a bucket of blood-stained towels on the floor by the sink.

"Janet? Are you okay?"

I tore up the stairs, shouting and nearly bumped into our neighbour outside the bedroom.

"Mr Sanders, your wife's had the baby," she whispered, taking my hands in hers.

I pushed past her and found Janet sitting up in bed cuddling a little bundle. I peeked under the blanket and felt a rush of joy at the perfect, peaceful face of our sleeping child.

"Boy or girl?" I whispered.

"A girl," Janet said.

"Mr Sanders..."

"She's beautiful," I said, kissing Janet. "Congratulations."

She didn't seem to hear me or even acknowledge I was there. I started to get an inkling something was wrong. The neighbour tugged at my arm and motioned for me to come out of the room.

"The baby's dead," she said gently. "I'm so sorry. I tried to tell you."

I realised now that she had but I hadn't let myself take it in.

"I know it's an awful shock, but these things happen. Perhaps it's for the best."

"I don't see how." I was choked by disbelief.

"We need to take it away from her now."

But I knew it wouldn't be easy. Janet clutched the baby, refusing to let go. The doctor who finally arrived was the no-nonsense type. I knew Janet's screams when he prised Ruby out of her arms would haunt me forever.

It took a long time to rebuild our lives. At first people tip-toed around us, trying to say the right thing but usually making it worse. The experience left us so ragged we found it impossible to be polite or patient, which drove people away when we needed them most.

We blamed ourselves, blamed each other, blamed other people, but all around us life went on. Neighbours pushed their babies in prams, took toddlers to feed the ducks, taught children to ride tricycles. They avoided us, probably because they didn't know what to say, or perhaps thinking our bad luck might rub off on them. Janet and I were locked together in a world nobody else seemed able to enter.

She became a smaller, quieter version of herself. She got upset more easily, lashed out when angry and became increasingly suspicious that I was going to leave her, no matter how much I tried to reassure her.

After some time, I tentatively suggested we try for another child, but she shouted, "How can you be so thoughtless? I don't want another child. I want the one we lost."

"Who's Giselle?"

Janet's face was white except for two red patches on her cheeks. She was standing in the kitchen as I came in from work clutching what I thought was a handkerchief but I gradually realised was a piece of paper. I hadn't heard Giselle's name for such a long time it caught me off guard. I felt my face flood with colour.

"Who? No one."

"Don't say that. Who is she?"

With a bitter smile Janet unfurled the piece of paper in her hand. "She's clearly not *no one.*"

My heart stalled. I held my hand out for the letter. Giselle must have got in touch at last. What on earth she could want? But catching sight of my own handwriting, I realised this was one of the letters I'd written a long time ago. It was humiliating to read. How pathetic and desperate I sounded back then. No wonder Giselle had run off.

"Where did you get this?" I asked at last.

"Does it matter?" Janet's eyes were taut and red. Her voice came out as a whisper.

"I suppose not. But it's not what..."

"Not what it looks like?" Her tone sharpened. "It *looks like* you're having an affair."

"No, you're wrong, you don't understand."

She shut her eyes. "I was tidying up, trying to sort out the mess in the spare room. Is this why you don't like me touching your things? Because you have secrets?"

"Of course not."

I could see she didn't believe me. "You've been behaving strangely for a while. When were you planning to tell me?"

"I promise you, there's nothing to tell."

"For once in your life be honest! Are you leaving me?"

"No. Of course not."

How could she think that after everything we'd been through our marriage could be threatened by a letter written years ago to a girl I barely remembered? "You don't understand."

"I do though, don't I?"

My face exploded in pain. I staggered backwards. Blood pooled in my mouth.

"What did you do that for?"

She smacked my face and head as I ducked.

I caught hold of her arms. "All right, stop. Stop now."

At last, the tension in her muscles subsided. She dropped her arms and turned away as though she couldn't bear to look at me.

"The worst thing about it is the lies. You're despicable."

I was wiping blood away from my mouth. "Look, you've got it all wrong. I wrote this letter years ago before I met you. I no longer know the girl. I barely did then."

"I don't believe you. If it means so little to you, why would you keep it?"

"I didn't realise I had." I tore it into shreds. "There you are, it's gone. Happy now?"

But I was starting to see that the letter was only a part of a much bigger problem, one we'd both been ignoring.

"That letter shows me everything that's wrong between us. When have you ever said anything like this to me?"

"It's different with you," I said in frustration. "I was young and stupid back then. I didn't know what I sounded like. With you it's real. It's what I want now."

"I don't believe you. Why did you change your mind about me? I've put on weight these last couple of years, is that it?"

"No. Look, if you have, I hadn't noticed."

"That's because you don't notice me! You're hardly ever here and when you are you avoid me."

"That's not true."

I was relieved when the telephone rang, and she went out to the hall to answer it. When she eventually came back said, "It was the Southgates asking us round to dinner."

"This evening? You said no?"

But as though the prospect of spending an evening with me was too awful to contemplate she replied, "No, Jack. I said yes."

It was an awful evening. Our friends must have wondered what was going on. Janet's face was blotchy and her eyes red, and my split lip was so swollen I had trouble talking. They shot us suspicious looks all evening, but no one said anything, and we got through it somehow.

But I knew that wasn't going to be the end of it. When we arrived home, we sat up for hours talking, with the fire smouldering and the mantel clock ticking. Janet came out with a string of questions about Giselle, which I answered as truthfully as I could without telling her about the murder because I didn't see how that would help. With the state she was in, she'd probably make the same assumptions as the police.

She listed every fault I'd ever had, from the way I left the tops off jars to the way I automatically disliked people when I first met them to the way I sometimes pretended to be listening when I clearly hadn't been, forcing me in the end to snap, "Perhaps you'd be happier if I did leave."

She raised her hand again, but I caught it just in time. "Don't. Don't hit me again."

But in the end, I told her I wanted to try and put things right.

"I do love you."

She closed her eyes. "You don't know what love means."

"Of course I do."

But all the things I knew it should mean like the sight of her making my stomach do cartwheels, making me forget time, making me want to punch the air and shout her name from rooftops were so wrong for what existed between us.

The awful realisation crept in that she was right. I didn't love her anymore, perhaps never had in the way she wanted, and had been too cowardly to admit it. I'd always prided myself on being basically honest but now I saw that even that wasn't true.

In the end all I could think of to say was, "This isn't getting us anywhere. We both need some sleep."

We lay awake in the dark like two figures on a tomb. I felt the bed tremble as this woman who'd done so much for me, rescued me from the brink of insanity, eventually cried herself to sleep. If only I could do something to put it right but every attempt I made seemed to make things worse.

We made up the next day, but she was quieter, more wary of me after that. I don't think she ever really believed me, and it's a sad irony that the row made me see what had been obvious to her but not to me. Our marriage wasn't working.

We never talked about Giselle again but bickered about silly things. It was easier when we were with other people, so we avoided being alone together as much as possible. Our diary filled up with social visits, treasure hunts and dinners. We probably appeared blissfully happy together but appearances can be so deceptive.

Janet became more suspicious, checking up on my whereabouts and hovering during my telephone conversations. Mindful of her violent temper, I became more defensive and secretive, concealing anything from her that she might misinterpret.

During the years that followed the atmosphere in the house was increasingly claustrophobic, but we probably would have managed if life hadn't suddenly changed for all of us.

Chapter Twenty

Talk about war had rumbled on for months but waking up on that bright, beautiful September morning in 1939, we had no way of knowing how it would unfold. As the Prime Minister's voice crackled out of the wireless, we looked wordlessly at each other. The tension of the past few days since the attack on Poland had been so unbearable it was a relief in some ways to know but still a shock.

We were at Janet's parents for Sunday lunch as usual, trying to keep things normal, discussing the weather, the quality of the potatoes and a new film that was coming out of *The Wizard of Oz*. The peaceful English scene through the window– golden leaves on the trees, a blackbird pulling at a worm in the middle of the lawn, the potting shed, the roller against the wall – made it difficult to accept we were at war.

I found myself looking at a picture above the fireplace that I'd never really noticed before.

"It's the village I was born in," said Bernardt. "You see the storks nesting on the roofs? They're thought to bring good luck because they have human souls. We used to celebrate their arrival every summer with cakes and music."

"The only year they didn't come was when the war started," said Marian.

An awkward pause hung between us. It seemed unbelievable that we could be at war again so soon after the last.

"All these houses they're building," she burst out. "They're all going to be bombed, aren't they? It's such a stupid waste!"

"It's hard to see how it could have been avoided this time," Bernardt said.

"I'm sure it could if women had been in charge," said Janet. "Thank goodness we have the shelter. Do you think it's strong enough? It doesn't look very—"

"Absolutely." said Bernardt. "These things are very well designed. They can withstand anything."

"You won't be called up, will you, Daddy? You're too old."

Bernardt laughed softly. "I don't think they'll want me."

It brought me up short, remembering my father-in-law was German. Officially, he was the enemy now.

"But they might want Jack."

It wasn't until the following summer when there was a sudden need for reinforcement that I was called up. Those months in between felt like the early years of our marriage. Knowing what was hanging over us, Janet and I made more effort, finding time to be together and paying each other compliments. It felt as though we were in love again.

We even talked about having another child, but it didn't seem fair to bring a baby into such an uncertain world or for Janet to have to bring it up on her own if anything happened to me.

"Don't go," she said when my papers arrived.

"I have to."

"You don't. I could shoot you in the foot."

"You could but you'd probably miss."

On the day I left I leant out of the train window and kissed her, and she clung to me so hard I nearly fell out.

"Don't volunteer for anything."

"What do you take me for? I've no ambition to be a hero."

As the train pulled out part of me wanted to jump off and run back to her because everything was so uncertain, and I had no idea if I'd ever be coming back.

Over the next few weeks at a training camp set up in the grounds of an old country house I pushed myself through assault courses, pack drills, route marches and exercises. I learned how to fire different weapons and throw grenades. I got used to being bawled at, herded around, and passing inspection at a moment's notice. It was relentless and punishing and often degrading, but as I drove myself forward, I kept thinking that if I got through this somehow, I'd make a much better go of my life.

The other men came from all over the country and all levels of society and living with them at such close quarters was a challenge in itself. I had nothing in common with any of them – or was just afraid to form attachments.

I was surprised by how many of the men couldn't read or write and found myself during the long periods of downtime when we were confined to barracks, writing letters for them, and reading theirs from home aloud, each of us trying not to show embarrassment at intimate sentiments.

Eavis who had the bunk below me picked something up off the floor as I handed him the letter I'd written for him.

"Is this your missus? What's her name?"

"Janet." But as I was putting it in my pocket, I realised with a jolt that it was the picture of Giselle rather than the one of Janet. I hadn't looked at it in ages but had taken it with me as well as the letters because I hadn't wanted Janet to find them and misunderstand again. Looking at the photograph now of Giselle on the boat brought back so many memories. I felt a sadness that I'd failed to find her. Now with the war, I'd never be able to. It was a chapter of my life I'd been unable to close.

Partly out of guilt, I wrote to Janet, telling her about things I'd been doing, the people I was with, the accommodation and the food. She wrote back with instructions to keep safe, eat well and get enough sleep.

Coming up with interesting meals with these blasted coupons is a challenge but I've become quite inventive. My figure's thanking me already. The broad beans we planted are magnificent – they end up in most of our meals. I'll turn into a bean at this rate! I've given some to Betty and Alfred and they've promised to give me some of their strawberries and cucumber when they're ready.

We keep ourselves busy in the factory. The other girls are a scream. When I have time, I give Mummy a hand with her raffles to support the war effort.

They're talking about internment again, but the tribunal said Daddy was C-category which means the lowest security risk, so that should be the end of that....

Shortly after I started my training the rules about foreigners changed.

...Daddy's been interned after all. It was a frightful shock. A policeman just turned up at the door at teatime and they took

him away. You'd have thought they would have more important things to do at a time like this than imprison a harmless old man! But he sounds happy in his letters and says he's being looked after well. We're hoping Mummy will be allowed to visit him soon and that they'll see sense and let the lowest risk people go again.

At the end of the training, I had a couple of days' leave. Those few days at home were idyllic but the thought of having to go back to the regiment hung over us like a shadow.

Chapter Twenty-One

After training, I was moved to various barracks around the country and only had the occasional afternoon off at short notice, but Janet and I wrote regularly.

December 13th, 1940

You're probably safer than us, Jack. I was doing a bit of Christmas shopping yesterday in C&A. This morning it doesn't exist anymore. The whole place blown to bits.

People ran for shelter in the pub across the road. But then that was hit, too – seven floors reduced to rubble. God only knows how many people were killed. It will take ages to get the bodies out. Some of them will probably never be identified...

Janet x

On one of my leave days, Janet wasn't able to meet me because her boss refused to let her have time off at short notice. Another time, leave was cancelled at the last minute so when I saw her in the New Year I felt nervous as though meeting a stranger.

The tearoom by the station was packed with other servicemen and their loved ones. The gramophone played patriotic songs, and the air was filled with perfume and cigarettes. Janet arrived flushed and breathless.

"Sorry I'm late. My boss is being very difficult today."

"It's all right, I've only just got here."

Sitting across the table from each other reminded me of the time Ellen visited me in prison. After ordering we sat looking at each other, not sure where to start. We both tried to speak at once, laughed, and apologised.

"You look very well," I told her.

"You, too."

"There's something different about you. What is it? You've done something to your hair."

She blushed and her hands shot up to the curls. "Do you like it?"

"I do. It suits you."

As she lowered her hands, she knocked her cup, slopping tea into the saucer. I swapped the cups around but a moment later she did the same thing. "Sorry. All fingers and thumbs today."

I asked about her father. She seemed relieved to have something to talk about.

"Mummy's been to visit. She said it wasn't nearly as bad as she expected. He's helped set up a school for the children. He's teaching them maths."

"That's good. I'm sure he's a great teacher. My sister's teaching too. A school for evacuees in a big house in Kent."

"Good for Ellen. It sounds fun. Better than factory work."

She blushed and laughed nervously. Her hand trembled as she picked up her cup, then put it down again with a crash.

There was something different about her. I hadn't imagined it. It wasn't just the hairstyle. Her face looked a bit rounder, cheeks rosier. It suddenly hit me, the last time she'd looked like that.

"You're not pregnant?"

All the talk and clatter around us faded.

Her face was red as she said in an unnaturally bright tone, "I... Yes. I was waiting for the right moment to tell you. Isn't it wonderful?"

"But how can you be?" I was calculating back to when we'd last made love during my summer leave, and looking at the size of her stomach, which wasn't very big at all.

"It doesn't show much yet because I've lost so much weight with all the rationing and I was very sick in the beginning which they say that's a good sign. You are pleased, aren't you, darling?"

I was aware of people looking at us and then away, questions mouthed, heads brought together. "When is the baby due?"

She looked down at the table, cheeks flaming. The waitress came to ask if we wanted anything else but took one look at us and melted away. I repeated the question.

"I'm not entirely sure," she mumbled.

She reached for my hand, but I snatched it away, aware that everyone was staring at us. "I was going to tell you, honestly, darling..."

"Were you? When?"

Most likely, she'd been planning to play around with the date.

"Or were you hoping I'd be killed so you wouldn't have had to tell me at all?"

"Don't. Please don't. It's been so lonely and horrible and with Daddy being taken away..."

I didn't wait to hear the rest. I kicked my chair back, slammed a handful of change on the table, pushed past all the nosy waitresses and gawping diners and got back on the train.

A few days later, I received a long letter from Janet saying it would never have happened under normal circumstances.

This beastly war's changed everything. I was so frightened and so lonely.

She didn't say anything about who this man was or how she knew him, nor whether she still had feelings for him but insisted she wanted us to stay married. Couldn't I see it might all be for the best?

It will be our baby, Jack. I did it for us.

For a long time, I didn't write back. But as the weeks passed and more people were killed, my anger subsided. I had to keep things in proportion. Who knew what the future had in store for us and our marriage? We could talk about it after the war was over. If it was ever over.

Although I couldn't bring myself to forgive what she'd done, I wrote to ask her how she was. A letter came back with news about life back home, the pregnancy, and plans for our future. She sounded happy and excited, as though she'd forgotten the baby was someone else's.

The little girl was born at the end of June soon after Bernardt's release. I had a day's leave at the end of the summer so was able to make it to the christening party.

Being back in Janet's parents' house, joining in the toast to our new arrival, felt surreal but after everything I'd gone through in the past year, it was hard to remember what normal felt like.

Chapter Twenty-Two

In December I joined a crowded train with no idea where it was heading. We arrived at the English port in icy winter rain and stood waiting with hundreds of other servicemen while lists were called. Ours was to board the boat for North Africa. Alongside the fear as I stood on deck watching the grey landscape disappear into the mist, I couldn't help a tinge of excitement. I was going somewhere I'd never have had the chance to see otherwise and hopefully doing something worthwhile.

As we slipped out of the port, I could just make out the murky shapes of other ships. With luck, the enemy would find it hard to spot us through the mist. I had a sudden memory of the last time I'd been on a boat. The day I'd met Giselle. I had a sudden vision of her in the ship's restaurant laughing, raising her glass, and saying, "To us!" Now I was being taken even further away from the possibility of ever finding out what happened to her.

The air in our cramped mess, several decks down, was rank with sweat, cooking smells, cigarette smoke and engine oil. The smells and the choppy sea had an immediate effect on some stomachs. I tried to take my mind off the boat's listing by reading the guidebook they gave us and concentrating on the lectures on how to identify the enemy.

I found it impossible to sleep the first few nights as the hammock swayed and twisted with each lurch of the boat. I lay rigid in the darkness, listening out for torpedoes.

The food was good but everyone succumbed to seasickness at one time or other. On the third day it hit me with full force. I staggered up on deck, skidding and falling as the boat pitched, grabbing anything I could hold onto. I slammed into the rail and clung to it as I emptied my stomach over the side, then collapsed onto the deck, sliding around in vomit. If the boat was hit at that moment I wouldn't even care.

But when I lifted my head, soaked through and shivering, my eyes met Giselle's. She was standing a short distance away, arms resting on the rail, looking back towards me, wearing that green coat, her hair and face picked out by the silver light through the storm clouds just as she had in the photograph I carried in my pocket.

She looked so real I almost called out to her but was so disgusted by the way I looked and stank I didn't want her to see me. I kept my eyes fixed on her but the image kept breaking up and reforming. Each time the boat rose she was there, talking, smiling. Then she dissolved into sea spray. Eventually my vision cleared, and I crumpled back onto the deck. I'd never felt so alone.

I swore I'd never think of you again, I wrote that night in my hammock to take my mind off the boat's movement and stave off the next attack. *But since I saw you, I can't get you out of my head. If you can get me through this, if you can keep me safe, I promise that when I get back, I will find you.*

It wasn't as if she could hold me to the promise but it gave me something to believe in.

After the chilly conditions in England, and the darkness inside the ship where all lights were forbidden, the heat when we docked was extraordinary and the streets ablaze with light. Local people gathered to stare at us. Catching sight of my reflection in a window, I saw why. My yellow skin was a shocking yellow.

"It's the malaria tablets," the sergeant said. "It won't show so much after a few days in the sun."

We moved on up to a camp near Cairo to acclimatise to the desert conditions and wait to be called forward for action. Our billet was comfortable although it was impossible to keep the sand out, and we were tormented by bugs. As fast as we roasted them with our blowlamps, more would arrive.

The fighting was worse than I'd let myself imagine. Apart from the searing heat, the dust was so thick and the light so blinding you couldn't see more than a couple of yards ahead and sweat made it impossible to get a proper grip on the gun.

The air was filled with the constant clatter of machine guns, shouts, and explosions so loud they made my ears bleed. Blazing shrapnel showered down around us. Robins, one of the young lads whose letters I used to write, was killed in the first few minutes. There was nothing anyone could do for him. Too shocked to register, I stumbled on through scorching dust, eyes burning.

Get through this. Stay alive. Who was that? Nothing you can do. Keep moving. Bodies exploding. Half a face. How is he still alive? Move on.

Afterwards when the guns stopped, the air was thick with smoke, petrol fumes, burning flesh and the screams of the dying.

Men were brought back on stretchers, limbs hanging off, insides out.

At night, my mind raked over it all. It struck me my father must have seen similar things in the Great War. It would explain his unpredictable rages. Did I ever really try to understand?

Mostly we were firing from too far away to see who we were killing but once amid the chaos, I fell sprawling into a crater. I might have passed out or just shut my eyes for a second but when I came to, choking on dust, gasping for breath, listening to bullets scream overhead, I felt a shadow creep over me.

I twisted my head to look up. Through the swirling dust a pair of red eyes stared down at me. An Italian soldier squatting beside me, gloating. I waited for the bullet, but it didn't come. It only gradually occurred to me that the man wasn't laughing but grimacing in pain from a wound in his side. I scrambled up and aimed my gun at him but couldn't keep my arm steady. The idea of killing someone at such close quarters sickened me.

Instead, I started to crawl away. But the sand shifted behind me. Something moved. Looking back, I saw that the soldier was less badly wounded than I'd thought. He launched himself at me. I tried to scrabble out of his reach, but he caught me from behind in a head lock, forcing my neck back until I thought it was going to snap.

My throat burned. My vision blanked. I couldn't believe this wounded man's strength. I also couldn't believe how stupid I'd been. But I couldn't let it end like that. I sunk my teeth into his arm and struggled free. We rolled over and over trading punches, fighting for our lives. He reared up raising his gun to smash it down on my face.

A bullet screamed. I was showered in blood and brains as he slumped on top of me. I felt a moment of immense relief followed by panic – a realisation that I couldn't get out from under the body. It was crushing the breath out of me. I could feel his blood soaking onto me. *Is this how I die?*

Someone hauled the body off me. I crawled away, retching and struggling to breathe, then dragged myself to my feet.

For ages afterwards, the incident haunted my dreams but over time the image distorted. Instead of the Italian soldier wielding the gun above me, it was Giselle.

Janet sent me photos of the baby, Matilda, and news of her first words, first steps and a lock of her hair. Despite my misgivings, it was somehow wonderful in the midst of all the death and destruction to hear about a new life, a perfect, pure little person who was the antidote to everything going on around me, and I found myself wanting to be part of her life. I wasn't allowed to send photographs or give away our location, so I told Janet about the people I was with, the heat and the magnificent sunsets.

My letters to Giselle were different because they were never going to be sent so didn't have to worry about them being read and censored:

I've made it this far. No idea why. It's easy to be brave if you have no hope. The trouble is, it sneaks back every so often, the thought that I might get through this. There might be a life after this madness. That's when the fear sets in. Because each time I go out there I'm calculating my chances of coming back alive based on the number of bodies from the previous day. There is no reason I should be luckier than anyone else. The randomness of it makes you realise how insignificant you really are...

Jack

The heat and the strictly rationed drinking water left me severely dehydrated. I spent hours under full sun on the lookout for movement. Sometimes, peering through the shimmering sunlight or the strange, melting, half-light of dusk, I saw things I knew I wasn't really seeing. I saw Giselle.

During leave in Cairo, she appeared quite often, always ahead of me, slipping down streets, disappearing round corners, jumping on a tram or melting into shadows before I could reach her. I saw her face in cabaret singers and belly dancers and waitresses in the tea gardens, in the shadows at the cinema-under-the-stars, even a young woman standing among the pyramids, but a turn of the head always broke the spell. I nearly made a fool of myself a few times but just managed to come to my senses.

Amidst the chaos of the fighting, I caught glimpses of her, an impression left in the bright light after an explosion or the swirl of sand whipped up by a desert storm. Perhaps it sounds fanciful but I started to think this was her response to the letters I'd written, as if somehow she was able to read them and was keeping me safe, protecting me in battle like an ancient goddess, although I had to remind myself that in those stories there was always a price to pay.

It was all nonsense, of course. I knew that. Was I losing my sanity? After all, I'd dismissed those mediums as cranks but now I was playing a similar game. Believing that someone's spirit, dead or alive, could help me was not only stupid but dangerous. I was making a pact with my own imagination. But I'd stopped believing in the ability or willingness of a higher power to protect me, so why shouldn't it be Giselle?

I keep thinking I see you. It's driving me mad. I know you're not really there. But if I am seeing you, does it mean that you're no longer alive? If I could only talk to you for a few minutes, there are so many questions I'd ask. Did you find love? Did you marry? Do you ever think about me? Do you even remember what I look like? Are you happy? Was it worth it?

Jack

I woke up in hospital, with no idea how I'd got there. In a cold panic, I opened my eyes in turn. I checked my limbs one by one. Above me was a tented ceiling. Around me, other beds. I ran my hand over my face, expecting to find a horrible disfiguring wound. My head hurt. I felt a sweep of nausea as I tried to sit up. A nurse rushed over with a bucket.

"You're awake."

"What happened? Where was I hit?"

"You weren't wounded. You've been ill. Been here for a few days."

Gradually it was coming back. We were forbidden to drink the local water but desperate thirst had got the better of me and I'd accepted a drink from one of the figures in flowing robes who often appeared at the roadside selling their wares. I woke the next day with a raging fever and excruciating stomach pains. When I'd tried to get out of bed, I collapsed.

I felt guilty taking up a place in this field hospital for something that had been my fault in the first place. I fell back to sleep but woke several times in a feverish state, thinking Giselle was standing by my bed. Sometimes seeing her made me feel euphoric. At others angry for everything her disappearance had put me through. Once, I felt her hand on my burning head. But gradually as my temperature returned to normal, I realised the hand belonged to a nurse.

You can't even leave me alone here, can you? You keep invading my thoughts, turning up in places I don't expect, making me think I'm going mad. Once you asked me, "What's the worst lie you've ever told?" And yet you lied to me about everything, didn't you?

I hate you. The problem is I love you, too, and I don't know which I feel more strongly. I'm not myself anymore. You left me with nothing...

Jack

"You don't really want to send this, do you?" A face swam in front of me. Young, tired, sun damaged. "Don't say something you'll regret," the nurse whispered as she straightened out my sheets.

I motioned for her to hand the letter back which she eventually did. After she'd moved on to the next bed. I folded it and put it inside a book with the others.

"You don't recognise me, do you?" said a voice from the neighbouring bed.

I lifted myself onto one arm and peered at the patient's face, at least the bit that wasn't obscured by bandages.

"Should I? Sorry—"

"You were staying at Mr Allerton's farm just before he was killed."

"Right." I fell back against the pillows, feeling my cheeks

burn. Was the incident going to follow me all my life? I dredged my memory, trying to recall the features of the younger policeman and the prison guards I'd known but none of them fitted.

"Name's Burris," said the man. "You helped me with the sheep when they were stuck in the snow."

Of course.

"That were a terrible business with Mr Allerton. Such a gentle person. For him to end up that way..."

"Yes, it was. Awful."

Did this man know I'd been arrested for Allerton's murder? Was he testing for my reaction?

"I knew Norland had a temper – he used to fly into rages – but it's hard to comprehend how a man could do that to another."

"Did you know him well?" I asked.

"Norland?" Burris shrugged. "He came over quite often. He'd have moved in if Gerald had let him."

He fixed me with a stare. "You were with that girl."

My heart quickened. "Giselle. You remember her?"

Burris snorted and then winced, putting his hand to his head. "Is that what she called herself? I recognised her straight away. Her real name was Grace."

"What do you mean? Recognised her from where?"

I thought back to Norland's letters. Had he been telling the truth about knowing who Giselle was? Had they all known?

"I used to work for her family on their estate. Recognised her straight away. Gerald was most interested when I told him. Thought her father would like to know she was back. He set those old folks up to keep an eye on you. They were quite happy to help. They were all for calling the police, but Gerald didn't want that. Said he wanted to do it himself."

I closed my eyes, thinking of the danger those busybodies

had put Giselle in. No wonder she disappeared. They must have frightened her off.

"What do you mean she was back – back from where?"

He looked surprised. "Back from the dead."

My head swam. "What are you talking about?" The man was obviously delirious. I asked him again but a scream erupted from a few beds down and the room filled with people running.

"No talking," ordered a nurse.

"What do you mean?" I asked more quietly. "Do you know what happened to her? Where she went afterwards?"

"Save it for the morning," said the nurse, coming over again.

"No. This can't wait," I said but she fetched someone to help and they wheeled Burris away.

"Where are you taking that man?" I shouted, trying to sit up. "I need to talk to him."

The matron stood over me, placing both hands on my shoulders. "Calm down. You're upsetting everybody else."

"You don't understand."

But she pushed me back down. Another wave of nausea swamped me, and I vomited and blacked out.

When I came to, a new group of casualties had arrived. I got out of bed and stumbled up and down the rows looking for Burris. I kept seeing men I thought might be him but each time I was wrong. I asked the nurses but the ones on duty that day were all different and no one knew who I was talking about. The following day I was discharged and sent back into action.

But at least I had something now to drive me on – a reason to get back from the fighting. I had a name. Grace. If I could just stay alive until I got back, there was a chance I could find her – or at least find out what had happened to her.

Chapter Twenty-Three

Despite promising Janet I wouldn't volunteer for anything; I joined the Italian campaign. After Africa it felt like we had a job to finish. Landing under smoke cover in Salerno, we made our way up the coast to Naples. The deserted, fenced-off seaside resorts around the coast with their spectacular cliffs and lemon groves and the view of Capri, reminded me of the trip to the Amalfi castle with the Cambridge set that Harry had invited me to join.

I tried to imagine how the place would have looked in peacetime with those young men and women swimming, taking boat trips, eating ice creams, and lazing in deckchairs under umbrellas. I wondered where they all were now.

As we fought our way inland, we discovered that everything that had made the country beautiful made fighting a war there almost impossible. Few roads remained that were suitable for trucks and tanks, making it easy for our enemy to guess which way we'd come. The jagged mountains gave them perfect vantage points so crossing each valley filled me with terror. They were full of rivers that needed to be bridged and mines that exploded all around.

"I don't see how can get across," I said once to the man behind me.

"Just keep going," he shouted as the ground erupted. I turned round but there was nothing left of him.

Yet there were strange glimpses of beauty, reminders of how things should be. From a distance the bombed villages looked like fairytale kingdoms. It was only when you got closer that you saw the terrified civilians picking for scraps amid the rubble, children dressed in rags with limbs blown off, fields full of crops and starving people unable to harvest them because of the landmines.

I saw an old woman stoop to dig a filthy apple core out of the gutter and eat it. It made me feel so angry, that the world could be so wonderful and yet this was what we were doing to it. I couldn't see how the country was ever going to recover. I'd arrived in Italy with vague hopes of doing something useful. Now all I wanted was to get back to my old civilian life and make a better go of it.

After the desert heat of Africa, the sudden arrival of winter hit hard. Mud and rain swamped our tents, roads turned to rivers and rivers swelled to torrents, washing away our Bailey bridges as fast as we built them. We inched forward through mud, blinded by mist and rain, coming up against stiff opposition all the way. It was clear by now we had no chance of capturing Rome this side of Christmas.

I received a letter from Ellen telling me her husband's plane had been shot down and he was being held as a POW. Not long afterwards Janet wrote to say my father's shop was bombed. "Thankfully, it was Sunday, so he wasn't there, but the damage is shocking."

When at last we moved forward to Cassino the following year, it was like entering hell. Bodies of troops who'd been before us were strewn around the mud where they'd been gunned down from the benedictine monastery in the hills above. Others had drowned in the bomb craters that filled with water when the Germans flooded the valley. Our chances of getting through this without encountering the same fate were pitifully small.

I'm scared. Walking over bodies – seeing things I'll never get out of my head. I don't want other people to see me like that. The smell of death everywhere. I don't think I'll ever get it off me. The only thing keeping me going is fear. It's become like a drug. I don't know how I'd operate without it. Today someone put their foot where I was about to put mine and got blown to bits. I've been lucky so far but I know I can't stay lucky forever.

The fighting was worse than I can describe. The last thing I remember was a blinding flash, a tremendous shock, and my vision slipping away. Blood rushed from my neck where a bullet had lodged. Why wasn't I dead already? I lay on the ground thinking about how Janet would cope and regretting that I wouldn't see Matilda grow up after all. I thought about what a huge mess I'd made of my life and the mystery over Giselle's disappearance that I'd failed to solve.

"Stretcher! Over here."

People were standing over me, examining my injury. "There's no point. He won't make it."

"He might. He's still breathing."

The next thing I registered was being in an ambulance bouncing and skidding over rough terrain, bullets flying from every direction. If the neck wound didn't get me, one of these surely would.

"Try and stay calm for me." The voice was Giselle's but it couldn't be her speaking.

But she was there when I woke in the hospital. And then she wasn't. And then she was again.

"Don't try to speak," a nurse said. "We can't understand you anyway. Save your voice and rest." I motioned for a pen and some paper so I could write down my thoughts.

1943

So, your name is Grace. It's hard think of you as anyone other than Giselle but finding this out gives me something to stay alive for. I will at least track Burris down after the war and get him to tell me about your family.

I won't settle for anything less than the truth. Whatever happened to you, however bad it was, I want to know. I'm a different person now. Nothing shocks me. If there's one thing, I've learned out here it is that life's too short to waste.

Jack

It turned out, I'd also broken a knee as I fell. The leg injury took several months to recover, during which time the Allies got control of Rome. I was sent there to do an administrative job, organising accommodation for troops on leave. I arrived in a storm but my spirits soared at the sight of domes and towers sparkling against the dark sky. I settled in quickly, exploring the city in my spare time, wandering through the squares, watching shows, and drinking in cafés and read Janet's letters. I imagined her in our old town pushing the little girl on a swing or taking her for a picnic and wondered if I'd ever get to do those things with them.

From a stall by the Vatican, I bought Janet a necklace and Matilda a figurine of the she-wolf suckling the twins Romulus and Remus, the mythical founders of the city. Someone called my name and I saw Douglas Fairley, the man who married Daphne, crossing the square. I limped over and we chatted like old friends. His regiment was about to move up, but we promised to meet for a drink when we got back to England. A week or two after, I learned he'd been killed.

From time to time, I saw Giselle. She was always ahead of me, just out of calling distance, slipping across a square or disappearing at the end of a long street. Once at the top of the Spanish Steps, I thought I saw her in the square below. On another afternoon, I was sitting in a café in Piazza Navona. As the wind drove the spray from the fountain into a fine mist, I thought I saw her sitting on the other side of the statues. I was so certain I leapt up and ran across the square, but when I reached the fountain, she was gone.

Chapter Twenty-Four

Coming back after the war was very different from how I'd imagined. The demobilisation process was lengthy and frustrating and due to a string of transport and communication problems I arrived home without having had time to let Janet know I was coming.

Walking up our old road, I had a sense of unreality. The houses were still standing but looked smaller and shabbier than I remembered. We'd won a war, but the country was in mourning. I hesitated before pressing the bell. Although we'd kept in touch, I had no idea how Janet and I would react to seeing each other. There had been so much left unsaid.

In the end though, I rang it, half expecting to find the house shut up and empty or for the door to be opened by people I didn't know. The little girl who answered stared at me for a long time. She wasn't recognisable from the bald, chubby baby I'd seen at the christening on my last leave visit. Her hair was fine and the palest blonde, almost white, unlike anyone in my family or Janet's.

"Matilda?" I asked.

She nodded but didn't say anything.

"Who is it, darling?" I heard Janet shout from the top of the stairs.

The child eyed me for a long time and said without turning round, "I think it's Daddy."

I panicked for a moment, wondering who Janet was expecting to see.

She came slowly down the stairs with that familiar smile of incredulity, then ran towards me and threw herself into my arms. "You're back!" It hurt my neck where I'd been shot but I couldn't help breaking into a smile.

"Yes."

"Why ever didn't you say?"

"I'm sorry. There wasn't time."

I dropped my bag and kissed her. The curtains next door twitched, and I caught a glimpse of our neighbour retreating behind them.

It was a shock to feel Janet's ribs when she hugged me. Her face had lost its plumpness, and some fine lines had appeared which suited her. She insisted on using the weekly ration to make a cake while I sat and watched, feeling like a stranger. Matilda stood silently in the doorway staring at me. I smiled at her. She smiled back and held up the wolf figurine I'd sent her from Rome.

"Do you like it?" I asked.

She nodded but ran off.

"She's shy," said Janet.

"It's all right, I understand."

Inside, the house was dingy and threadbare. Over tea Janet filled me in on the lives of the other people in the street, several of whom wouldn't be coming back and some who had moved away.

"It felt so empty when the children were evacuated – like they'd been led away by the pied piper. Some of them came back before the bombing started but others stayed away the whole time. Beth Parker went to fetch her boy from the station but he'd changed so much, they walked right past each other on the platform."

A rustling noise made me look down. The little girl handed me a picture she'd drawn. "Did you do this, Matilda? It's very good."

"We call her Tilly," said Janet.

The drawing was of three stick people, one a child with a triangle dress, a larger person with bubbles for hair going down to her feet labelled Mummy and the other with short hair labelled Daddy. I caught Janet's eye. She looked away and stroked the child's hair. "Why don't you go and play in the garden while Daddy has his tea?"

"She thinks I'm her father," I said, watching through the window as she played on a swing.

Janet coloured. "Of course. What else would I have told her?"

"Won't that get complicated? What does the real father think?"

She shook her head and shivered. "He was killed. A long time ago."

"I'm sorry."

She got up and busied herself clearing the tea things. "It wasn't meant to happen."

"All right, let's not go through it again."

"No, I want you to understand. They'd just taken Daddy away and I was worried sick about you. Everyone was being sent to France and it was all so terrible. I didn't think I'd ever see you again. We thought we were going to be invaded like everywhere else. He'd lost a brother and his best friend. He'd just received his call-up papers. He was so frightened. We only meant to comfort each other..."

I nodded. "Who else knows?"

She looked up at the ceiling as if she couldn't quite believe I was asking the question. "No one."

"Did you love him?"

That was obviously a bigger question. Tears pooled in her eyes. She caught them with her fingers. "God, Jack, do you have to ask?"

"Yes."

I was expecting the answer so it shouldn't have surprised me when she nodded.

After a long pause she asked, "Do you think it's true that there's one special person in the world for each of us?"

"Yes," I replied at last. "I think it is."

She nodded. "So, what do we do now? Do you want to stay?"

I shrugged. "For now, yes, if you don't mind. I've nowhere else to go."

"Stay then. We can see how it goes." She ran the hot water and rinsed the cups. "Probably best if we have separate rooms, at least to start with."

I agreed, partly because I was too tired to argue. We were alive. The war was over. I kept telling myself that was what mattered.

Dressing in my old clothes again was one thing. Fitting back into civilian life turned out to be another. Finding a job was easy now there weren't many people to fill them. But after living with constant fear and glimpsing exotic worlds, I found myself restless and frustrated back home. It was hard to settle. No wonder some returning soldiers turned to crime.

Janet found the adjustment difficult, too. She'd got used to living in a certain way and although she never said so, she must have been wishing Matilda's real father had been the one to return safely.

Insomnia, bad dreams, and pain from my injuries kept me awake at night but surviving the war gave me a new sense of purpose. I was more determined than ever to solve the mystery of Giselle's disappearance. There were more private detectives about after the war, with so many people looking for lost husbands and relations, either because they wanted them back or they wanted a divorce. Now, finally I had the means to pay, and something I hadn't had before the war – her real name.

A light rain fell as I walked down a road of three-storey, bay-fronted Victorian houses looking for number seventy-four. There was nothing on the building to show that it was a detective agency. I knocked and waited. At last, the door was opened by a housekeeper with a severe face and hair scraped into a bun.

"Mr Snow's expecting you. He won't be long."

She invited me to leave my umbrella in the stand and showed me up the stairs to a waiting room. Sitting in an armchair, I glanced at a newspaper but found it hard to concentrate. There was no one else waiting which was a relief as conversation would have been awkward but I kept thinking about all the people who must come here – wives looking for husbands, husbands looking for wives, parents looking for children, businessmen with scores to settle. All the evidence locked away in those filing cabinets next-door – compromising pictures, receipts, tickets, newspaper cuttings, diaries of movements. What sort of person did this for a living? Digging out other people's secrets, turning up rocks and exposing what seethed underneath?

Ten minutes later I heard a muffled goodbye and feet scuttling down the stairs. The housekeeper reappeared and showed me into a large, book-lined office with polished floorboards and a leather-topped desk. Mr Snow, a tall, angular figure, was standing at the window, where I imagine he'd watched me come down the road while listening to his previous client. He turned as I came in, closed the shutters, and smiled.

"Mr Sanders. I'm sorry to have kept you waiting."

He reminded me of a bird with his bony face, hooked nose, and widow's peak. The skin on one side of his face and down his neck was raised and pink, probably the result of a severe burn. A few years ago, it would have shocked me. I wondered if he'd sustained the injury in the war or in this job.

"Please sit down. Take your time. Tell me how I can help."

His chair creaked as he settled back to listen to my story. He stuffed his pipe and puffed on it watching the swirl of smoke travel up to the ceiling. I told him everything right up to the soldier who recognised me from the farmhouse and told me Giselle's real name was Grace.

Mr Snow took notes as he listened, underlining words and occasionally stopping to clarify something. Cars swished through the wet streets below, their headlamps briefly brightening the room through the crack in the shutters.

Eventually he put down the pen, and steepled his fingers. "Why is it so important to you to find this lady?"

"I want to know if she's alive."

"And then what? I hope you don't mind my asking."

"I want to hear from her lips what happened on the train that day – why she disappeared."

"And that's all?"

The secretary appeared with a tea tray. Mr Snow waited until she'd poured the tea and left the room before continuing.

"I'm sure it's occurred to you that after all these years, it's probable that Giselle – or should we say Grace – is married with a family. If so, she won't welcome someone turning up from her past."

"I realise that."

I'd been through every scenario during those long nights in Africa and Italy, from Giselle being married to another member of the aristocracy to her being a spy. In most cases she wouldn't want to know me.

"And of course with the war..."

He took the tongs and dropped a couple of sugar cubes in his tea, stirring thoughtfully.

"I understand."

He went through his notes, tapping his pen at certain words.

"It would be unfair of me to offer false hope."

"Are you saying you won't take the case?"

It was a blow. Something I hadn't really considered up until now.

He shook his head. "No. I just want you to be aware there are no guarantees."

"Understood."

I liked the fact he wasn't exaggerating the likelihood of success. He seemed a man of integrity. Although the fees were higher than I'd hoped I wasn't going to back out now.

Over the next few weeks, I jumped every time the telephone rang, or the letterbox rattled. I went over everything the detective had said and wondered how I'd react if he found Giselle, but she refused to see me. Now that the search was more real, I was suddenly less sure.

Chapter Twenty-Five

I'd all but given up hearing from the detective when I received a letter which I opened over breakfast. Could we meet? He'd found something that could be of interest.

"What is it?" Janet asked, looking up from cutting Tilly's toast into soldiers.

"Nothing. Just business," I said, putting the letter away.

My heart was thumping. Part of me wanted to cut off the past and start anew. To be that better person I had promised myself I would be all those nights in the war, and make things work with Janet. But a small, irrational part still clung to the hope that, despite everything I'd been told about Giselle, there had merely been a mistake, and she was still alive. Perhaps even still cared.

If this works, if the detective can find you, will you agree to see me? Will you even recognise me? Or will we talk like polite strangers? That would be the worst thing of all.

. . .

I arranged for Gilbert Snow to visit me in my office the following afternoon. I had difficulty concentrating on anything while waiting for his arrival and spent most of the afternoon looking out of the window at the cars rumbling around the edge of the park below, but in the end, he arrived without me noticing.

"Take a look at this," he said, slipping a slim file from his briefcase and putting an old newspaper cutting on my desk. "Tell me what you think."

My heart stopped. I felt my face flush.

"It's her. That's Giselle."

I looked for a long time, taking in every detail. But then the words in the headline and the date on the page sank in.

"Except that it can't be, can it?"

Death in the Alps

Tragedy struck the fashionable ski resort of San Moritz yesterday when a cable car ripped away from its cables during a storm and plunged 260ft into a ravine. It is thought the accident might have been caused by a tree falling on the line during high winds and snapping it.

Among the victims were Lady Lorna Hamden, wife of English baronet, Sir Hugh Hamden, their daughter, Grace, and an unborn baby. Lady Hamden had been expecting a child.

She and her daughter had taken the cable car up the mountain to a beauty spot on a sightseeing visit with fellow hotel guests American sisters Miss Amanda and Miss Ida Cartwright, retired Indian civilian Mrs Felicity Dempster, Italian architect Mr Mauro Arnolfi and experienced Swiss guide, Stefan Hartmann.

They are believed to have been on their descent when the accident happened at quarter past five in the afternoon. There were no survivors. Witnesses report seeing the cabin swinging and hearing a noise as it broke away from the cable.

Grief-stricken Sir Hugh was at the hotel when the accident struck. He is being comforted today by friends at the Hotel Carlotta where the family had been staying.

Rescuers worked throughout the night to recover the bodies, but their efforts are hampered by the severe weather and danger of avalanches.

The owner of the hotel Maxime Häberli, said, "We are all in mourning today. No one could have predicted such an awful thing happening."

February 1931

I read and re-read the article. I tried not to think about what it would feel like, being tossed about in a cable car in a storm, to hear the cables snap, and feel the car plunge. But I looked again at the date. Horrible as the story was, it had obviously happened to someone else. Not Giselle, who I'd met several weeks after this accident happened.

"It can't be her," I repeated.

Gilbert frowned. "You're saying it's not the same girl?"

"Can't be, not unless she's come back from the dead." But Burris's words replayed in my head – the man I'd met in the war hospital. He'd recognised Giselle, and he'd known her name.

Gilbert placed the photograph I'd given him of Giselle on the boat next to the one in the newspaper for comparison. I wanted to believe this was a different girl. And yet the girl in the paper was Giselle. Looking into her eyes I was sure of it.

"Newspapers make mistakes," he said gently. "But they can't have got the date on the page wrong, can they?"

I agreed it was unlikely. My heart was still racing. Something Harry had said a long time ago filtered back into my mind

– something about a tragic accident. Why hadn't I listened to him then? All the time I could have saved...

Gilbert produced a steel ruler from his bag and held it against the faces, comparing measurements. He studied the eyes and earlobes but sat back, shaking his head in frustration.

"It's impossible with the faces being at different angles. And we don't know how recent this photograph of Grace is. It might have been taken a few years before the ski trip in which case there would be a difference in age between these two girls which could explain why this one is slightly rounder faced. But I must say they do *look* remarkably similar."

"Might she have had a twin sister?" I wondered but then remembered Giselle saying her sister had died. "One that perhaps even she didn't know about?"

Gilbert turned his hands up. "It's possible. But it's more likely to be a coincidence. This is simply another girl that looks like her. After all, it's been fifteen years since you saw her and you only knew her for a few days. Can you honestly say you'd recognise her now?"

"But Burris, the soldier who used to work for Mr Allerton, he recognised Giselle as Grace."

Gilbert smiled patiently. "Yes, but he could have made the same mistake we're making. He knew Grace and when he saw Giselle jumped to the conclusion she was Grace. Remember, he hadn't seen her for some years either."

We sat in silence for a few moments, thinking.

"What if..."

"I suppose..."

"Sorry, after you,' I said.

"If just for now we suppose it is the same girl, why would she give you a different name and pretend she was at finishing school?"

I shrugged. "She told me her life was in danger. She had to

get away from her father. Perhaps she wasn't killed in the accident but ran away in the confusion."

He lit his pipe and puffed out smoke. "Hmm, the problem is a witness reported seeing mother and daughter getting into the cable car. Unless she was lying, but why would she lie?"

My secretary looked in again to ask if she was needed any more that evening and I said she should go home. It had grown dark outside. I got up and closed the shutters. I offered Gilbert a brandy, but he said he needed to keep a clear head.

"If the story she told you was true it might explain why she vanished from the train that day. She might have seen her father or one of his associates and jumped off the train to avoid them."

"Or she might have been taken."

I was recalling the men who had peered into our carriage on the way up to the farmhouse and Giselle's fear when she saw them. And what had Burris the shepherd said about the owner planning to tell her father she was there?

"We need to find out more about the baronet," I said. "Now we have his name that should be easy."

"I've already made enquiries," said Gilbert. "Sir Hugh and Lady Lorna Hamden lived in Swan Hall in Lancashire. The family made their fortune through the cotton mill Hugh's grandfather built.

"They took the child in when she was six years old. She came from a modest family in a Welsh mining village. She was a relation of Lady Hamden, a niece, I think. It seems the couple weren't able to have children due to Sir Hugh's injuries in the Great War. Grace's real mother was a war widow struggling to bring up four children while keeping the family drapery business afloat, so the adoption gave her one less mouth to feed. I imagine the money they offered would have been enough to save the business."

For a moment I thought I'd misheard. "She sold one of her children?"

"I'm sure she didn't think of it like that. It meant she could give Grace a better life. The Hamdens were a very wealthy family. Grace would be brought up as a lady, presented in court as a debutante. She'd have been well-placed to find a husband."

"It still doesn't make it right."

He shrugged as though the morality of the thing wasn't relevant right now. "The house was requisitioned by the army during the war. It was left in a sorry state, from what I hear, but according to neighbours, Sir Hugh had let the place go after the accident in the Alps. Within a year he'd dismissed the staff, shut up the house and moved abroad – somewhere near Antibes.

"However, I've managed to track down his wife's lady's maid, Alice Carter. She was staying with them on the skiing holiday and saw the pair getting into the cable car."

At last, we were getting somewhere.

"Unfortunately, she's in a specialist nursing home, suffering from mental trouble. I spoke to the manager, but she refused to let us talk to Alice. She's in a very vulnerable state."

It was a blow. Every opportunity that was dangled before us seemed to get snatched away.

"She has a teenage daughter, however. Iris. She may have pictures of Grace and be able to tell us a little about Alice's time with the family. It might help us establish if the Grace and Giselle are the same person or if they could be related."

"Of course. When?"

He held up his hand again. "I've written to the school, but I should warn you, from what I hear Iris hated Grace. She blames her for her mother's condition. Grace was a very difficult child."

"But we must talk to Iris – if only to rule Grace out."

"Please don't get too excited about this," Gilbert urged. "The most probable outcome is that there's no connection between these two girls. And if Grace turns out to be the person you knew as Giselle, she lied to you – and we have to ask ourselves why. Solving the mystery might lead to further disappointment."

I understood but having come so close to finding her after all this time I wasn't about to let her go now.

Chapter Twenty-Six

The headmistress of the convent school in Berkshire agreed to let us talk to Iris in her presence. Her office smelled of polished wood, old books and roses arranged in a tall vase on her desk. A large window, slightly ajar, looked out onto the playing fields where a group of girls were playing lacrosse, their shouts carrying across the crisp air.

Iris was short with straw-coloured hair pulled into a ponytail save for a few loose strands she kept tucking behind her ears. She came in looking pink and nervous as though expecting to be told off but relaxed when she found this wasn't the case.

"My mother was a lady's maid," she told us. "Not really a servant, more of a companion. She joined the family as a housemaid before the Great War. But when Sir Hugh took over the estate and the dowager moved to the London flat, taking her maid with her, my mother became lady's maid to the new Lady Hamden.

"It's not an easy job. She did everything for her – kept her rooms tidy, brought in her breakfast tray and helped her dress. She went with her on visits and helped her choose clothes and hats, so she had to study the magazines to keep up with what was fashionable."

She turned to the headmistress. "May I fetch my photographs?"

The headmistress nodded. As Iris scampered off, she called after her, "Don't run!"

The girl walked very properly out of the room, but we heard her clatter down the corridor. The headmistress rolled her eyes and laughed.

"It's very good of you to let us come," Gilbert said.

"I hope you'll find it helpful. But please do bear in mind that Iris has been through a lot. It isn't easy having a mother who's been in service, let alone one in an institution. Girls can be quite unkind."

"Who pays her school fees?" I asked.

She frowned. "We don't know, but they're always paid on time via an arrangement with a third party."

"What do you know about Grace Hamden, the baronet's daughter?"

"I believe she was Lady Lorna's niece," said the headmistress. "Came from a small place in Wales. Being adopted was an excellent opportunity for Grace."

"Being packed off to live with people she didn't know?" I said, ignoring Gilbert's cautionary look.

The headmistress gave me a condescending smile. "You'd be surprised how quickly children get used to a new environment, Mr Sanders. I've seen girls arrive in tears but in no time at all they've settled in as though they've lived here for years.

"And Lady Hamden wasn't a stranger. She was a relation. Her beginnings were just as humble as Grace's, but she adapted to life in the big house extremely well by the sound of things, which shows how easily it can be done."

"But that's different," I objected. "Lorna chose to marry Sir

Hugh. She knew what she was taking on. The child had no choice in the matter. Did she even know what was happening?"

Gilbert cleared his throat as Iris's footsteps sounded in the corridor. She came in catching her breath, clutching an envelope, which she shook out onto the headmistress's desk, scooping up a few photographs as they fell to the floor.

She handed me a picture that showed a family with their staff outside a grand country house with towers and gables and dozens of different chimneys.

"That was Sir William and his wife and the boys. Hugh's this one at the front with the fair hair and striped blazer."

Looking at the building, my heart flipped over. It took me back to sitting in that train carriage with its rain-streaked windows on our journey up to Northumberland, Giselle sketching the house. Swan Hall looked exactly as I remembered from her drawing.

Iris picked up another picture showing a handsome couple seated in front of a much-reduced staff assembled at the same house. She pointed to a small girl with a round face and dimples who looked like herself but with darker hair. "That's my mother, see? The dress she's wearing used to be Lady Hamden's. She used to let her have some of her old ones to adapt for herself."

She sifted through the pile, picking out one of a distinguished couple with a young girl. It was clearly the same building but taken at the back on a veranda. The man was tall and leaned on a stick. A spaniel sat in front of him.

The girl looked about ten. She was wearing a white dress and had long hair tied with ribbons. Behind her stood her mother – or adoptive mother – petite with dark curls and a bright birdlike face. They looked like a happy family but studying the picture more closely, I was struck by the child's haunted expression and the mother's hand resting on her shoulder looked as though it was there to stop her breaking away. Perhaps I was reading too much into it.

The next picture was a studio shot showing the same girl a few years older with her hair pinned up and her face resting on clasped hands. My heart thumped. Looking closely at the girl's hands I couldn't be sure but the ring she wore looked like the one Giselle had owned, the one with the pink diamond solitaire that I'd found at the farmhouse after she'd gone and gave to Janet without meaning to.

"I imagine your mother must have got to know Lady Hamden quite well," Gilbert said.

"Oh, she did. Lady Hamden came from a different background to Sir Hugh. My mother was the best friend she had. She used to talk to her about everything when Mother was dressing her hair and always called her by her first name."

"Did your mother enjoy working there, would you say?"

Iris scowled. "She did until Grace came. Grace made her life hell."

The headmistress made a disapproving noise.

"She wasn't right, you know. Up here." Iris tapped the side of her head. "The family were tricked into taking her. Nobody warned them what she was like."

"And what was she like?" I asked.

Her eyes widened. "Evil. She hated everyone, especially Lady Hamden because she blamed her for bringing her there, and Mother because she was Lady Hamden's maid. My mother still has scars where Grace pushed her into a fire. She couldn't fight back or even complain because Sir Hugh wouldn't listen."

"Did your mother go with the family on the skiing holiday?" Gilbert asked.

Iris nodded. "She's never got over the shock. Says the cable car was swinging about like washing on a line. Then it dropped like a stone. Some of the bodies were thrown out as it fell. It's the screaming she can't get out of her head."

I could understand that. I had a sudden vision of someone screaming on the battlefield. I had to walk over to the window for a few moments and compose myself.

"It caused her breakdown. She blames herself, you see."

"But it was an accident. No one's to blame for these things," said Gilbert.

Iris blushed. "Lady Hamden asked her to go with them up the mountain, but she had a headache that day and asked if she could be excused. She walked into the village to buy some post-cards and someone in the shop warned her about the storm coming but she didn't take much notice.

"When she got back to the hotel the baronet asked to see her about something and it wasn't until they noticed how dark the sky was and he mentioned that the others were going out in the cable car that she remembered about the storm.

"She ran to warn everyone, but they were already getting into the cable car, and they couldn't hear her. All she could do was wait and hope.

"She stood on the hotel balcony watching the sky change colour and the clouds sliding over and feeling the temperature drop. Then the first drops of rain appeared, and the wind started whipping the snow.

"She and Sir Hugh went out in the storm to look for the others but by then it was so hard to see anything, and they could hardly stand upright."

"She definitely saw both Lorna and Grace getting into the cable car?" I asked.

Iris looked surprised and nodded. So, Alice had seen them go up, but it didn't prove that they had both come down – although as Gilbert pointed out the chances of surviving a fall like that, let alone surviving long on a mountainside in those conditions were tiny. I wanted to question Iris more closely, but Gilbert shook his head.

"How is your mother at the moment?" he asked gently.

"I don't know. I'm not allowed to see her."

The mistress cleared her throat. "Not for the moment. It's for Iris's own safety. During her last visit her mother tried to attack her. She was very distressed. She doesn't realise what she's doing but it's upsetting for Iris. However, she's receiving excellent care. She's in the best possible place."

"Who pays the bills?" I asked.

"I have no idea. Now, I'm sorry, we must go. I have lessons to prepare, and Iris is missing French."

She walked purposefully to the door and stood holding it open. I noticed Iris stoop to pick up Gilbert's card that had fallen to the floor and put it in her pocket.

A few days later Gilbert sent me a parcel. Inside was a diary and a letter in neat schoolgirl handwriting.

Dear Mr Snow,

I found this diary in a box of my mother's belongings the last time she went into hospital. I don't know why she didn't finish it but it tells you a bit more about Grace so you might find it interesting. There is nothing more I can tell you. Please don't disturb my mother. She's very ill and bringing up Swan Hall and the accident could make her worse.

I hope this is of some help to you.

Best wishes

Iris Carter

I slipped it into my pocket on my way out to work. I was certain that Iris had told me all she knew but that her mother held the key to Giselle's disappearance.

Chapter Twenty-Seven

Alice's Diary

Grace was trouble from the moment she arrived. We'd been looking forward to her arrival. We made her room look lovely with new clothes hanging in the wardrobe, toys in the toy chest and cheerful pictures on the wall.

A house that size needs children. The staff used to talk about how it had been full of noise and laughter in the old days when the family was growing up. Hugh was the fourth son – the handsome, indulged baby of the family who spent his time partying in London and travelling to exotic places with his friends, shooting elephants, crossing deserts, and digging up forgotten cities. But the Great War took all that away.

The third brother died at school – he'd been born with a weak heart. The second was killed in the early days of the war, I'm not sure where. Hugh was wounded in Ypres. He was sent to a big house near Cardiff which had been turned into a hospital for officers. He wasn't expected to make it through the night, but over the following weeks and months he recovered.

Not that it was easy, so I've been told. He went from feel-

ings of euphoria and relief that he had survived to rage that he was so damaged and useless and deep feelings of guilt that he had been given a chance while others hadn't. He was still grieving for his brothers and friends and he suffered terrible nightmares.

Lorna often read to him, pushed his chair around the grounds and very gradually she helped him take a few shaky steps. She knew nothing about his position in society.

He spent a year in the hospital and fell in love with her although it took a while for him to voice his feelings. Whereas the old Hugh had been full of confidence, his disability had made him self-conscious and self-loathing. He couldn't believe anyone would find him attractive, especially not someone as young and pretty as Lorna. She kept her feelings to herself too because relationships between nurses and patients were forbidden.

One afternoon Lorna was summoned to the matron's office. Afraid she was in trouble, she smoothed down her uniform, straightened her hat and knocked on the door. To her surprise a well-dressed, middle-aged couple sat staring at her.

"Do come in, dear, we don't bite," said the woman.

They asked her a series of questions and she began to think she was being interviewed for a different nursing job. It was only when they saw her confused expression that the woman laughed and said, "Hugh has written to us to tell us about the girl he wants to marry. We wanted to see you for ourselves."

"And you pass with flying colours," said the husband.

In the old days they wouldn't have approved, but he insisted he owed his life to Lorna. They knew he wasn't the catch he would have once been. Whomever he married would have to be his carer as well as his wife.

Even when she found out Hugh was the son of a baronet it never crossed Lorna's mind, she would one day live in the big house. It wasn't until after the war ended that his elder brother died. It was a dreadful shock for the family and meant a different future for Hugh, although it seemed a long way off.

Sir William had a London flat that Hugh used and a villa in Antibes. It was all very romantic – the couple spent a year on the Riviera to aid Hugh's recovery. Lorna used to push him in his chair along the front and she'd read under the umbrella pines while he painted.

I think he would have happily stayed there, hosting parties, and holding exhibitions. But it all changed when his father died suddenly of a heart attack. The estate passed to Hugh, and suddenly he had an estate to run.

As with so many big houses at the time, life at Swan Hall wasn't as rosy as you'd imagine. Keeping up with the outgoings was a constant struggle, there were too many staff, and repairs had been left for too long.

On top of that he was still recovering from his injuries. But with Lorna's help and encouragement he made better progress than any of us thought he would although he tired easily and got dreadful headaches and mood swings.

He still used the wheelchair most of the time when he first came back but put himself through a gruelling regime of physiotherapy. Gradually he walked further with sticks although there were setbacks, and his frustration made him furious.

The only thing missing from their lives was a child. We assumed Sir Hugh's injuries were to blame. Lorna was adored by visiting children. She'd play hide and seek, organise quoits tournaments and set up treasure hunts for them around the grounds but it seemed such a shame she didn't have any of her own. After they'd gone she'd withdraw to her room or go for a long walk. It must have been unimaginably painful to have everything money could buy but not the thing you wanted most in the world.

So, when we were told they were going to adopt, we thought it was wonderful, and so noble of Sir Hugh to bring up someone else's child but he said that he'd been lucky to survive the war and wanted to help a family whose father hadn't come back.

Reading Alice's words, I could sympathise with Sir Hugh. I was reminded every day of the people we left behind. Why them and not me? I wondered if the guilt would ever leave. They invaded my dreams, turning up when I least expected to see them, and revealing their wounds before I had a chance to cover my eyes. Sometimes I didn't see them at all, just heard their cries.

I took the diary home with me and after reading Tilly a bedtime story and waiting for her to fall asleep, sat by her bed, catching up with Alice's story.

They brought Grace home late one night. They'd been travelling all day and she was tired and disorientated by the journey, her cheeks all red and swollen from crying. We stood at the front of the house to greet them, but she was half asleep, so Sir Hugh carried her inside. He set her down gently but as soon as her feet touched the floor, she went wild.

I smiled, picturing Giselle as a child. Tried to imagine what it must have been like for her to be taken away from her family. Arriving at an imposing old house full of strange faces, realising her life was never going to be the same. I thought about the little girl in the pictures with the haunted expression.

She looked from one to the other of us, her eyes huge and terrified. Then she ran back to the front door, hammering on it and screaming, "Let me out!"

I wanted to give her a big hug and tell her everything would be all right, but I caught something in those eyes – a glint of hatred. Lorna tried to coax her away from the door, but she smashed her fists into Lorna's face, making her fall backwards, blood trickling onto her hand.

While I was seeing to Lorna, the child slipped past me and tore through the house, looking for another way out, punching and kicking anyone who stood in her way, screaming, "I want to go home."

She rattled the French doors back and forth, kicking the panels and slamming her hands against the glass. She turned over chairs and swept a vase off a table. Shards flew everywhere.

Sir Hugh caught her, holding her arms out in front of her and saying, "Steady on." He grimaced as she kicked his bad leg.

"Overtired, that's all. She'll be fine after a good night's rest."

We took her up to her room but she wouldn't stay there. In the end, Sir Hugh locked the door. "Come away. Leave her to settle."

But that's when the screaming started. It sounded like an animal being slaughtered. It went on all night. My room was directly above the child's and I lay rigid in my bed, hardly daring to move. The silence that followed was so thick and ominous it was almost worse than the screaming. I was terrified, imagining what we'd find in the morning.

It was even worse than I'd thought. The child had wet the bed, ripped the feathers out of the pillows and shaken them all over the room, pushed over the washstand, cutting herself on the smashed basin, and she'd smeared a disgusting word on the mirror in what looked like blood.

But where was she? At first there was no sign of Grace. Lorna rushed white-faced to the window, but it was secure – there was no way she could have got out. At last, we found her cowering inside the wardrobe. She looked so small and frightened, her face swollen and burned with tear trails, it was hard to believe this little mite could have done so much damage.

"When can I go home?" she asked.

"Now look," said Sir Hugh, "this is your home now. We didn't bring you here as punishment. It's really not such a bad place to be."

"I want my family."

He sat on the bed next to her as I dressed her cuts. "I'm sorry to have to tell you, my dear, that it won't be possible to see them any longer. But I think you're going to get along fine here. When you've calmed down, why don't you come and have some breakfast?"

We spent the day sorting out the room she'd destroyed, and moved her things upstairs to an attic room where she could do less damage. Later, as I was passing the drawing room, I overheard Lady Lorna say, "What on earth have we done?"

And Sir Hugh's reply: "She'll get used to us. Give her time."

I didn't hear any more because he closed the doors with a thud.

"That was a long story." Janet looked up suspiciously as I came down from Tilly's room, the diary safely back in my pocket.

"She wanted me to stay until she fell asleep. I don't like leaving her awake in the dark."

Janet smiled. "You mustn't spoil her. She needs to get used to it."

But Alice's story about Grace was still going round in my head. I wasn't sure that being strict with a frightened child helped and hated to think of Tilly in that situation. I'd already become more attached to her than I'd expected. Was this private investigation fair on any of us? And yet at the same time I had to know what had happened to Giselle – or Grace as I had to think of her now.

"Someone telephoned for you. A Mr Snow. What does he want?"

I hesitated. "Ah. It's about that case in Berkshire, I expect. He must have more information for me. I may need to go away again for a few days."

She shot me a suspicious look but didn't argue. I waited until she was out of earshot before picking up the receiver in the hall.

"I just wanted to make quite clear," said Gilbert, "that I don't want you to visit Alice. Iris lent us her mother's diary on the strict understanding we wouldn't involve Alice personally. I gave her my word. Please leave the investigation to me."

"Of course."

Was he forgetting who was paying who? I hoped a visit wouldn't be necessary as I could find out what I needed through the diary, but I couldn't rule anything out.

Chapter Twenty-Eight

Alice

Despite Sir Hugh's optimism things didn't get easier. If anything, they got worse. Grace refused to speak to anyone for the first few weeks. If you touched her, she screamed. The only time I managed to get an answer from her was when I asked if she wanted anything.

"Yes," she said each time. "I want to go home."

"This is your home now," I told her, as gently as I could.

But I was fearful saying it because she was so unpredictable. Sometimes she'd behave as though she hadn't heard. At other times she'd lash out, grab my hair, and twist it round her little fist until I saw sparks.

The doctor told us it would make the transition easier if Grace wasn't surrounded by memories of her old life so we were forbidden to give her any letters and instructed to throw her belongings away. Most of her things were poor quality anyway but I rescued a doll just before it went on the bonfire. It was a china one with golden hair, a torn dress, and a chip on the nose. Valueless but it had obviously been well-loved. Grace was overjoyed when I gave it to her. She threw her arms around me, which took me by surprise. After that she never let the doll out of her sight. Although she refused to speak to most people, she talked to it as though it were real.

"Is it true?" she asked me once when I was tying a ribbon in her hair. "Did my family all catch Daddy's illness and die in the night? Was I the only one found alive in a house full of dead people?"

My heart dropped. This wasn't the story I'd heard in the kitchen. Surely, they would have told us if Grace had been in close contact with a deadly illness? I was shocked by the lie but they must have thought it would be another way to help her break with the past.

"I suppose it must be true," I said, although I hated myself for doing so.

Her eyes were huge and filled with fear. "What if I've got it, too? Am I going to die?"

"No. No, of course not. We'd never let that happen. Doctor Collins examined you, didn't he, and said you were fine. He's an excellent doctor."

She frowned, considering this. "Daddy's doctor told him he'd be all right and he wasn't."

I drew her towards me. For once she didn't resist. She felt so small, squashed up against me and she let me stroke her hair and tell her everything was going to be all right. She clung to me for ages, crying. I began to think I'd been wrong to be frightened of her. Sir Hugh was right – she was just a small, terrified child in need of love.

Jack

Reading Alice's diary, I felt anger swell up inside me. How could those people have thought it fair to take everything away from a child and tell such a monstrous lie? Alice had been kind to save the doll for Grace. She must have risked getting into serious trouble. But if the maid could see the injustice of it all, why couldn't everyone else?

Alice

Grace could be sweet, snuggling up for a story, or playing cards and boardgames. But you never knew what might set her off. A kitten that scratched her when she tried to stroke it was found drowned in the fountain, some spectacles belonging to a guest were found in their case, smashed. They looked like they'd been stamped on. A maid was dismissed for stealing a necklace but we later found Grace's doll wearing it. And a pair of devil horns and glasses were drawn on a portrait of Lorna.

"You're supposed to be keeping an eye on her," roared Sir Hugh. "What were you thinking of, letting her run amok?"

The only thing Grace seemed to care about was the doll. She would tuck her up in bed and sing to her, read her stories, and pretend to be a nurse, making the doll well from a variety of diseases. She kissed the doll so tenderly and took it with her everywhere but went mad if anyone else touched it.

As the months went by she set one servant off against another, unmaking a fire that had already been made, scratching a car that had just been polished, throwing handfuls of mud into the soup that was cooking, tearing clothes down from the washing line and trampling them into a puddle.

And yet despite the things she did I felt sorry for her. Everything at Swan Hall was different from what she was used to. She asked for Welsh cakes, barabrith, cawl, and each time was told there was no such thing. It was like telling her she hadn't existed before.

No school would put up with her behaviour so the decision was made for her to be educated at Swan Hal with a governess. While cleaning the rooms, I'd hear Grace practising her elocution over and over, choking back tears as she recited Camelot, the Kubla Khan and The Highwayman. I heard the thwack of the ruler every time she forgot a line. When she swore, the governess washed her mouth out with soap, which made her sick.

But hardly a day went by when she didn't cause tension in the family. Lady Hamden was at her wits' end. Things were so different from what she'd imagined when she offered to adopt Grace. She became thinner and hollow eyed. With all the weight she was losing, I had to make alterations to a couple of her dresses. After one of the doctor's visits, I found sleeping pills on her bedside cabinet.

Once when I went into Lorna's room in the morning, I could see her bed hadn't been slept in. She was sitting on the window seat, her face wet with tears.

"What did I do to deserve this?" she said. "Why didn't Ellie tell me what her demon daughter was like? Why didn't she send the other sister? Do you think it's too late to ask her to swap?"

I had no idea how to answer. All I was thinking was that if Grace's mother and sister were still around, the story about the family dying from an illness must be untrue.

"All I wanted was to give a child a loving home and help someone I loved. How could Ellie deceive me like that?"

"I'm sure things will get better," I said.

A sharp laugh escaped her. "I'd send her back if I could, but

Hugh won't hear of it. You know what men are like. It hurts their pride to think they can't solve a problem. She behaves better when she's with him, so he has no idea how bad things are."

I didn't dare comment. Hearing her criticise her husband put me in an impossible position. But I'd also noticed Grace adapting her behaviour according to who she was with, which made me think she must have some control over her outbursts.

"We're doing the right thing," I heard him say while I was dusting the bookshelves in the library later that morning. "She'll appreciate it one day. It's bound to take a while for her to settle in."

Lady Lorna's voice, high and hysterical, shot back. "A while? How long's a while? I can't stand another day."

Sir Hugh sounded tired and irritable. "Please don't be so melodramatic. This is what you wanted, isn't it?"

There was a pause. Then Lorna's voice shook. "What I wanted? Is that what you really think? What I wanted was a child of our own. If you'd been able to give me that, we wouldn't be going through this."

A terrible silence followed and then a smash and a splintering of glass. He must have hurled his glass into the fireplace.

It was the first row I heard between them, but certainly wasn't the last. Wherever you went there were whispers, exchanged looks, people turning away, doors closing. The house seemed to be holding its breath, waiting for the next eruption.

Jack

A sense of unease trickled through me as I read Alice's words. Where was all this leading?

Chapter Twenty-Nine

Alice

Sir Hugh had little to do with Grace at first, but he occasionally took her out with him for walks around the estate. Grace was a different child when she was with him.

From Lorna's bedroom window, I used to see the two of them out in the grounds, him with his sticks, Grace pushing the doll in its pram. He was convinced she'd be better behaved if she was allowed to let off steam outdoors the way he and his brothers had, climbing trees, making dens, rolling down banks and splashing in the lake.

She'd scamper back and forth with little finds to show him, play house in the rhododendrons, they'd spot deer and collect conkers. I think she was happiest on those walks when she had him all to herself.

She liked watching him paint. He produced some lovely pictures of the estate in different seasons, the walled garden when the wisteria was out, the rose garden in summer, the statue garden in winter and the lake in the mist. Grace would stand beside him for hours asking about the colours he was using, the techniques, the thickness of the paint, the type of brush. He did several paintings of Grace in the gardens and the woods. She looked adorable – like a little flower fairy.

"There's nothing wrong with the child," he used to say. "She just needs to be managed the right way."

And she'd stand there looking like butter wouldn't melt but as soon as he was out of earshot, she'd start up again.

As time went on you could feel the distance growing between the couple. Lorna's disappointment in Grace and her belief that she'd been deceived over the adoption was so huge.

Hugh clearly felt she was managing Grace wrongly and was dismissive of her complaints. He still behaved like a gentleman in front of other people but in private he was short with Lorna, as though he found the things she said petty and embarrassing.

They rarely made eye contact and when they were alone in the house each seemed anxious to fill up their time, living separate lives under the same roof. Sir Hugh would retreat to the orangery with his paintings or the library to sort out paperwork, Lorna to the morning room. I suppose Grace saw this, too.

When Grace became older, she stopped playing with the doll. It sat in her room, but occasionally I'd still hear her whispering to it as though to another person.

The tantrums never stopped altogether but very slowly, Grace accepted her situation. Things got better for a few years, at least on the surface. She managed to get her temper under control, achieved good academic results and behaved nicely in front of guests. From the outside you'd have thought they were a perfect family, but I sometimes caught a look that reminded me she hadn't forgiven Lorna for snatching her away from home and then rejecting her.

The real problems started when Grace reached her teens. She attracted a lot of attention wherever she went and could hold people spellbound.

One of Sir Hugh's paintings made me feel uneasy. It was a very exuberant picture of Grace reclining against some cushions in a boat on the lake, wearing a floaty dress. It was lovely in a way with the light dappling through the willow branches but the way the dress was rucked up and something in her expression didn't seem right on a girl so young.

A group of Hugh's old London friends gathered at the house at weekends. They'd roar up in their cars, often in theatrical fancy dress, and dance wildly for hours, drink champagne under the stars, sprawl on the grass talking about paintings and poetry and travel, their music and laughter rippling out over the lawn long after most people were in bed. It wasn't always easy to tell what gender they were, let alone who was in a relationship with whom.

They hung around all weekend, getting up late and doing things on a whim such as painting an entire wall of the drawing room with a trompe l'oeil Mediterranean landscape, and the morning room walls with a menagerie of fantastical beasts. Lorna was horrified when she saw it. She thought it an act of vandalism, but Hugh snapped, "When did you become an expert on art?"

Whereas Grace was thrilled and asked if she could help.

By the time she reached her late teens, Grace became the centre of these weekend parties. She'd drape herself over the guests, share cigarettes, and discuss art and poetry late into the night. They could hardly conceal their adoration. Lorna tried to keep Grace away, which only led to rows.

"It's hardly Grace's fault if people find her charming," I heard Sir Hugh say one afternoon. I'd been carrying a tray of lemonade through the library and froze halfway across the room. It was a sweltering day and the French doors to the veranda were open, but the curtains were closed to protect the furnishings from the sun, masking me from view.

"If I didn't know you better, I'd think you were jealous."

"Jealous?"

"Of the attention she gets. It's normal for someone of her age. You must stop being bitter about it."

"Are you mad?" Lorna's voice was high and indignant. "I'm concerned, that's all."

He snorted. "Is that what it is?"

"Can't you see what's going on?"

I heard his newspaper rustle. "All I see is you getting hysterical."

Not long afterwards something happened at one of those weekend parties. It was a bright, warm evening at the end of a scorching afternoon. People were lazing on the lawn, playing croquet, or sipping gin and tonics. One of the guests said they fancied a walk and Grace said she'd go with him to show him the way.

I was collecting the empty glasses when I heard splashing and giggling and the click of a shutter. Peeping through the rhododendrons, I saw a male guest taking photographs of Grace sitting by the lake. I retreated, walking briskly back across the lawn but before I reached the house the man's wife pushed past me at such a rate, she almost knocked me over. Voices erupted – swear words, protestations. A slap rang out.

When the couple left, Lorna went out for a drive. She still

wasn't back by midnight. Sir Hugh was in a dreadful state, pacing up and down but it wasn't until the next morning that she arrived back in a taxi. He followed her up to her room but she wouldn't let him in and stayed there for days afterwards refusing to see anyone.

After that, the tension in the house soared. It was Michael, one of the other staff, who alerted me to Lady Lorna's drinking. He was having to top up the decanter in the drawing room more often than he used to. Lorna would often mix a cocktail in the evening before dinner but these days she was drinking a second or third.

She sometimes took her drink back to her room and wouldn't come down for meals. To prevent the gossip below stairs I removed the evidence, washing out Lorna's tooth mug that smelled of brandy, clearing up a broken perfume bottle she'd thrown across the bedroom and washing stained clothes. I thought I was helping but now, looking back, it feels more like colluding.

As time went on, the drinking became harder to hide. Sir Hugh made excuses for his wife but Michael told me about a disastrous lunch party where she asked him to refill her glass but he was under instructions not to.

"Are you deliberately ignoring me? Or has my husband told you not to serve me?"

The laughter around the table stopped. Michael had no idea what to say.

"It isn't up to him. What's the matter, Hugh, am I embarrassing you?"

"You've had enough," murmured Sir Hugh. "You'll make a fool of yourself."

Ignoring him, she thrust her glass at Michael. "Fill it up."

He glanced at Sir Hugh who nodded wearily, then poured a small glass.

She threw the drink in Sir Hugh's face.

Michael froze. He lost control of the spoon he was holding and watched in horror as a potato fell off and rolled across the table.

People started making excuses about leaving. Sir Hugh hissed something in her ear, but it only made her laugh.

"I know what you all think – that Hugh made a mistake marrying me. He could have done better."

"You know that's not true," he muttered.

But she ploughed on. "I told him at the time he'd regret it, but he insisted he never would. I've seen the way you look at me. And I heard you, Mary and you, Ava, saying how I got ideas above my station. Well, guess what? It's me who made the mistake. I hate it here. I didn't ask for any of this. I was tricked into living here. Just like I was tricked into having her."

She pointed her glass at Grace. One of the women gasped and took Grace's hand.

"None of you can see it, can you?" Lorna shouted. "You think she's charming but she's laughing at the whole bloody lot of you."

There is something else I really should say here but it's difficult to admit to even inside my head, let alone see it written down. It's something I would prefer never to talk about. And yet if I don't, I won't be telling the whole truth.

I always admired Sir Hugh. I believe he had good intentions and he loved his wife but with his marriage problems and everything the war had put him through, something made him snap.

I loved Lorna, and I loved my job, but if things continued as they were between her and Sir Hugh, I knew I'd lose them both.

Sir Hugh started to pay me attention. I should have stopped

him. At the time that seemed impossible but I've thought a lot about my feelings for Sir Hugh and whether I might have unknowingly given him the impression it would be all right. I could say I was still young – in my twenties – and how could I be expected to stand up to the man of the house? But I wonder sometimes if that was an excuse.

At the time I thought Sir Hugh was a sad, broken man who needed some comfort. If someone were to provide that discreetly there was a chance that he and Lorna could eventually get past the problems they had, and their marriage would be saved. I don't know if I've said it clearly enough now. I can't use the words. But he used to summon me to a guest room sometimes and I... well, I hope it's obvious without me having to write it.

What went through my mind each time was that I was doing it for Lorna, to make her life easier. I tried not to think at all when it was all going on. Afterwards he would leave without a word and each time I'd hope it would be the last.

I always waited a few minutes after Sir Hugh had gone before leaving the room just in case anyone was around. On one occasion I opened the door and, seeing the corridor was empty, thought it was safe to leave. But as I turned the corner at the end I nearly bumped into Grace. The look she gave me – so cold, so triumphant – made me certain she'd guessed what was going on.

I did my best to look unconcerned, but it would break Lorna's heart if Grace told her, and I would lose everything. The fear hung over me. Every now and then I'd catch a look from her and be reminded that she knew.

For a while, things seemed to get better. In June, Lorna and

Hugh spent a few days away together in Paris to go to a wedding and when they came back, she had a glow about her.

"It was so lovely to visit galleries and churches and sit in parks and for once not have to worry about all this," she said, gesturing around her at the estate. "Hugh seemed like a different person, more like the man I married."

For a few weeks after, they seemed closer than they'd been for a long time, but I knew it wouldn't last. The financial worries hadn't gone away, and Sir Hugh spent long hours with his accountant going through the ledgers, which put him in a bad temper.

Lorna complained of feeling unwell one evening and went to bed early. In the morning, she looked pale and asked me to take her breakfast away. She'd been sick and blamed the mushrooms they had had for supper. A few days later she reacted badly after eating crab. When it happened a third time, she was convinced she was being poisoned. She started coming down to the kitchen, questioning the cook about how the food was prepared which caused some bad feeling. She gave the staff strict instructions to keep Grace out of the kitchen.

"I don't suppose it could be anything else, could it?" I asked, although I was embarrassed doing so.

"What else could it be?" But I looked at her face and saw it dawning.

"Oh." Colour flooded her face. She clapped her hand to her mouth. "I can't be," she kept saying. "I mean, it's not possible, is it?"

But the doctor confirmed a baby was on its way.

"You were right," she said, her face pink with excitement. "I daren't say a word to Hugh yet, it's still so early, but I had to tell someone. I still can't believe it's happening."

She produced a bottle of champagne and two glasses. "Come on, help me celebrate."

"Oh no, I couldn't," I said, but she insisted. "You must! You're the best friend I have here, the only one who understands what it's like for me."

I blushed at her words. We clinked glasses. I'd never drunk champagne before. The bubbles got up my nose, making me laugh.

"Will it all right for the baby?" I asked.

"I don't know." She froze, the glass halfway to her lips. "No more after this then."

It felt strange, drinking champagne with Lorna, sharing her precious secret. It was all wrong and yet it was such a perfect moment. My head was fuzzy. I felt as though stars were exploding.

"I hope it's a boy," she said, suddenly coming to her senses. "I couldn't bear another girl, not if they turned out anything like Grace."

We looked at each other wildly as a floorboard creaked outside the room and a shadow passed under the door. Someone was standing on the other side of the door. Whoever it was had heard everything. Lorna made two quick steps across the room, but the door opened just as she reached it.

"Oh! Grace. You gave me a fright."

I'll never forget the look on Grace's face – so cold, so terrifying. But she forced a smile as she walked into the room and poured herself a glass of champagne. "What are we celebrating?"

Gradually, the truth sank in. Male or female, the new child would be a blood relation, a baby that properly belonged to Swan Hall. Where would that leave Grace?

Jack

So, just as Grace had got used to living at Swan Hall, her future was threatened all over again. What would that do to someone? I thought about all the secrets Giselle and I had shared at the farmhouse. Remembering how convincingly she'd lied to the other guests that first night, I also now wondered to what extent she'd also deceived me and what she was capable of.

Alice

It was coming up to Christmas. Lorna asked me to accompany her to London by train to visit a dressmaker who specialised in clothes for ladies who were expecting. She was pleased when Grace asked to come too. We visited a gallery, had afternoon tea, and saw a ballet in the evening. They were both on best behaviour, looking like any mother and daughter, happy in each other's company.

But on the way back as we squeezed our way along a crowded platform to catch our train, a scream made me freeze. Lorna who had been closest to the edge of the platform had been knocked off balance. Panic broke out around me. A train was approaching. I tried to get to Lorna but there were too many people in the way, pushing me back. At the last moment, a man lunged forward and caught her, dragging her back onto the platform.

"Thank you. Thank you so much." Grace was already there, hugging Lorna. "Are you all right? What happened?"

Lorna thanked the man and laughed it off. "Someone pushed past and I lost my footing."

She wasn't seriously hurt, just bruised and shaken, but the

terrified look she cast me as we boarded the train confirmed she was thinking the same as me. Had Grace pushed her?

"You have to tell Sir Hugh," I begged her when we got home.

She shook her head. "He won't listen. He always says I'm ill or tired or just imagining it. Promise me you'll watch out for her."

I promised. And from then on, I stuck as close to Lorna as I could. She, became increasingly anxious, locking her door at night and jumping whenever Grace came into a room.

The doctor diagnosed pre-natal anxiety. "It's very common. She must rest and not worry about anything or it could harm the baby."

He recommended taking a holiday away from the worries of managing the estate. The next thing I heard, Sir Hugh was taking Lorna away on a trip to the Alps and I was to go too. It seemed like a good idea – anything to get away from the atmosphere in the house. But to my surprise, Sir Hugh told me Grace was coming too. "It's important for us all to spend some time together as a family before the baby arrives."

If I'd had any idea what would happen on that holiday I'd never have gone.

Jack

I turned the page. It was blank. Looking more carefully, I saw several pages had been ripped out. My heart beat fast. What had Alice written that she didn't want anyone to see? What had Grace done on that holiday that needed to be covered up?

A knock on the door made me jump out of my skin. "Telephone call for you," said Janet. "That Mr Snow again."

I put down the diary and went downstairs to the telephone in the hall. Gilbert's voice crackled down the line.

"I've heard back from the owners of the house near Cardiff that was used as an officers' hospital. They've given me an address in Daffyd's Well for Lorna. I thought I'd go down there and see if I could track down Grace's original family."

"And?"

"They've all left unfortunately. But there's a sister – Evangeline Clements. Used to be Evangeline Lloyd. She's married to a farmer, lives in Somerset."

"What address? I'll go and see her."

"No. Let me go first. She might not welcome the intrusion. There's no reason to suppose she can shed any light on Grace's disappearance. Most likely, she has no idea what happened to her sister after she left the family at six years old."

"All the same, I'd like to speak to her."

"Please, Jack, leave it to me."

I was getting closer all the time to finding Giselle although I was having to push back doubts about who she really was and what she'd done. Perhaps Gilbert had been right all along, and I should leave the past in the past where it belonged.

And yet I couldn't leave things as they were. Without answers, I couldn't go on.

Chapter Thirty

Alice Carter sat in an armchair, hands clasped in her lap, staring out of the window onto the nursing home lawns. She was frail and birdlike with iron grey, bobbed hair. Her head shook minutely and she took a sudden wheezy breath.

"She's like this most of the time," said the nurse.

"I won't upset her. I promise."

Introducing myself, I sat in the tub chair beside Alice, asked after her health and commented on her surroundings and the view. She didn't respond. The nurse stood over us for a while but eventually slipped away to deal with another patient.

"I've been speaking to your daughter, Iris," I said.

Alice's small, dark eyes brightened. I passed on some of the things Iris had told us at our meeting about a hockey match she'd scored the winning goal in and a prize she'd won for an essay. Alice smiled, looking much younger than she had when I first saw her.

"We were looking through some photographs," I said. "There were some taken when you worked at Swan Hall."

She stiffened and clamped her lips closed like a small child.

"Do you remember much from your time there?" I showed her the picture of the staff outside the house. "Is this you here?"

She nodded. Her finger reached out and traced the faces.

"Do you remember Lady Hamden?" I asked, pointing to her.

A small smile formed again. "And her daughter, Grace?"

Alice's head snapped back to the window. I tried again. "I'm looking for Grace. People say she's dead, but I don't think she is. Do you?"

Alice looked resolutely ahead, trembling. I glanced around and lowered my voice.

"You aren't going to get into any trouble. I'm just trying to solve a mystery. The thing is, I've been reading this diary you wrote..."

I held it up for her to see but she lunged for it. Caught off-guard, I toppled back in my chair. I held tight to the diary but she bit my hand.

A nurse appeared by my side. "Whatever's going on here?"

"I don't know," I said, still shocked by the violence.

"I must ask you to leave. Now."

I could still hear Alice's screams as I backed out of the room. Something had obviously terrified her. During the confusion when the staff were trying to calm Alice, I slipped into the office and stole a look at the accounts. A few moments confirmed my suspicions – that Alice's fees were paid for by Sir Hugh Hamden.

Next, I needed to visit Grace's sister, Evangeline Clements. I found the village Gilbert had mentioned without much trouble and locals directed me to an ivy-clad, brick farmhouse a few miles further on. I rang the bell a few times, unable to believe my bad luck when nobody came to the door. No sign of anyone round the back of the house but a full line of washing billowed in the wind so the place was obviously lived in.

I was about to get back in my car when a voice called out, "Can I help?"

A woman's head appeared between sheets of washing. "If it's my husband you want, I'm afraid he's out in the fields."

"Actually, it's you I came to see – that's if you are Mrs Evangeline Clements?"

"That's me, yes. But do call me Evie."

She held out her hand. I shook it and introduced myself while fighting back bitter disappointment. With her square face and dark colouring, this woman looked nothing like Grace. There was no way she could not have been mistaken for her. Still, I was here now. I may as well press on.

"I'm looking for someone. A woman called Grace Hamden. I believe she's your sister?"

"My sister?" Evie looked startled. "I'm afraid you're mistaken. I don't have a sister."

I wished I hadn't blundered in. Of course, she thought Grace had been killed in the cable car accident.

"But you did once." I showed her the picture of Giselle. "Could this be her?"

She took it from me and gazed at the face for a long time. At last, she glanced up at me, eyes wide. "Who are you?"

"I'm sorry, I'm making a mess of this. I'm looking for a girl I knew. She called herself Giselle, but she looked identical to your sister, Grace. And I'm wondering if she could have been the same person."

The woman shook her head. "That's not possible. My sister died, Mr Sanders, in 1931. It was terribly sad news, but we weren't brought up together. I hadn't seen her since we were children."

She pulled another shirt out of the basket and pegged it on the line. I found myself staring at her hand. Without meaning to I reached out, my fingers straying towards the sparkling pink stone. With a gasp, she snatched her hand away. "What are you doing?"

"I'm so sorry, I didn't mean to alarm you. It's the ring. A pink diamond from Australia? The girl I knew wore one identical to this one."

She cocked her head, frowning.

"But the thing is, I met her a month after the skiing accident in which your sister's supposed to have died."

Evie's tone sharpened. "Well, it can't have been her then, can it? You must have got it wrong."

"The girl I met told me she was in danger. And then she disappeared. I've blamed myself for it ever since and now I feel I owe it to her to find out what happened to her."

"I'm afraid someone's been lying to you." The woman's features softened a little. "Look, come inside. I don't think I can be much help, but I'll tell you what I know."

She picked up the basket and led me through a boot room into the house. I followed her through an untidy hall with a chequered floor to a comfortable sitting room with a crackling fire. "Take a seat. I'll make us some tea."

"Oh, please don't bother."

"It's all right. I could do with a cuppa anyway."

Her footsteps disappeared down the hallway. I could hear teacups rattling and a kettle being filled. Looking around the room, some photographs on the piano caught my eye. I got up to study them. One in particular drew my gaze. Two little girls, one dark, one blonde, sitting on the grass with a baby between them wearing a christening gown. My heart beat faster as I picked it up.

"I still think of her like that."

Evie's voice made me jump. She nodded to the picture in my hand as she set down the tray. "Silly, I know. It was taken just before Grace disappeared."

"What happened?"

"I just woke up and she'd gone." She sat down in a wing chair, collecting her thoughts. "Grace and I went to bed as usual the night before. In the morning, she wasn't there anymore. Must have been lifted out as she slept beside me."

It was hard to believe. "You had no idea it was happening?"

She shrugged helplessly. "I've asked myself so many times how they could have done it without waking me. Grace wasn't the sort to go quietly. She could fight like a cat, and I was a light sleeper. I can only think they must have put something in our milk that night to make sure we didn't wake."

"What did you think had happened?"

She poured the tea and handed me a cup. "Nothing at first. It took a while to be certain she wasn't hiding somewhere waiting to spring at me. I remember running through the house flinging open doors and shouting at the maid: 'When I'm upstairs you say she's downstairs and when I'm downstairs you say she's upstairs! Where is she?'

"My mother told me Grace had gone away. At first, I thought she meant she'd died. I'd already lost my father and baby sister, so it made sense."

I murmured my condolences. She flicked me a grateful smile and shook her head.

"We thought we were lucky, making it through the war. My father came back in one piece but then he went down with the Spanish flu. He seemed to recover but it left him with a weak heart. Months later, I went to fetch him for breakfast and couldn't wake him up. He was only in his thirties."

She drew her cardigan around her shoulders, remembering. "Our baby sister, Bella, died soon after him. You know what people were like back then – they told us Bella had 'gone to play with the angels.' It took a while to work out what they meant. Made me so angry! I didn't see why the angels should have my little sister to play with – and why hadn't they taken Grace instead?" She brought her hand to her mouth. "I'm sorry, I know that sounds awful. Scone or lemon drizzle?"

I took a slice of the lemon cake. "Why do you say that about Grace?"

She closed her eyes, biting her lip as though trying to hold back a flood of hurt and anger that she'd harboured over the years.

"I'm being unfair. Sisters fight, don't they? It would have been different if we'd had the chance to grow up together."

"What was she like?"

Evie puffed out her cheeks and laughed. "A terror! Never did as she was told. Barely a day went by when she didn't get herself into trouble. Sneaking into the shop and dressing up in the fabrics. Knocking my mother's best jug off the dresser and turning it round so you couldn't see the crack. Tricking me into climbing inside a wooden chest and then slamming the lid down and running off. Saying the wind had changed while she was pulling a face, and it would never change back."

That last memory pulled me up short. Hadn't Giselle told me a similar story?

"Grace was four years younger than I was," said Evie, sipping her tea. "But she was stronger and so determined. She had a terrible temper. I sometimes provoked her just to see what would happen, she was so easy to bait. She'd fly at you – bite, pull hair, pinch, kick. She pushed me down the stairs once and I broke my arm. I've still got the scar – look."

She drew up her sleeve to reveal a raised ladder climbing upwards from her left elbow.

"Grace always had to get her own way. If she didn't, she'd hold her breath until her face went blue."

"Sounds frightening."

Evie frowned. "It was a little."

"What sort of things did she get angry about?"

"Oh, I don't know. She was jealous of the attention our father gave me. She seemed to think she had to make up for the extra time I'd had with him before the war. She'd clamber onto his knee when I was already there and push me off. I cracked my head on the floor once. Came up in a huge bump. When he died, she didn't stop crying for days.

"She was jealous of the baby too. Not at first. She loved Bella when she was born. Treated her like a doll but she soon got fed up with her crying and resented the time my mother spent with her."

Bella? Where had I heard that name before?

Evie was quiet for a moment. "My mother put it down to Grace being a middle child. Gethin, the next one down, was a boy so even when Bella came along, he was still special, but Grace had to fight even harder to be noticed. My mother was so busy trying to keep the business going she had no time to spend with us and Grace was too young to understand."

She frowned. "I'm not getting this quite right. Grace could be sweet and affectionate. She'd cuddle up to listen to a story and she loved sentimental songs like *Don't Go Down to The Mine, Daddy*. She wasn't as bold as people thought – she was frightened of so many things – the dark, earthquakes, volcanoes, wolves, poison gas, falling through cracks in the pavement. She had nightmares and I always had to reassure her.

"Eventually I got my mother to admit that she'd gone to live like a princess in a grand house in England. I asked when she was coming back, and she said 'Never'."

"Did she explain why?"

Evie chased some crumbs round her plate with her finger. She shook her head. "She never discussed it with us, but she was grieving for my father and struggling to feed us all. She'd just managed to keep the business afloat during the war but we were left with so little."

"So, your aunt offered to adopt Grace?"

"She was a cousin, actually, but yes – to adopt one of us. To tell the truth I never understood why Mother chose Grace. She was prettier, obviously, but such a difficult child."

Even now after all these years, Evie seemed stung by the unfairness.

I stirred my tea. "But don't you think that's why your mother chose to send Grace away rather than you? Because she was the difficult one?"

Evie rested her cup on the arm of the chair. "I never thought of it like that. I always felt I'd failed in some way. But after what Grace did to Bella, I think you could be right."

I felt my skin prickle. "What did she do?"

Evie sighed. "I had a china doll which Grace adored. She was always asking to play with her, but I wouldn't allow it because she was careless, and I knew she'd break her. She'd already dropped her once and chipped her face. I used to hide the doll but Grace always found it."

I remembered what Alice had said in her diary about the doll that went everywhere with Grace and how upset she'd get if anyone took it away from her.

"Our house was four storeys high," Evie said, "with a long garden at the back leading down to a river. One afternoon—it must have been early summer—I looked down at the garden and noticed the clothes had been tipped out of the laundry basket which stood empty at the end of the lawn.

"Grace's gold hair glinted in and out of the foxgloves. She was staggering along, carrying something heavy. When she reached the basket, she knelt down, put in whatever she'd been carrying, and pushed the basket towards the river.

"I wondered what she'd put in that basket in place of the laundry and then it struck me. My doll! I was sure she had her. I checked in all the usual hiding places – on top of the wardrobe, under the bed, behind the curtain, but there was no sign of the doll.

"I couldn't let her get away with that. The doll's face would be smashed in, and her clothes spoiled. I banged on the window, flung it open and yelled, "What are you doing?" Grace looked up and saw me but pretended not to hear. I clattered down the stairs, tore open the French windows and raced down the garden screaming, 'Give her back!'

"Grace dropped the basket and took off around the garden. My mother, the maid and a neighbour heard us. Suddenly they were all shouting and running down the garden. It was only when they brought up the basket that I saw it wasn't my doll in there at all. It was baby Bella."

"Was she all right?"

"She seemed to be." Evie shivered. "But she died that night."

We sat in awkward silence. I played the scene over in my head. "But what happened? You said she was all right."

She shrugged. "The doctor said although she hadn't drowned at the time, her lungs had probably taken in too much water."

"Grace was very young. Do you think she knew what she was doing?"

Evie closed her eyes. "At the time I thought so. She said she'd been playing Moses in the bulrushes and hadn't meant to harm Bella. I didn't believe her." She gave a long sigh and turned away. "Now, if I'm honest, I'm not sure. Perhaps I was unfair. I've thought about it a lot over the years. People kept asking me exactly what I saw. If I hadn't insisted on my version of events Grace might never have been sent away."

"You were only children," I reminded her. "And Grace sounds very mischievous."

Evie smiled. "She certainly was. She got worse after Bella died. Used to make up terrible stories. Once she told me she'd been down to the graveyard when I was asleep and dug up the baby and played with her. She pretended she could see Bella and talk to her. It used to drive me mad!

"Whenever she did something wrong, she'd say Bella did it or Bella told her to do it. And I remember shouting at her 'I wish it had was you who died, and not Bella!'"

Evie suddenly became brisk, tidying up the tea tray. "I've often wondered if Grace remembered me saying that."

"You can't blame yourself," I told her. "If you had any idea how many things I've said that I regret... But I have to ask, did you ever see Grace after she moved away?"

Evie stood up and walked over to the window. "Never. I thought about her a lot, but didn't dare mention her name because it upset my mother so much. She'd been ill since giving birth to Dylan, my baby brother, retreating into herself staying in bed for days or sitting hunched in a chair as if she'd suddenly become very old. It must have all got to her – losing my father, then baby Bella, and then Grace. Even though she must have thought she was doing the right thing sending Grace away, it must have made her feel awful."

"She never spoke about her?"

"For a while I used to come across reminders – Grace's name scrawled inside the cover of *Mary Poppins* or a ballet shoe at the back of a cupboard still moulded to the shape of her foot; an item of clothing or a mark on the wall where we'd recorded our heights – but gradually everything of hers was removed. It was as if she'd never been.

"I'd have dreams of spotting Grace running ahead of me but when she turned round, she had no face – just a mask like the ones the soldiers wore when they were horribly wounded.

"There were times when I wondered if my mother had lied about where Grace had gone. She could as easily be dead or in a poorhouse, or in prison." Evie offered me more cake, but I declined.

"As I got older, I thought about her less often but it's the milestones that get to you. I'd find myself thinking she'll be blowing out her birthday candles today, sitting her exams today, leaving school today."

"Weren't you able to keep in touch?"

She shook her head. "I tried at first. I wrote but I never heard back which didn't surprise me – Grace hated writing. One year my mother sent back all her Christmas presents because she refused to do her thank you letters.

"When Mother died, I thought Grace would want to know so I wrote with details of the funeral. I received flowers and a formal letter from Lorna regretting they wouldn't be able to come but heard nothing from Grace. That clinched it for me.

"I married Freddie in 1930 and moved here. We invited Grace to the wedding, but she didn't even acknowledge the invitation. We read about the cable car accident in the newspaper the following year. It was such a shock even though I barely knew her anymore.

"Freddie and I went to the memorial service for Lorna and Grace. It was very moving. Sir Hugh was very gracious and welcoming. I had so much admiration for him."

He didn't sound like the man Giselle had described. I told Evie what she'd said about her father and how frightened she was of him.

She listened to the end and smiled, shaking her head. "It doesn't sound like him at all. He obviously loved them both very much. This person, whoever she was, can't have been telling the truth."

"I'm told he lives abroad now. You wouldn't happen to know where?"

Evie looked surprised. "I don't think that's true either. He's still in Swan Hall as far as I'm aware, but losing his wife and Grace left him a broken man. My guess is that he wants to be left alone to grieve in peace."

There was something in her expression that convinced me she had more to tell.

"You did see Grace again, didn't you?" I said gently. "Was it after the accident?"

She looked wretched but was no better at lying than Janet.

"Please, I need to know. Did she really die in that cable car? And if she didn't, why would she want people to think that she had?"

The telephone made us both jump. I cursed whoever was ringing.

"Excuse me, I must get that." Evie jumped up. "I'm sorry, there really is nothing more I can tell you. I'm sorry you've had a wasted journey."

She was hiding something, I was sure of it, but there was nothing more I could do.

"Thanks anyway. I'm sorry to have brought up bad memories."

I'd taken up enough of her time. Besides, there was someone else, I needed to see.

Chapter Thirty-One

The name Swan Hall was only just legible on the lichened gateposts as I drove between them. The gates had presumably been removed for the war effort. Dried leaves and beech seed cases crackled under the tyres as I followed the twisting drive through a tunnel of tall trees. On through parkland shrouded in mist, over a bridge with a broken balustrade, past a dry fountain coated in green mould to a gravelled forecourt sprouting waist-high grass and a lawn studded with Nissan huts.

Swan Hall appeared at last, forlorn and neglected. The windows were shuttered, and the chimneys gave out no smoke. Thinking that Evie had made a mistake after all and the house was abandoned, I almost turned round but the road was too narrow and now I'd come this far, I had to be certain.

It was drizzling as I climbed the steps to the front door under the cold gaze of a pair of stone griffins. I pulled the bell several times, but no one came. I walked around the building, checking for any sign of life. At last, I found it – a chink of light in one of the downstairs rooms at the back. I put my hand up to the French doors and peered in.

I sprang back as I met the furious glare of an unshaven man with a shock of white hair. The doors rattled.

"What do you think you're doing? This is private property."

"I'm sorry. I rang the bell. I wasn't sure if you'd heard."

"Are you from the National Trust? I've already told you—"

"No, actually I was hoping to have a word with Sir Hugh."

The old man raised his eyebrows. "Do you have an appointment?"

"No."

"Then you've had a wasted journey."

He tried to shut the doors, but I pushed my foot inside. "It's important. It's about his daughter."

"You're rather behind the times. The baronet's daughter died some years ago. Didn't you know?"

"Well, that's just it. I don't believe she did."

He flinched. "What on earth are you talking about?"

"I take it you are Sir Hugh?"

He glared at me again. "You're a journalist, is that it?"

"No. I'm a lawyer."

He took my card and studied it before at last stepping back to allow me in. "Whatever it is, get on with it."

The room was filthy. It smelled of damp and dust. Paraffin hissed from an enamel stove in the corner. Cobwebs clung to the decorative plasterwork on the ceiling and the curtains were tide-marked with damp. Panelling had been ripped off the wall – perhaps used for firewood – and someone had drawn moustaches on the carved figures on the fireplace.

The bookcases around the walls suggested this room had once been the library but the shelves were empty now. The blankets on the chaise told me the baronet lived in this one room. In a corner stood an easel. The half-completed painting of a Mediterranean coastal village reminded me of the ones around Amalfi.

"Do you like it?" he asked.

"I do, it's very good."

Other canvases were stacked against the wall. A conglomeration of crates and boxes stood on the floor, with stuffed animal heads balanced on top. I wondered what condition the other rooms were in.

I remembered Alice mentioning the library in her diary and the conversations she'd overheard in this room. Giselle had been here. She'd sat in this room. Gazing around, I felt a jolt and found myself staring at her. Although amateurish and coated in dust, her face in the portrait propped up on the fireplace was unmistakable.

With the aid of his stick, the baronet crossed the room to a desk covered with unopened post and overflowing ashtrays. Unwashed mugs and plates sat on a pile of dusty ledgers. He lowered himself into a chair, indicating that I should sit opposite.

"Well?" he said in a clipped tone, as though I were holding up important business.

I set down the newspaper cutting in front of him. His body tensed and he nodded but pushed it away.

"Do you know where Grace is?" I asked.

I saw a flicker of fear before he laughed. "Good God, man, I take it you can read?"

"I've met her. It was after the accident."

He looked at me, his ice blue eyes round and hard. "Why on earth are you digging up this business now?"

"Because I'm interested to know why you told everyone your daughter was dead when you knew perfectly well, she wasn't."

He studied me. "What do you want?" Before I could answer, his eyes lit up with barely disguised triumph and, I suppose, relief. "I see. You're in love with Grace, aren't you? You thought she loved you too but one day you woke up and she was gone. Is that it?"

He laughed softly. "Well, I'm sorry to break it to you but you're not alone. Just one in a long line of men she's made a fool of. It's a game she plays—making people fall in love with her. Picks them out, the weak ones, catches them at a low point, plays on their vulnerability. And when they're no more use to her she moves on. You're no different from all the rest."

He leaned forward. "So, if you've come here to claim back money you were stupid enough to spend on that girl you're going to be disappointed."

"I'm not interested in money."

"Good. Then get out."

But I hadn't come all that way and waited so many years to be sent packing like a schoolboy. "I'm not going anywhere until you tell me..."

His eyes blazed with indignation. "If you don't leave, I'll call the police."

"Go on then. I'm sure they'll be very interested to hear that you killed your wife."

He laughed but couldn't disguise his shock. "Killed my wife? Where did you get that idea from?"

Eventually, he reached for a whisky bottle. He offered me a glass, but I said no. Apart from its sticky appearance, I needed to be able to think straight. He shrugged and poured himself one with shaking hands, swirled it around and threw it down his throat, slamming the glass back on the desk.

"Well, to answer your question, I have no idea where Grace is. Dead, for all I know. Hope to God, I never see her again."

I couldn't let him leave it at that. "How can you talk like that about your daughter?"

"She's not my daughter."

"You adopted her. You're her legal guardian."

I pushed the newspaper cutting towards him. He appeared to steel himself before reading it. Staring at the picture, he seemed lost in thought.

"Whatever you might think we adopted Grace with the best of intentions. My wife never felt she deserved all this." He flapped his arm around him. "It made her feel guilty. She felt duty-bound to share it with someone less fortunate. She was an amazing woman, Lorna. Took me on despite my injuries, put up with my moods and the stress of running this place. It might look like an idyllic life to you, but you haven't seen the bills. If we hadn't tried to help someone out, my wife would still be here today."

Rain hissed at the windows. The branches of a horse chestnut tree thrashed in the wind, dropping conkers onto the ground with a series of thuds.

Sir Hugh was quiet for a few moments, deep in recollection. "It was a baby Lorna wanted, not a child. Someone she could love from infancy. When we married, she asked a cousin's little boy to be our pageboy and the woman's two daughters to be bridesmaids. The cousin was a widow. She came to the wedding with a baby in her arms and three older children."

He smiled ruefully and poured himself another glass. "We felt sorry for her, trying to manage a young family and run a business while grieving for her husband. A while later, when we'd given up on having children of our own, I brought up the idea of adoption and Lorna reminded me of the widow.

"We offered to take the baby off her hands but she wrote back, saying the baby had died. Lorna suggested taking one of the older girls instead to help the poor woman out. So, we took that child out of a miserable little pit village and gave her everything she could wish for." He slammed the glass down and closed his eyes. "And I've regretted it every day of my life."

He rubbed his hands across his face. "No wonder her

mother wanted rid of Grace. If she'd been honest and told us she was pregnant again, we'd have insisted on waiting for the new baby. Instead, we got Grace.

"We realised straight away there was something wrong with the child. It was like a switch that went off in her head. She could be sweet and meek until some tiny thing set her off. Then she'd act like she had the devil inside her."

"Is it so surprising given what she'd been through?"

"Lorna was all for sending her back, but I felt we had a duty to see it through. There was so much I didn't see at the time." He rubbed his eyes. "I wish I'd listened to my wife. She told me Grace was dangerous, especially when she found out we were expecting our own child. I thought it was the pregnancy making Lorna hysterical. If only I'd paid more attention."

He drained the glass again and poured another. I hoped he wasn't going to drink himself senseless before he got to the end of his story.

"We were happy until Grace came along. But she had to get in between us and turn us against each other." He pressed the thumbs of his clasped hands to his forehead. "I was stupid. I should have seen through her. If it wasn't for her..."

"Grace was a child," I said. "You can't blame her for what happened."

He threw me a bloodshot glare. "You've no idea what she was like. Right up until the end she was up to her spiteful games. Told me a pack of lies about Lorna seeing another man in London, made me think it might be his baby she was carrying."

I tried to make sense of what he was saying. "You killed your wife because Grace told you she'd been unfaithful?"

He looked at me aghast. "No! For God's sake, man, haven't you listened to a word I've said? I'd never harm Lorna. She was my world."

His voice took on a hard note as he said, "I'm sorry to disillusion you but the person who killed my wife was Grace."

The shock hit me like a punch. "Why would she do that?"

"To punish me."

"Why?"

"Because she was jealous." He smiled, a gleam of triumph in his eyes. "The only man she ever loved was me."

Chapter Thirty-Two

"You're saying Grace killed your wife out of jealousy? Because she wanted you? I don't believe that."

"Believe what you want." The baronet fixed me with a glare, let his eyes travel over me. "You didn't know her. You don't know anything about her. You spend a few days with her, and you think that gives you the right to come here and bring all this back up?" His voice shook.

I was determined not to show how sick his words made me feel. I had to calm the situation somehow if I was to learn anything useful. "I'm just trying to get to the truth. I know Grace didn't die in the accident. What really happened?"

He sighed and slumped back. "I thought she had. Everyone did. Lorna and Grace had planned to go up the mountain with some other people from the hotel. They were both out when I got back from the lower slope in the afternoon. The weather had been fine, no sign of trouble. The storm came out of nowhere. It was terrible – hailstones the size of pennies, you couldn't see a thing.

"Some people told me they'd seen my wife and daughter

heading towards the cable car. There was nothing I could do but wait."

He stared into the distance, then rubbed a hand across his eyes.

"It was an awful thing. The gondola smashed to pieces. Never crossed my mind anyone would have survived. We recognised the first body they brought back – he belonged to the party they had been with. The search went on for several days, but it was obvious by then they were only looking for bodies.

"Eventually they found what was left of Lorna down a ravine that had filled up with snow. They said Grace must have fallen further down. It wasn't safe to explore any further in those conditions."

"So how can you say Grace killed your wife? You weren't there."

He gave a short laugh. "Because it turns out I was wrong. They took the cable car up but they never took it back. The maid, Alice, went out looking for them in the storm before it happened. She saw them arguing – Lorna trying to walk away from Grace, Grace running after her, grabbing hold of her, Lorna breaking away, Grace catching up with her and dragging her. Lorna fighting back."

He closed his eyes. "Alice saw Grace shove Lorna and kick her over the edge. I didn't believe her at first – Alice was another piece of work, always making things up. She and Grace never got on. But now I feel awful. I left my wife alone with Grace so I could spend an afternoon with my friends. After all the things Grace had done I should have known better."

He swallowed more whisky. "Grace didn't know anyone had seen her. She must have taken the opportunity to run off under cover of the storm. I wish we'd never gone to that damned place."

But something still didn't add up. There was something he wasn't telling me.

He lit a cigar and drew on it, then let out a long sigh. "Grace was a very disturbed young woman. She'd started saying things to get attention, embarrassing us in public. Making accusations."

"What sort of accusations?"

He continued as though he hadn't heard. "Lorna was convinced she was trying to kill her. She'd reached the stage when it wasn't safe for her to live with us any longer, not with the baby coming. Lorna gave me an ultimatum – either she would leave with our baby or Grace would have to go."

"So, why did you take her skiing with you?"

"I'd heard from a friend about an asylum not far from the ski resort that specialised in troubled young women. I arranged to take Grace there during our trip. Told her we were going to look at a finishing school."

"You lied to her?"

He looked at me scathingly. "She'd hardly have come otherwise, would she? But unfortunately, she must have discovered the paperwork and blamed poor Lorna."

I was still digesting what he was saying. "You were going to stick Grace in a madhouse? So, you could make a fresh start with your new family? How could you do that?"

"It was for her own good." He banged his fist on the table. "If Alice hadn't left the paperwork lying about when she unpacked Lorna's things Grace would never have found out. One more day and she'd have been receiving the treatment she needed and my wife – and our unborn child – would be safe."

We were both silent for a moment.

"You really had no idea Grace had survived?"

"None. I didn't imagine anyone would survive a night in those temperatures. The first I knew was when she turned up here after I'd got back. Just walked in. I had the fright of my life

– thought I was seeing a ghost. She was pregnant. Did you know?"

My heart stalled. I tried not to show any emotion. I wasn't going to give him the satisfaction. "When was this?"

He turned his mouth down. "I don't know – late summer. A few months after I'd got back. The evenings were still light. I'd been out in the garden, left these French doors open. I walked back in and there she was standing where you are now."

He was out of his chair now, walking around the room, leaning on his stick. He stood looking out at the wilderness beyond the window.

"She blackmailed me. Wanted money for the little bastard she was carrying. Said if I didn't give it to her, she'd go to the newspapers, make out I was the father of her baby. I could have called the police, got Alice to tell them what she'd seen, and had Grace arrested for murder, but I didn't. Despite everything she'd done, I gave her the money. But that wasn't enough. After the birth she came back. Kept coming back for more until I had nothing left. Until she knew this place was finished. Oh, she enjoyed it, found it tremendously funny."

"Why would she want to tell people the baby was yours?" I asked, struggling to keep my breathing steady. "Could it have been?"

He shrugged dismissively. "It's unlikely – the dates don't fit. But she could say anything she wanted, couldn't she? People always believed Grace."

"You bastard."

His face turned red. "How dare you! What business is it of yours?"

"She's your daughter, for god's sake."

His voice shook as he said, "She was not my daughter."

"I don't mean literally."

"She's not related to me in any way." I snapped my head

back as he thrust his walking stick in my face. "You're making it sound worse than it was."

"Worse? How could it be worse? You're disgusting."

I ducked as he smashed the cane down. It missed my head but I hunched over, clutching my shoulder, determined not to cry out. I heard a drawer slide open and when I looked up, he was levelling a gun at me.

"The police will understand," he said. "We're on very good terms. I'll tell them I disturbed an intruder, had to act in self-defence."

I felt sweat break out over my forehead. I had one chance to do this right.

"All right. I'm leaving."

I made a slow movement to get up, then kicked the gun out of his hand. I waited for the explosion, but it didn't come. He laughed quietly, watching my expression.

"Did you think it was loaded? Sit down."

He leaned back against the desk as I caught my breath. "Look, it was nothing like you're suggesting. It was Grace who made the advances if you must know, and she was plenty old enough to know what she was doing."

"Even if that's true it doesn't make it right."

I forced myself to ask the question I didn't really want to hear the answer to. "Were you in love with her?"

The silence was painful. He turned and looked out of the window again, drew in his breath and said quietly, "For a short time, yes. I was stupid like all the rest. She manipulated my feelings just as she did yours."

He came over to me and stood holding both arms of my chair, his face close to mine. I could smell his unwashed skin, the cigar, and the whisky. He laughed. "You think you meant something to her? Do you think she even remembers you? She was with you for – what was it – a week? Two?

"Perhaps it was your child she was pregnant with. Some poor little bastard's out there somewhere as the result of your sordid little affair. But for God's sake, man, if you think her interest in you was anything close to love, you're very much mistaken.

"She singled you out, spotted your weakness. Don't you see? For me it was vanity, for you – greed? You thought Grace was your passport to a grander life, did you? Thought you might end up getting a slice of all this?"

He laughed, shaking his head. "You were nothing to her." He jabbed his finger into my face with each word. "Nothing."

I tried to ignore him, but he kept saying it. My head tightened and filled with blank noise. I slammed my fist into his face.

He staggered backwards. With a crunch he caught his head on the fireplace. I watched in horror as he slumped to the ground, a stream of blood trickling onto the hearth. He groaned, put his hand to his head and stared at me in confusion.

I had to get out. I could call an ambulance anonymously once I was away from the house. I turned to go but before I reached the doors I registered movement behind me reflected in the glass. With a roar he grabbed me around the knees and brought me crashing down, splitting my lip as I hit one of the boxes.

I twisted round just in time to see him grab his walking cane. He brought it down across my face with a crack. My eye felt like it was going to explode.

Through blurred vision I saw him in silhouette raising the stick again. Blinded by pain, I wrenched it out of his grasp and hurled it aside, pinning him down to the floor.

He kept taunting me, laughing at me.

"Shut up," I told him. "Shut up!"

But he wouldn't. I stuck my hand across his mouth to stop him speaking but he bit me. I pressed my arm down across his throat. His eyes were huge and bloodshot, glaring. I kept picturing his filthy hands all over Giselle. I could feel his spit on my face. I pressed down with the weight of my whole body. I just wanted it to be over.

When he was still, I stood up, shakily, catching my breath, knotting my hands in my hair. I stepped round him to get to the French doors again, tripping over the boxes. He groaned and twitched. His hand groped for the stick again. It wasn't over. I would have to hear those taunts all over again. He would never stop. My eyes fell on the coal shovel. I picked it up and smashed it down on his head.

This time there was no doubt. The silence that followed slammed through my body. I became aware of my own ragged breathing as I backed away, skidding in blood, wiping my face on my sleeve. What had I done?

I wrenched open the French doors and crashed across the overgrown rose gardens through thistles and waist-high nettles to the lake. I caught myself on something hard which I realised later was a croquet hoop and sprawled face-down, scrabbling in wet mud and leaves. I lay there, my breath coming in short gasps, pain searing through my injured leg, watching the scene play out in my head, hoping each time it might end differently. I couldn't stop trembling.

I'd become the person I'd always dreaded, the one I'd once been accused of being, the monster who had invaded my dreams. I vomited into a heap of leaves and knelt there for ages shivering violently, trying to think straight. Part of me wanted to close my eyes and pass out.

What was I doing? I must get up. It wasn't safe to lie there. I'd left the car at the front of the house. Anyone arriving would see it. I had to get to it before they did. Ignoring the agony in my leg, I forced myself onto my feet, scrambled up the bank and round the side of the house. The French doors were banging in the wind, drawing attention.

Round at the front the car stood on the forecourt for anyone to see. Dragging my leg through the gravel, brushing twigs and mud and vomit off my clothes, I prayed I wouldn't meet anyone coming up the drive.

I threw myself inside, gasping for breath, trying to control the shaking in my hands. I was fumbling so much I kept dropping the keys. My lungs felt like they had a knife stuck in them. I hoped to God the engine would start. In the rear-view mirror, I flattened my hair. The stick had left a dark red mark on my face and my eyeball had swollen up like a golf ball.

Come on – start!

The ignition turned over, but it had been raining all afternoon and the engine was damp.

"Hey!"

A figure running towards the car, one arm raised. "You, there! Stop!"

Where did he come from? What did he see?

At last, the ignition caught. Cursing, I swung the car round, engulfing the man in a cloud of chippings, forcing him back against the wall. I tore down the driveway and swung out onto the road. I drove as calmly as I could to avoid suspicion, but my throat was dry, and my stomach twisted each time I saw a vehicle that might have been a police car. I kept checking the mirror, sure someone would come after me. It must be only a matter of time.

Had the man on the forecourt seen enough of me to recognise me and give a description to the police? Images kept swimming back as I drove. I wiped my face, still unable to believe what I'd done. It was as if I'd been watching rather than taking part. But already I was making excuses. After all, I'd killed before on the battlefield. Was this so different?

Yes. This wasn't some anonymous figure, and I hadn't been carrying out orders.

But it was self-defence, I reminded myself as I drove through the hills, past farms that looked like the one I'd stayed in with Giselle. He attacked me with that stick first. Then again, he was older than I was. He was drunk and disabled.

But he'd goaded me into it. Perhaps he wanted me to do it – didn't want to live anymore but was too cowardly to take his own life so he tricked me into doing it for him.

No. I should have left him alive. Left him to relive his memories, to suffer over what he'd done. And yet if I'd done that what would have happened? He'd have had me tracked down and arrested. Then he'd have won and justice would not have been done.

I hardly noticed my surroundings as I drove. Arguments and counter arguments slammed through my mind. I got back in the depth of night.

"Where have you been?" Janet poked her head out of her room.

Her expression changed as I walked towards her. "What's the matter? Are you ill?"

I thought about asking if I could get into bed beside her. I needed to feel the warmth of her live body against me, but was afraid my shivering would give me away, so I lay in my own room going over and over it in the darkness. I knew I wouldn't sleep. I wished I could tell Janet everything. I needed her strength, her reassurance. But how could I expect her to forgive what I'd done? How could I expect her to go on living with me if she knew the truth?

I must have fallen asleep at some point because I dreamed I was back there. If only the dream could end differently but I couldn't stop it unfolding. I felt myself pick up the coal shovel and bring it down on the baronet's head again and again. I woke with my heart crashing against my ribs. Would I ever be able to sleep without reliving that scene?

The doorbell rang. They'd come for me. I leaped out of bed and started pulling my clothes on. But moments passed and I heard Janet's voice and the milkman whistle as he went up the path. It would be the next time. Or the one after that.

In the morning, I caught Janet staring at me over breakfast. "Your face! What in heaven's name did you do to it?"

I raised my hand to hide it. "It's nothing."

"Nothing? You look a fright!"

She drew her daughter towards her, but Tilly kept staring at me wide-eyed and silent.

"A drunkard attacked me in the street."

"But that's outrageous," she said peering. "Did you go to the police?"

"No."

"Well, you must. If you don't ring them I will."

"Please! Leave it, it's nothing."

She stared at me askance. I had to say something convincing. The last thing I wanted was for her to draw attention to my absence or my injuries.

"There really is no point. It happened so suddenly. I wouldn't recognise him again."

She wanted details – where, when, what was said, what he hit me with, who else was around. I lost patience.

"Can we please stop making a drama out of this? It looks worse than it is."

She closed her eyes and gave a long shuddering sigh. "Why don't you tell me the truth, Jack? I know this isn't a normal marriage and we're not like other couples, but I'd like to think we could still support each other."

"For God's sake there's nothing to tell."

"I don't believe you. Whatever trouble you're in, don't you dare get me and Tilly mixed up in it."

She swept up the child and walked away. I should have pulled her back, said something – anything – to allay her suspicions but I couldn't make myself do it.

A terrible tiredness engulfed me. I telephoned my office to say I was sick, then slept for hours. No dreams this time but I woke with a jolt, thinking of all the things I must do that couldn't wait. I burned the clothes I'd been wearing and bought new ones. Even if they hadn't been blood-stained, I couldn't have gone on wearing them, being reminded each day of what I'd done.

I examined my face in the bathroom mirror, helping myself to some of Janet's powder to mask the scar from the baronet's walking stick. I thought about going away for a few weeks, keeping out of sight until my injuries had healed, but that would only make people suspicious.

I checked the newspapers and listened to the wireless. When there was no mention of the baronet's murder, I let myself hope it might go unnoticed for a while. Perhaps the man who'd tried to stop me hadn't been into the house after all, hadn't seen the body. The longer it took for the death to be discovered, the more chance I had of getting away with it.

I wrote a final letter to Giselle and hid it away with the others.

Do you realise what you've done? What you made me do? I sold my soul for you. Do you even care?

I stopped. How did I expect her to react? With gratitude? Not if the baronet was to be believed. Giselle had loved him—

been in love with him. However unpalatable, it might be true. Anger and hatred swept back through me despite my exhaustion and for a moment I saw it all clearly. I'd done it because I had to. I'd done it for her.

Yes, I thought. The awful truth was, if I could go back and relive the moment I would kill him again.

"Gilbert, this is a surprise. I wasn't expecting you."

The detective looked different – older and greyer. I was surprised he had travelled so far to see me in my office without an appointment.

"I'm sorry, Jack. I can't work for you anymore."

A frisson of fear coiled through me. "What do you mean? Why?"

He placed a copy of the newspaper in front of me. The baronet's face stared out at me under the headline *War Hero Brutally Murdered.*

I thought I was having a heart attack. In the picture the baronet looked younger, stronger, and more handsome than when I'd met him. I read the article, trying to ignore the sweat that trickled between my shoulder blades. Sir Hugh Hamden, a distinguished gentleman who had won a medal for his bravery in the Great War, had been the victim of a violent robbery.

Mention was made of the tragedy he'd suffered in the past, losing his beloved wife, daughter, and unborn child in a skiing accident. A policeman described the murder as 'despicable and cowardly'. They were doing everything they could to bring the perpetrator to justice.

"Awful," I murmured.

"I told you not to visit Alice Carter and you did anyway," said Gilbert, struggling to keep his voice calm. "Now this."

I'd known what he was leading up to, but it was still a shock to hear him say it, as though that made it all real. "What makes you think I had anything to do with it?"

"Please don't insult my intelligence. I had Sir Hugh under surveillance. I was going to ask him in my own time where Grace was. My man saw your car arriving at the house on the day the baronet was murdered. He also saw you leave in a blinding hurry. He thought you were going to run him down."

A vision of the man pinned to the wall shot through my mind. "Even if I was there, it doesn't show I killed him."

"No," he said in a low voice, hardly able to contain his anger. "But the method of killing – so similar to one you were associated with in the past – and the information you would no doubt have obtained from a conversation with Sir Hugh, combined with your *obsession* with his daughter, would be enough reason to arrest you."

"But I—"

"I understand why you did it," he said, meeting my eyes for a moment, "but that doesn't make it right. Why couldn't you have stayed away and left me to do the detective work? What was the point in employing me if you were going to go and sniff things out for yourself?"

He took a breath. "Have you thought about the consequences of this – not just for yourself but for others? Who's going to pay for Alice's care now? Who's going to pay Iris's school fees?"

I had a sudden vision of Iris telling me proudly how she intended to try for Oxford. I felt myself crumple. "Gilbert, please—"

He drew himself up and turned away as though he could hardly bear to look at me.

"I can't take the risk of being associated with you. I will destroy every record of meetings and correspondence between us. You are not to call me or write to me or ever mention that I worked for you. Do I make myself clear?"

He turned back as he reached the door and his features softened as he said, "And I'd advise you as a friend to abandon this search. It will destroy you."

After he left, I slumped over the desk. If Gilbert had worked it out, how long would it take others? His employee had seen me clearly enough to give Gilbert a description. How long could I trust him to keep quiet?

For weeks, months afterwards, I waited for the knock on the door, a voice behind me, a hand on my shoulder. I jumped every time the doorbell or the telephone rang, especially late at night or early in the morning and scanned the newspaper feverishly before Janet had the chance to see it.

I didn't sleep until exhausted and appalled myself with thoughts about how the only way to be sure I was safe would be to find Gilbert's employee and kill him to keep him quiet. But then of course I'd have to kill Gilbert too. Afraid to look into the future, I found myself frozen in the present.

The scar on my face faded but didn't disappear, reminding me every day of what I'd done. And yet life carried on. I continued living with the same woman who had no idea what I was capable of. Because if I lost Janet, I'd lose everything. She'd saved my sanity once and was the only person who could do so again.

The only way I could block out the fear and the guilt and the self-hatred was when I was with her. Keeping up a show of a perfect marriage was my only hope of escaping justice.

As week after week passed, I began to allow myself a flicker of hope. After all, there was nothing to connect me to the baronet's death as long as Gilbert kept quiet. Nothing to say I'd been there or that I had any connection with the household. But hope was dangerous. Hope made people careless. I knew that.

To continue the search for Giselle now would be stupid and could cost me my life. Gilbert's words kept sounding in my ear.

It will destroy you.

Chapter Thirty-Three

"There's a Mrs Clements to see you," said my secretary.

I had to take a few moments to compose myself. Gilbert's visit had left me feeling shaken and sick. Why was Evie here now? Had she read about the baronet's death and worked out that I killed him? I tried to look unconcerned as I rose from my paperwork and shook her hand.

"How can I help you?"

"The thing is, I wasn't quite honest with you when you came to see me."

"You mean you already knew about Grace?"

If only she'd told me the truth, I needn't have gone to Swan Hall to find out more. I'd never have met the baronet and it wouldn't have ended in the awful way it did. But I couldn't hold Evie responsible for everything that happened.

"Do you know where Grace is?"

She shook her head. "No. But I shouldn't have lied to you. I've been feeling guilty ever since. And I know you feel bad about Grace's disappearance but you shouldn't. I could see how much she meant to you, but to the truth is, you had a lucky escape. I want you to know what sort of person she is. I hope it will set you free."

"Go on," I said, although I doubted anything she had to say would surprise me.

She took a deep breath as she sat down.

Evie

Grace turned up on my doorstep eight years after she was supposed to have died. It was Sunday teatime in the autumn of 1939. The last thing I was expecting. I looked out of the window and saw a smart young woman in a belted red coat getting out of her car. I assumed she wanted directions or had come to report an accident.

Freddie answered the door. It was an age before he came back, and I wondered what could be going on.

"I'm afraid you're mistaken," he was saying.

The woman was slim, elegant, mid-twenties with long hair in soft curls. She looked tired and a bit anxious. I wondered if she had news about one of my brothers.

"Evie?" she said. "It is you, isn't it?"

I studied her face. "I'm sorry. Do I know you?"

She laughed. "It's me. Grace."

It still didn't register. Grace is quite a common name. It didn't occur to me she could be *that* Grace. After all, she was dead. We'd been to the memorial service.

"I'm your sister."

My heart raced. The Grace I remembered was a little girl with long golden hair, a button nose, and cat's eyes. I couldn't see what she had in common with this aristocratic young woman. She had a clipped, educated English voice, no trace of the Welsh accent.

She said, "I should have written, but I just found out where you lived and didn't want to waste any time. We jumped in the car and came straight here. Was that too awful of me?"

I was starting to think she must be mad and wondering how we were going to be able to get rid of her.

"*We?*"

"Oh yes, didn't I say?"

The car door opened, and a small figure clambered out. A skinny little boy with sandy hair and huge, dark eyes. He walked towards us shyly. He'd obviously been asleep in the car because his hair was all messed up, his clothes were creased, and he looked about him, blinking in confusion.

'This is Billy, my little boy,' she said, drawing him to her. 'He's been dying to meet you. Shake hands, Billy.'

The child did as he was told and said 'how do you do' in a small, gruff voice.

"Hello, young man." Freddie bent down to talk to him "How old are you?"

"Seven." That was a surprise. He looked much younger.

"Well, it's lovely to meet you both," Freddie said to the woman, "but I'm afraid you've had a wasted journey. You can't be Evie's sister."

Grace's expression clouded and then cleared. "Oh, you mean the ski accident? I had a lucky escape. I'd have come and found you years ago, but didn't know you were still alive. They told me the whole family had died."

"Who did?"

"The Hamdens. Oh, Evie, you're still wearing your bridesmaid ring. I lost mine."

. . .

I looked again at the distinctive ring on Evie's little finger, identical to the one Giselle had worn and that I'd unintentionally given Janet.

"We were given them at Lorna and Hugh's wedding," she explained to me. "We thought they were pretty but had no idea how much they were worth. Mother put them away in a drawer for when we were older, but Grace was always getting hers out and wearing it on her thumb. She must have been wearing it the night they took her."

My heart speeded up. I couldn't think where she could have heard about the rings if she wasn't Grace but I had to be sure. I asked her what else she remembered about our childhood.

She said, "Not much but I remember the shop with all the fabric. And the garden with the foxgloves and the river at the bottom. And your doll. I didn't mean to take it with me. They must have thought it was mine."

That convinced me. It was such a relief to know she was telling the truth. For years I'd dreamed about Grace coming back into my life. But things never happen exactly as you imagine, do they?

It was so unexpected. I was all fingers and thumbs hanging up her coat. Grace was wearing an elegant woollen dress which made me horribly aware of my scruffy old blouse and skirt.

Freddie and I normally ate in the kitchen, but we brought everything through to the dining room on the best china. I'd always thought of it as quite a formal room but following Grace's gaze I was suddenly aware of the faded wallpaper and moth-eaten curtains.

"It must seem awfully shabby compared to what you're used to," I said but she replied, "It's lovely. So homely. And it has a happy feel."

I filled her in on the rest of the family. "Dylan's at Cambridge. His college is beautiful – it must be like living in a hotel. He's very clever but I expect he'll be called up at any moment which I'm dreading."

Grace looked confused. "Dylan?"

"My – our – brother. Oh, you've missed so much. Dylan was born after you left. You'll love him. I practically brought him up myself because Mother was ill after his birth. She was still grieving, and she never really recovered from you going away."

Grace gave me a strange, cold look. "Neither did I."

Freddie was still studying her, baffled. "How did you find us?" he asked.

"Billy was asking where I was born so we took a trip to Dafydd's Well. I was afraid I wouldn't recognise the house, but I knew it immediately. It brought back memories – the miners swaying down the street under our window on their way back from the pub after their shift, their faces all black from coal dust, singing those rude songs and having fights. And the carriages taking the ladies and gentlemen up to the castle for house parties. We used to watch it all out of the window, didn't we?"

Her memories were so accurate and specific that I didn't see how she could be making them up. I was still getting used to the idea that all these years we'd each believed the other to be dead.

But Freddie wasn't convinced. "It seems strange you haven't tried to contact us before," he said.

Grace smiled patiently. "We went down to the chapel to look for the graves and couldn't find them. I asked around and someone told me Evie was still alive and married to a farmer in Somerset. They found someone who remembered the name of this village and we made our way here. The lady in the dairy gave us directions."

Her little boy ate in silence, cramming two rock buns into his mouth in quick succession before touching the ham. I thought Grace would tell him off, but she didn't seem to notice.

His dark eyes lifted to the window as he ate. He stared at the fields in amazement. "Why aren't the cows in their cages?"

My heart clenched. "Haven't you ever been to a farm before?"

"There aren't many in London," Grace said, lighting up a cigarette.

I reached down the Coronation ashtray for her. "You live in London? How glamorous."

She grimaced. "This is so much nicer. And safer."

Billy spotted our marmalade cat on the window seat and without asking to be excused wandered over to stroke him.

"Evie, I must ask an enormous favour," Grace said in a low voice. "Will you look after Billy for me until this war's over?"

Freddie cleared his throat.

"Goodness," I said. "I'm not sure. We'd have to talk it over."

"I'm so worried about him in London. I know he'd be happy here. He's very well behaved – won't be any trouble."

"Isn't there a government scheme?" I started to say but she closed her eyes.

"I couldn't send him off to people I don't know."

"But you don't know us," Freddie pointed out. "You haven't seen Evie since you were children."

"You're the only family I've got. And Evie was always so kind to me."

It wasn't quite the way I remembered our relationship, but I felt touched.

"Are you sure this is the best place for him, though?" Freddie said. "Farms can be dangerous places and we don't have a lot of spare time. Wouldn't Billy be happier in a family with other children to play with?"

She shook her head. "He doesn't get on well with other children. He's much happier with adults."

"Can't they have him at Swan Hall?"

Grace shuddered. "Never. I'd never let him go there, not after what I went through. In any case, the staff have all gone now and it will probably be requisitioned."

I was a bit shocked to hear her talk like that about the home she'd been given. It seemed so ungrateful. But looking over at Billy sitting on the window seat with the cat while we argued over his future, I thought how awful it must be to part with your child and that must account for her brittleness.

Her eyes glistened with tears, and she looked helplessly at Freddie. He shrugged and said of course Billy must stay.

"What about you, Grace?" I asked. "Don't you want to stay for a few days to help Billy settle? We've plenty of room and you can't drive back tonight. It will be blackout soon."

"Just tonight if it's not too inconvenient. I'd love to stay longer but it's out of the question, unfortunately. I have too much to do in London but I'll come and visit at weekends. You'll be sick of the sight of me before long."

"Oh, I'm sure that's not true."

It did seem like a good way to re-seal the bond between us. If Billy stayed with us Grace would surely keep in touch.

We stayed up talking until late while Billy played with the kittens. I wanted to know everything about him, the routine he was used to, the things he was capable of, and the things he liked doing.

"What time does he go to bed?"

Grace shrugged. "Oh, just when he's tired. I don't believe in silly rules like that. It seems so artificial, expecting a child to fall asleep just because it's a certain time."

"But doesn't that affect his behaviour?"

She looked at me blankly as though she couldn't think why.

"I hope you don't mind me asking but is Billy's father still around?"

She looked away. "No. Not anymore."

"Oh, I'm sorry to hear that."

She nodded. I wanted to ask her more, but didn't feel I knew her well enough yet, despite us being sisters. It was hard to get past that defensive wall she'd built around herself. But I told her I'd thought about her such a lot over the years. "I used to wonder where you were, what you were doing, if you were happy. I wrote hundreds of letters."

She smiled apologetically. "I never saw them. They must have thrown them away."

"I envied you, living in that big house, becoming an aristocrat."

She said, "I envied you, too, for being the one Mother chose to keep."

The hard note that crept into her voice made me uncomfortable.

"How funny," I said. "I saw it the other way round. Mother chose to give you a better start in life. Surely you were the lucky one, living in that grand house – it sounded like a fairy tale."

She let out another harsh laugh. "In case you hadn't noticed, fairy tales can be very dark under the surface. There's no woodsman to save Red Riding Hood in the original story, Sleeping Beauty is raped and the three bears rip Goldilocks to shreds and eat her."

It was so like her. She'd been obsessed with unhappy endings as a child. Made me tell her the tale of Beddgelert over and over again before we went off to sleep. You know the one? About the prince who unwittingly killed his dog, believing it had killed his baby son. He only found out too late that the real killer was a wolf.

I asked her about it. She drew on her cigarette and replied, "If you must know, it was hell. If we're talking about fairy tales, Lorna was the wicked stepmother. She was jealous and cruel, and in the end, she lured me out into the snow to get rid of me."

I looked for a trace of a smile but there wasn't one.

"What do you mean *get rid of you?*"

"The ski trip. It was all a trick. Lorna suggested we go out in the cable car. I was surprised but pleased because she so rarely wanted to spend time with me. Since she found out she was expecting the baby she had lost interest in me altogether. But when we were about to get into the car, I realised I'd left my gloves behind. I ran back to the hotel. And that's where I found the papers for the asylum with my name on them. It all fell into place. They were going to have me put away so they could play happy families with the new baby."

I was shocked. I didn't know whether to believe her.

"I didn't know how long it would be before the others came back so I just picked up my things and left. I found some kind people in the village who helped me get away."

It was such a shock. I couldn't believe her life had been so different from the one I'd always imagined. Grace just shrugged. She told me about the years in between, scraping a living, a series of unhappy relationships. Having a child made it hard to find a husband or a good job but she said, "As long as Billy's safe I can put up with anything."

"He'll be safe with us," I assured her. "We'll look after him."

I went to make up their beds and put out towels for them but when I looked out of the window I got a shock. Grace was out there by the summerhouse talking to Freddie. I saw her put her hand on his arm and then reach up to touch his face and bring it towards her own. It was a few moments before Freddie stepped back with his hand raised, as though keeping her at bay.

"I didn't know what to do," he said to me afterwards as we were getting ready for bed. "I don't think she meant anything by it."

But that sort of thing's hard to misinterpret. Despite everything we agreed we should still take Billy, but I already knew I'd be glad to see the back of Grace.

Jack

Listening to Evie, I was disappointed in Grace. But given everything she'd gone through, perhaps it wasn't so surprising. I wished I could explain to Evie what I'd learned from Sir Hugh but that would mean admitting I'd been to see the baronet. It wouldn't be hard for her to guess where that visit had led. Nice as she was, I didn't know her well enough to trust her.

Chapter Thirty-Four

Evie

Billy clung to Grace as she was leaving but she stood him upright and shook his shoulders. "Be brave. You'll be fine. I'll be back to visit before you know it."

He stayed with us throughout the war. To begin with, you'd hardly have known he was there, he was so quiet. You'd turn round and find him watching you with that puzzled frown. His solemnity reminded me of my little brother Dylan but made me afraid of getting too attached to Billy because we had no idea when Grace would take him back.

When he was getting undressed on that first night I noticed some marks on his trunk and legs. Nasty, dark pink scars. "How did you get these?" He said he couldn't remember. This must be what Grace meant about him not getting on well with other children.

It made me fiercely protective of Billy and anxious about him going to the village school, but the teacher assured me she'd keep an eye on him. The responsibility of caring for this gentle little person frightened me. It wasn't just the school bullies but all manner of accidents he could have, coming from the city and not being used to the farm.

One morning, I woke up and found his bed empty. Afraid he'd run away or had an accident, I searched all over the farm, getting frantic until I eventually found him in the barn with Freddie.

"One of our cows got into a field of clover once,' Freddie was telling him. 'She swelled up like a barrage balloon. Never seen anything like it. If I didn't do something quick, she'd explode."

Billy's eyes were wide. "Did you call the vet?"

"There wasn't time. She was swelling up before my eyes. But I'd been to a talk once by a vet about what to do in that situation. He said to put a knife in just here in the hollow of the flank, like bursting a balloon. You've got to get it right—an inch to the left or right would kill her. I was terrified I'd get it wrong. Only had seconds to decide."

Billy put his small hand on the cow's side where Freddie had indicated. "Did you do it?"

"I did. The smell was awful but all that gas came out."

The child waved his hand in front of his nose and giggled. It was the first time I heard him laugh. Then he looked serious again. "Did she get better?"

"She did. She became our prize milker."

He smiled. "Can I help with the milking?"

"If you like."

He soon got the hang of it and when he saw me, he held up a bucket of foaming milk, his face flushed with triumph. After that he used to go out with Freddie in the van. He took enormous care measuring the milk out for customers and they got to know him.

But it was always there in the back of my mind. One day Grace would take him back.

Jack

"What did Billy tell you about his mother?" I asked Evie. "Where had they been living? Who with?"

She bit her lip. "He said he didn't remember much. I think the truth is, he didn't like talking about home. She never had much time for him. His main memory was watching her get ready to go out at night, doing her hair, trying on different dresses, and putting on her powder and lipstick. He used to try all sorts of tricks to make her stay – claim to feel sick or have a bad stomach. Grab hold of her skirt or wind himself around her legs, but she always shook him off. He spent whole nights on his own waiting for her to come back."

"Where did she go?"

"He didn't know. Sometimes she'd disappear for days on end. Billy had to forage for food in the cupboards and scrump apples from neighbours' gardens."

"Do you think that's true?" It seemed the sort of thing an imaginative child might say for effect but Evie was certain.

"When Grace was at home, she had regular male visitors – he'd wonder why they left money for her when they went. They don't seem to have stayed anywhere for long. They moved in with a succession of Grace's lovers. One of them treated him badly."

"The marks?"

She nodded. "I should have realised they were too serious to have been inflicted by another child."

I sighed. It was getting harder to make excuses for Grace. How could she turn a blind eye to someone harming her child? Unless that's why she sent Billy to live with Evie – to give him a safer and more stable upbringing. Such an unbearable decision for any mother.

"And where is Billy now? Are you still in touch?"

She turned away, pressed a hand over her nose and mouth and let out a choking sob.

"Are you all right? I'm sorry. I didn't mean to upset you."

"Grace didn't deserve him," she whispered. "Didn't deserve to have him back."

"What do you mean?" A chill crept up my spine.

Evie got up and walked over to the window to compose herself. "We hardly heard from her from the moment she left. Letter after letter that said things like:

I'm sorry I can't visit you yet, but I can see from your last letter how happy you are. I don't think it would be wise for you to come back just because there haven't been any bombs yet. We don't know when they might start. I can only be happy if I know you're safe.

Or

I'm sorry I won't be able to pop down after all on Saturday. Something's come up. I hope you're not too disappointed. I'm sure you have plenty of other things to do so you won't miss me.

"I kept inviting her down. Each time she made excuses – the restricted trains or she didn't feel well, or she had some commitment. Or she agreed to come but didn't turn up. There was always a reason but Billy would get excited and I couldn't bear to see the look on his face when he realised she wasn't coming after all."

I offered Evie a handkerchief. She cleared her throat. "But the worst rejection was after the war ended. She wouldn't take him back."

"Why ever not?"

"When she didn't get in touch after the armistice, we thought she might be ill. Or worse. They were still finding unexploded bombs and buildings sometimes collapsed on people because they weren't safe. Freddie and I did everything to track Grace down. The police were no help. They told us they had no record of a Grace Hamden. Only one who'd died in 1931."

She sighed and shook her head. "But eventually I received a letter from America."

Dear Evie,

I must thank you for everything you have done for Billy. He's obviously happy, living with you so I think it best if he stays. He's quite grown up now and capable of looking after himself. I wouldn't even recognise him!

I have some wonderful news – I've got engaged! I've moved out here to be with my fiancé but it wouldn't suit Billy. The last thing he needs is to be uprooted again now he's settled.

I'm sure you'll agree it's all for the best.

Grace

I digested the words Evie had recited. "I can't believe she'd do that," I said at last, although I was starting to see it was just the sort of thing she would do. "And you never saw her again?"

"Oh, we did." Evie's voice hardened. She tried to light a cigarette, but her hands were shaking too much and I had to do it for her. "Eventually. But as I say, by then it was too late."

I felt my blood chill. "Too late?"

She looked at her hands. "Billy died." And she looked straight into my eyes, confirming my own thoughts. "I'm sorry, Jack. I wish you could have met him. You'd have been so proud."

"How? When?" I felt my voice crack.

Because the truth was, I'd been sitting there thinking that even if Giselle was lost to me, I could do something for our son to make amends for the life he'd had. Now that could never happen.

She shuddered. "He hanged himself in his bedroom. We found Grace's letter in his pocket. That final rejection was too much for him."

I sunk my head into my hands. But I tried to cling to the one positive thought. "You say she did come back for him, eventually? Even if it was too late."

Evie shook her hair back and turned her gaze to look out of the window. "Yes. A few months after he died. Turns out the engagement didn't last. Grace wasn't capable of loving anyone. She turned up at the house one evening as if nothing had happened and asked to see Billy."

I handed Evie another handkerchief and she squeezed my hand.

"At first, she didn't believe me when I told her. Then she went to pieces. I reminded her, she hadn't sent us her address when she emigrated, so we had no way of letting her know. Said some awful things. I should have been more sympathetic, but it made me angry, knowing it could have all been avoided if she'd been less selfish."

I felt my eyes fill with tears.

"So that was the last I saw of her. You'll understand why I want nothing more to do with her now. And if you take my advice, neither will you."

Chapter Thirty-Five

1948

When I saw Giselle again it was like finding myself in an old, familiar dream. After Evie broke the spell, I'd stopped looking.

I was down in London to see some clients. It was a bright, sticky day in July and the sun lent an element of cheer to even the grimy, bomb-ravaged streets. Despite the shabbiness and poverty, the banners for the Summer Olympics created an air of hope.

Although there had been much debate in the press about the need for a huge sporting event so soon after the war, it made more sense to me now, I was here in the capital. The sense of pride lifted my spirits.

I'd had a meeting in the morning near the Empire Stadium where workmen were busy laying a cinder athletics track over the old greyhound track. At the Empire Pool nearby the ice rink had been dismantled to turn it back into a swimming pool but blackout paint was still being removed from the glazing.

On the way to my second meeting, in Shaftesbury Avenue, I was about to hail a taxi when I saw Giselle standing at a bus stop. She was wearing a yellow sprigged dress that rippled in the breeze, and shielding her eyes from the sun's glare so she could read the number on an approaching bus.

I was used to my eyes playing tricks on me. I'd seen her everywhere over the years and told myself this was the same trick of the light. But when she turned towards me, pulling her hair away from her face, I found myself gazing at those familiar, honey-coloured eyes. I stood transfixed, waiting for the image to fade and dissolve into the drab surroundings, but it didn't.

She hadn't changed. Didn't look a day older than when I'd last seen her. It was as though those seventeen years hadn't happened. I walked slowly towards her, not wanting to startle her. She did startle though when her eyes met mine.

"Giselle," I said. I couldn't stop my smile from spreading.

She looked back at me with suspicion in her eyes. "Who are you?"

"I'm Jack. Jack Sanders. You must remember,"

She took a step back. "I'm sorry, I don't know you."

For an awful moment, I thought I'd made a mistake. Her voice sounded flat and empty. Closer up, she had more freckles than I remembered. But I couldn't walk away without being sure. I caught up with her again but she dodged me and took off in the other direction.

"Don't go."

She pushed through a line of people queuing for a bus, collided with a woman pushing a pram, weaved through a knot of people gathered outside a theatre, and stepped off the kerb and narrowly avoided an encounter with a cyclist.

"Giselle!"

She glanced over her shoulder and crossed the road, ignoring horn blasts and shouts. On the other side, she turned off down a side street, looking behind her and picking up speed. I followed her past empty shops and blackened buildings with broken windows, trying to keep her in sight despite the mass of bodies that kept getting in between us. Once or twice, I lost her but then glimpsed her again. A bus trundled up and she jumped on the back. I ran, grabbed the rail, and swung aboard behind her. I was aware of people staring, but didn't care. Panicked now, she leapt off again. I jumped, too.

"Don't. Please don't run away."

Her eyes searched mine as I caught her arm. They flickered back and forth, as if she was wondering whether to scream or run. "You're mixing me up with someone else," she said at last. "My name's not Giselle."

"All right, Grace if you prefer. Or whatever you call yourself these days. Come on, you must know who I am. You must remember."

The bus rumbled away and she started walking again. I kept pace, no idea where we were heading. She kept giving me little looks. I started to wonder if she really had forgotten or if I had got this wrong after all.

"You came with me to a wedding only we never got there because of the snow. You told me you were running away from your father. You vanished, and I got arrested. All I needed was for you to tell the police I was with you and had nothing to do with Mr Allerton's murder. You owe me an explanation."

Her face flushed as recognition dawned. "Jack," she said, some of the magic creeping back into her voice. "Of course I remember."

"Can we talk? Look, it was a long time ago and I don't want to interfere in your life. I just want to know what happened. One conversation and I promise I'll never bother you again."

She looked away, weighing things up. I hardly dared speak.

"Please?"

When she turned back, the old smile was like the sun bursting through clouds.

"But I can't stay long. I'm supposed to be at work. I only popped out on an errand for my boss."

As we walked, making stilted conversation about the heat and the state of the streets, I had to keep reminding myself that this was Grace, not Giselle. Everything I'd been told by the baronet and Evie played through my head. She wasn't the person I once thought her to be, and I mustn't let her persuade me she was. But I wanted answers.

The flaking gold lettering above the coffee shop sparkled in the late afternoon sun. I pushed open the door into an elegant, dark-panelled interior smelling of coffee, cigarettes, and wood polish. After the hot streets it felt deliciously cool. A waitress in black and white uniform greeted us and showed us to a table next to a faux marble pillar.

Giselle seemed ill at ease. She sat very properly, taking in her surroundings and flicking her gaze over me.

"How did you find me?" she asked.

"I wasn't expecting to. Not today. I gave up looking years ago. But I couldn't miss you. You look just the same."

If anything, she looked lovelier. I almost resented her fresh, unmarked face, the softness of her skin. It was stupid but I couldn't help feeling a bit insulted that she'd come through everything unscathed. Catching sight of myself in the mirror behind her, I was shocked by how old and haggard I looked, with shadows under my eyes and lines at the side of my mouth.

She shook her head and laughed. "I can't believe this is happening."

"Neither can I."

"So many people I knew were killed in the war."

I smiled. "I suppose I was lucky."

She studied my face for a long time and then reached up to touch the scar under my eye. "How did you get this?"

"Shrapnel."

"And this?"

I tensed as she ran her finger lightly down the mark left by the baronet's stick but mumbled something about hand-to-hand fighting.

"The bastards. What else did they do to you?"

"It doesn't matter. I don't want to think about that now. Let's talk about you. I can't believe I found you after all this time. I thought for an awful moment back there you really didn't remember me."

"Of course I remembered. I just couldn't believe it was happening. I'd given you up for dead like everyone else I knew."

She told me she'd made herself forget because that had been the easiest way to deal with things. With everything I knew about her, it made sense. She'd adopted this way of coping throughout her life, forgetting about Evie when living at Swan Hall, forgetting about Billy when he was living away from her.

"I had to make a new life for myself," she said.

I told her I understood, although I didn't completely.

"What do you call yourself these days? I'm not sure I can get used to calling you anything other than Giselle."

She smiled. "So, call me Giselle."

"All right. Do you live in London?"

She nodded. "I stayed here all through the war, working as an ambulance driver. It was grim at times, but I felt I was doing something worthwhile. Now I work in an office which is much less interesting."

The waitress came and I ordered tea for us both. Giselle still looked nervous, and I was afraid she was having second thoughts. I looked at her left hand.

"You're married?"

"This?" She touched the ring and smiled. "I bought it off a market stall. It helps ward off unwanted attention. She looked down. "But there is someone. You?"

"Yes."

"Children?"

"A daughter."

She smiled. "I see. Congratulations."

I didn't tell her that Janet and I rarely spoke to each other these days. There was so little left to say. Janet had moved back to her mother's house with Tilly soon after my visit to the baronet. I missed them both but could hardly complain. We'd just about managed to stay on civil terms. There was a lightness about her recently that made me suspect she was seeing someone else.

We sat in silence for a moment. "You won't believe how hard I tried to find you," I said.

I recounted everything from the day she'd disappeared from the train carriage to my visits to the hypnotist and the psychic evenings, engaging the private detective and my arrest for Mr Allerton's murder. But I couldn't bring myself to tell her about the hallucinations during the war and didn't have the courage to tell her about my encounter with the baronet or what I'd learned from Evie.

"So, tell me, what happened that day on the train?" I said at last. "Where did you go?"

She took a deep breath, lit a cigarette, and waited for the band to start on their next song, frowning as she tried to get her memories in order. As they launched into *Isn't This a Lovely Day?* she said, "You remember what I told you about my father?"

"Of course."

"When you were out of the carriage talking to the guard, I saw a man on the platform walking along the train looking into all the windows. I recognised him at once. He worked for my father, chasing up people who owed money. I knew he'd seen me. There wasn't time to let you know what was happening.

"He got on the train. I jumped off but he followed. I pushed my way through the people on the platform, but he was getting closer. The other train pulled in. I had no idea where it was going but I climbed on."

She closed her eyes, remembering.

"I sat there willing the train to leave. The door opened and he stood there, looking straight at me. Luckily, a couple of elderly women noticed and came to my aid. They told the guard he was making a nuisance of himself, and he was thrown off. They were very kind and insisted on taking me back with them to their house for the night. In the morning, I told them I was going to the police. But really, I went back to the guesthouse to ask for your address."

The waitress appeared bearing a tray and started to unload the silver teapot and tiered platter. Giselle's eyes lit up at the array of cakes.

"I really shouldn't," she said, but I insisted so she helped herself to a fruit tart. Watching her, I was fighting back feelings of confusion. I ought to hate her. I should at least be angry. But all the resentment I'd built up over the years, all those questions I'd stored up suddenly seemed unimportant. I remembered the baronet's words about her sensing a weakness in people and exploiting it, but it wasn't as if she'd found me and persuaded me to buy her tea. It was the other way round. I was in control of this situation.

"No one came to the front door," she said. "The house was so quiet. As if we'd never been there. I walked around to the back. The kitchen door was hanging open. I pushed it. That's when I saw the blood.

"It was such a shock. I'm sorry, Jack, but I thought you must have done it. His trousers were undone and there were pictures scattered everywhere. Pictures of you. I remembered how angry you were when you suspected he was spying on us. I thought you must have walked in on him and poured acid into his eyes as punishment for being a Peeping Tom."

"You thought I could do that to someone?"

She looked into my eyes. "Not anymore, but I was confused. Scared."

My stomach knotted. As the man I was then, it was unthinkable. I'd never have harmed the landlord. But I was no longer that person. How would she react if she knew I'd since killed the baronet?

"I felt it in a way it was my fault. If I hadn't left like that you wouldn't have gone back and taken out your anger on him. It was only much later when I read that Norland had done it. And by then it was too late to find you. I'd discovered I was pregnant. I couldn't turn up on your doorstep in that state. You'd have thought I was trying to trap you into marrying me."

"I wouldn't," I said. "I already know about the child. And I know what happened to him. I'm sorry."

She looked startled, then crushed. "I'll never forgive myself for what happened to Billy," she whispered.

I took her hand. "You weren't to know. I just wish you could have trusted me."

Because if she had, none of it would have happened. I wouldn't have to spend my life looking over my shoulder, wondering when the police would catch up with me. Our child could have grown up in a proper family and would still have a future ahead of him.

"I thought you'd be happier without me," she said. "And I had Billy to remind me of you."

I could have pointed out that she hadn't kept Billy either but just managed to stop myself because nothing could be done about it now. Although I had to bite back my frustration and anger that she'd chosen to emigrate with another man instead of being reunited with our son, I had to accept she believed she was doing the best thing for him by leaving him in Evie's care. How was she to know he'd kill himself as a result?

"But I don't understand why you went back to see your father," I said. "You said he'd kill you if he found you."

My heart sped. I had to hear it from her.

"I had to. I wanted to show him I'd survived. He couldn't get rid of me that easily. I wasn't going to spend my life in fear of him. I promised him I wouldn't tell anyone I saw him hit Lorna and throw her body down the ravine. He'd found out she was seeing someone else, and the baby wasn't his. I promised I wouldn't tell how he turned and saw me and came after me and that I was terrified, pleading for my life. And I wouldn't tell anyone how he'd mistreated Alice as well as me.

"All I wanted was for him to look after Alice now. I'd heard terrible things from Burris about him sending people after her when she left Swan Hall. I don't know what they did but they made sure she'd never speak about what she'd seen. I wanted him to promise he'd pay for her to be looked after. At least it would go some way to putting things right."

I nodded. Perhaps one day I'd be able to explain to Giselle that I'd taken over the payments for Alice's care, albeit in a much lesser establishment, telling myself it was a kind of atonement for killing the baronet. I wished I'd been able to afford to cover Iris's schooling as well.

"But he wouldn't listen. He said I'd have to agree to be certified and have my baby aborted or he'd put the blame for my mother's death on me and see me hanged."

I thought he couldn't stoop any lower than he already had. "But he's dead, Giselle. He can't harm you now. You don't need to worry anymore."

She nodded. "I read about it in the paper. A robbery, they say."

A frisson of angst ran through me as she caught my eye. It

felt like an invitation to open up and admit it was me who killed the baronet, but I couldn't be sure I trusted her enough. I'd become so used to hiding the truth. But I hadn't forgotten what the baronet told me about Giselle being in love with him. Repugnant as I found this story, I wasn't certain he was lying. And if her relationship with her stepfather was more complicated than she'd told me, Giselle would hate me for what I'd done.

We left the café and found a telephone box so Giselle could call her boss and say she was ill. We walked to a park where we sat on a bench for a long time by the bandstand, watching squirrels running up trees and people buying ice creams and lazing in the sun, talking until it grew dusk.

"All those moments where things could have turned out differently," I said. "So much time wasted."

She smiled. "Maybe it's for the best. Who knows how it would have worked out for us? At least we both have a perfect memory."

It was extraordinary how comfortable it felt to be with her even after so much time had passed and with everything that had happened.

"You're different from how I expected," she said at one point.

"What do you mean 'expected'?"

Her cheeks flushed. "I mean you're not exactly as I remembered. But we're bound to have changed, aren't we? My memory of you was always so special. I was afraid if I ever met you again, I'd be disappointed."

"And are you?"

She smiled. "No. Not at all."

She'd changed too. Who hadn't during the war? She was gentler, quieter. Life had made her less idealistic. But every now and then I caught glimpses of the old Giselle, which made me feel nostalgic for the people we'd once been.

Eventually I looked at my watch and saw I'd missed the last train. "I'll have to find a hotel for the night." And then I surprised myself by saying, "Come with me?"

She laughed. "I can't."

"You can."

She hesitated, biting her lip. "I'm not sure it's a good idea."

"It is. It's the best one I've had in years."

She started to raise other objections, but I kissed her to shut her up.

"Just tonight then," she said at last.

We found a room on the top floor of a blackened Victorian guesthouse with dingy wallpaper and a curtain hanging off its rail. The room was stuffy with the window closed but when we opened it the roar of traffic and petrol smells invaded. But the surroundings weren't important and making love to Giselle after so long was incredible – gloriously familiar in some ways, new and different in others.

"You won't believe me," I said afterwards, "but every woman I've kissed was you. It was easy to convince myself when I was drunk, but when I woke up and looked at the person beside me, I always felt cheated."

I trained the lamp on her face, studying it. She screwed up her features and pushed me away.

"You didn't used to mind," I said.

"I was younger then."

"But you look even better now. You have cheekbones."

"You're saying I was fat-faced?"

"Not at all."

She hit me with a pillow, and I hit her back.

When I woke up the next morning, I reached for her, but the bed was empty. I sat up, furious with myself for not noticing. It saddened me that she hadn't stayed long enough to say goodbye, but I felt a sense of completion. I'd found her. I knew why she'd left and the guilt I'd carried with me for so many years had lifted. I'd never understand everything about her, but I wouldn't torture myself anymore, wondering what happened to her. It was also a relief to hear her version of events and realise she wasn't the callous person I'd been led to believe.

Hearing the front door below me shut, I looked out of the window. I saw her look back up at our hotel before hurrying across the road. I pulled on my clothes and rushed downstairs. She turned round as she heard my footsteps in the road but this time didn't run away.

"Is that it?" I asked. "Don't we get to say goodbye?"

"Last night was goodbye," she said gently. "I don't think we should see each other again. As you said, we both have different lives now."

"My marriage is over," I told her.

She looked anxious. "Don't change your life for me, Jack. You'll only regret it."

"I won't. I know I won't."

"Go back to your wife," she urged. "You can still make things right. And remember this for what it was. A perfect moment. It can't be anything else."

"Please, we can't leave it like this," I said, aware I was breaking all the rules I'd set myself. "Let me know how I can contact you."

Eventually she sighed and wrote down an address. "But don't contact me yet. Wait a few weeks and think about whether this is what you really want. Don't throw away what you have unless you're certain."

I kissed her for the last time and watched her walk down the road, swinging her bag, before turning back to catch my tube. On the train home I checked several times that the piece of paper with her number on it was still there.

We met for a day and then a weekend. I confessed about the misunderstanding over the bridesmaid's ring, which Janet now wore but she only laughed.

"She's welcome to it. It only had bad associations for me."

Over the next few months, we began to see each other regularly in guesthouses, hotels, car parks whenever I could get away. We spent a weekend by the sea, chasing each other along the beach, skipping stones and strolling along the pier. We fell back into our old habits, conjecturing about people and questioning each other.

"Do you believe in luck?"

"What's your favourite quotation?"

"If you could change one thing in your life, what would it be?"

"You must know the answer to that," I said. "I wouldn't have left you alone on the train for those few minutes. My whole life would have been different."

Occasionally we'd stay at a friend's house. It felt like we were playing at being a normal couple, cooking and eating together, falling asleep and waking up next to each other, going to the pictures and walking hand in hand.

But the more you anticipate something, the less likely it is to be exactly as you picture it. There were moments when she surprised me with things she said or did that made me feel as if I was with a stranger. The closer we got to being able to spend our lives together, the more I found myself questioning things that would have been better left alone. Small things that once observed, wouldn't go away, like the way she threw back her head when she laughed or nibbled her lip when thinking, tiny discrepancies between the person in my memory and the person I was with.

At first, she was intrigued when I pointed these things out but it started to annoy her. "You have to accept me for who I am now, not who I was once," she said in frustration.

It was hard sometimes to avoid an accusatory note creeping into our questions.

"Why didn't you believe me about my father?"

"Why couldn't you have given me a choice about Billy?"

"Why did you give up so easily?"

"Did you ever think we had a future together?"

But at other times I'd catch a glimpse of how she had been, and it seemed only a matter of time before this new Giselle merged into the old one.

Of course, I was worried about the life she'd dropped for me. And it was always at the back of my mind that she might disappear again. It wouldn't surprise me to wake up one day and find her gone. When she was with me, was someone else looking for her as desperately as I once had?

I had moments of panic when I thought our happiness hung by a thread and could be whisked away at any moment. If she discovered I'd killed her stepfather, what would she do?

As I was watching her get dressed one afternoon something shifted in my memory.

"The scar," I said. "It's gone."

"What scar?"

"It was just here. You said it was from a riding accident."

She frowned. Then her face cleared. "Oh that. Yes, I had it a while. I didn't realise it had gone."

As I picked her coat up for her at the cinema one evening

her ration book dropped out of a pocket. I picked it up and opened it without thinking.

"Who's Isabella Matthews?" I asked.

She snatched it off me. "How should I know?"

"How did you get this?"

"Well, I can hardly have one that says Grace Hamden, can I? The only thing you'll find with her name on is her death certificate. If you must know I took it from a patient I'd gone to help in the ambulance. By the time we got there, the ration book was no use to them. Don't look at me like that."

"But this is a serious crime. You could go to prison."

She rolled her eyes. "It has nothing to do with you. Why do you always have to be so suspicious?"

The funny thing is that until that point I hadn't been suspicious, just curious. But now as I looked into her eyes, I had that sudden, awful feeling again that I didn't know her at all.

She turned away. I caught her, held her face in my hands, studying it. I started to get alarmed. "Who are you? Who are you really?"

"I'm who you want me to be."

"Don't give me that. Tell me the truth. Have you been lying to me all along? Were you ever Grace Hamden? Did your father really kill your mother or did you make that up along with everything else?"

She struggled to get out of my grip, scratching my face in the process. "You chose me, remember?" she shouted, her eyes full of anger and hurt. "It was you who invited me to the wedding. You who wouldn't leave because of the snow. And you who followed me to London and begged me to come back. You were always free to get on with your life. But this is what you chose."

We stood staring at each other, trying to make sense of things. "You're right," I said in a desperate bid to stop things slipping away. "I'm sorry."

"You asked why I left you. The answer is because it was the right thing to do. The only right thing I've ever done. I didn't want to spoil your life the way I'd spoiled everyone else's."

"Well, you did anyway!"

A slow, painful silence hung between us.

"Don't you understand anything, Jack? I'm not a good person. My life is complicated. It's not like other people's. I don't deserve you. I'm not who you think I am."

I drew her towards me. Something wasn't right. I didn't understand it but now I'd finally found her, I wasn't going to lose her again. "I don't care what you've done. I just want to be with you."

Chapter Thirty-Six

The divorce was Janet's idea. She said she didn't see the point in us staying married any longer, and besides, she'd met someone who was more understanding at her amateur dramatics group. When I asked Giselle to marry me we came up against a problem – her identity.

She had no papers to prove who she was, only the ones that belonged to the deceased Isabella Matthews. I offered to help her prove her identity as Grace Hamden, but she shuddered at the suggestion.

"Grace Hamden has a death certificate. Why resurrect her now? Giselle Sanders is who I want to be. Can't you arrange some paperwork to prove that?"

I was worried about the consequences of her marrying under a false name but the last thing I wanted was to re-establish a link in people's minds between me and the dead baronet so decided it was better to keep quiet.

We spent our honeymoon on the Amalfi coast, fulfilling the promise I'd made to myself during the war to come back to the area in peacetime. We hired a car and took the twisting coastal road from Sorrento with dizzying views of towering cliffs spilling with olives and lemons, tumbling villages of pastel houses and glittering sea. We stopped wherever we fancied and found rooms with cool, brightly tiled floors and bougainvillea-draped balconies.

During the day we explored quiet, sunlit fishing villages, visited markets, rented a boat, and chugged around the rocks to hidden coves, and swam in the emerald waters of a grotto. In the evenings we strolled the ancient paths in citrus-scented air, discovering restaurants and eating mozzarella baked between lemon leaves and *spaghetti alle vongole.*

For our last few nights, we rented a tiny, whitewashed house cut into the rocks on different levels with a series of terraces shaded by pergolas and arbours leading down to the sea. Lying in bed you could hear the waves crashing below and the pine branches rustling and if you left the shutters open you could see the bay lit up by a string of lights.

On the final evening, we followed the rocky footpath above the house for miles, marvelling at the plunging views down to bays and gullies, watching the sea turn from azure to liquid gold to mauve as the sun set and the first stars pierced the sky. We stopped and sat on a rocky ledge that seemed to hang in mid-air, watching the waves thunder onto the rocks.

"I want to tell you something," I said.

It seemed the right time. I was sure enough of her now we were married, to be able to admit to what I'd done. So, I told her the whole story, how I'd gone to Swan Hall and rowed with her adoptive father and, in a blind rage, killed him.

"Those things he said about you. What he did to you. The way he thought you dispensable... I didn't mean to do it. But I told you when I first knew you, I'd always been afraid of this flaw inside me, that one day I'd make a huge mistake."

I realised as I said it that what I was really hoping for was some reassurance, if not forgiveness but she drew away from me, folding her arms around herself. Her face was pale in the moonlight. She didn't speak for a long time.

"Say something."

"You should have told me," she said.

"I know. I was afraid of losing you."

I should never have said anything. I wished so badly we could go back a few moments to before. "Would you still have married me if I had?"

"I don't know," she said at last. "You're not who I thought you were."

We stood in silence while she battled with her emotions. There was no getting away from it – I'd killed someone and kept it a secret and married Giselle pretending to be one sort of person when I was another.

"You shouldn't have done it, Jack," she said at last. "But I understand you didn't go there with that intention. You're a good person. You're still good."

I drew her towards me and kissed her. It felt like an enormous weight had been lifted. We pushed further out to sea, not saying much, still letting the enormity sink in. She knew the truth and she still wanted to be with me. She'd forgiven me. Now all I needed was to find a way to forgive myself.

After a while she said, "While we're telling each other things, there's something you should know about me."

But I already knew what had happened in the Alps. Much as I hated her father, I'd come to believe his version of events, that Giselle – or Grace – had killed Lorna. It made sense. She would have been horrified, finding those papers for the asylum. She would have challenged her stepmother Hadn't meant to push her, but it had happened.

"You don't have to tell me."

"No. I do."

But I wished afterwards she'd told me she killed Lorna. It would have been easier to hear than what she did say.

"The thing is, you see, I'm not Giselle."

I smiled. "I know that."

"No. I mean I'm not Grace either."

I felt the smile die on my face. I must have looked like an idiot. "I don't understand."

Up until that moment I think I'd managed to persuade myself that I was wrong about the missing scar, wrong about the unmarked face, wrong about those little facial expressions and turns of phrase, wrong about the ration book. Of course, I should have put them all together. I'd already guessed she was incapable of telling the truth. I just wouldn't admit it to myself.

For a while she didn't speak. Then she said, "Yes you do. You do understand."

"Then who are you? Her twin sister?" I still hoped she was joking.

She screwed up her face. "You know, Jack. You've known for a long time. I'm Isabella Matthews."

"No, you're not."

"I'm Bella. Grace's baby sister. The one she tried to drown? It wasn't safe for me to stay there anymore after she put me in the river. If they hadn't sent me away, she'd have done it again and succeeded. When Dylan, the next baby, was born, my mother must have worried about what Grace might do to him, so when Lorna and Hugh offered to adopt a child, she sent Grace."

It was starting to make sense. "You're not the girl I met on the boat-train. Not the girl who came with me to the farmhouse."

"No."

"But how did you...?"

She stared out to sea, folding her arms around herself. The

lights had come on in the little villages like a glittering necklace strung along the bays. "I grew up in Chippenham. Had no idea I was adopted.

"I saw a picture of Grace in a magazine once. One of the society titles. It was a piece about a debutantes' ball with a close-up of Grace in a beautiful dress. The hairdresser spotted it first. She held the page up next to my face and everyone in the shop was struck by the likeness. They were all pulling my leg, saying we must be related. My mother laughed it away and said she couldn't see the similarity but we left in a hurry. Afterwards she said the hairdresser was being ridiculous, but I wished I'd kept the picture.

"Over the years I started to wonder about things – like why I was so much younger than my siblings, why I was blonde when they were all dark. Eventually she told me the truth, said I had a right to know. It was a shock, but it made sense.

"Years later when I was at secretarial college in London, I met Grace. It was just by chance. Someone mistook me for her and told me she worked in a theatre. I went there out of curiosity and saw her face on a poster. She belonged to a dancing troupe.

"Eventually someone arranged for us to meet. I knew nothing about her background – the big house, the privileges – but we hit it off straight away. I didn't tell Grace I knew about how she'd tried to drown me. I didn't think it was fair to blame her for that – she'd been so young. All she remembered was waking up in a car with some strangers. The things she told me about that place – I felt so sorry for her.

"She introduced me to people, showed me London and we ended up sharing a room. I used to babysit Billy in the evenings. He was a lovely little boy. She told me all about herself. Told me about you, too. The way she talked made me envious. I realised she didn't know how to love someone properly, but you were the closest she came."

My own voice sounded distant in my ears. "Where is she now?"

Bella exhaled, reached out to touch my arm but I drew back.

"We fell out. Grace never paid her share of the rent, and I didn't like the people she brought home. The theatre closed when war broke out. I found her living on a diet of drink and drugs and working as a prostitute to fund her habits. Billy wasn't getting the love he deserved. I told her I'd report her to the authorities if she didn't sort herself out. The next thing I knew she'd disappeared, taking Billy with her.

"I heard nothing from her until after the war when she turned up at my digs without Billy saying she had nowhere to go. I hardly recognised her, she was so thin and drawn.

"I was reluctant after what had happened, but she swore she'd changed. She was determined to get back on her feet, get Billy back and look after him properly this time. All she needed was someone to help her, give her somewhere to stay, show her some kindness. I remember the day she went down to see him, and I remember when she came back."

Bella bit her lip in that way Giselle never had.

"She said she was going out for a drive. Somehow, I knew I wouldn't see her again."

I had a sense of everything closing in. "What did she do?"

Bella shivered. "She drove onto a railway crossing. The police said it was probably an accident, but I never believed that. The train driver said he waved and shouted to her and braked as hard as he could, but she sat there looking straight at him."

A sharp wind cut across the cliff. The place suddenly felt cold, hard, and alien. I couldn't believe what I was hearing. I tried not to think about Grace being so alone and so distraught.

All I could think of to say was, "You've been lying to me all this time."

She shook her head. "I didn't lie. Just let you believe what you wanted to believe. I told you at the start I didn't know you. Told you I wasn't Giselle. But you insisted. In the end I decided to go along with it."

She was like a different person. She was a different person. "Why?"

She sighed. "Because I thought you looked..."

"What? A mug?"

"No. I thought you looked kind. And handsome. And when I worked out who you were I thought why not?"

"So, you decided to make a fool out of me?"

A tear made its way down my cheek. I brushed it away.

"It wasn't like that; I promise I never meant to hurt you. It just seemed a bit of fun."

I struggled to digest this. "But later. Later you could have told me. All these months. You let me marry you believing you were someone else. You realise that's a crime?"

"Is it? I didn't kill anyone. You're the one who did that. So be glad you married me because I'm the only one who knows what you did, and they can't make me testify against you. That's right, isn't it?"

I nodded weakly. She tried to touch me again, but I pulled away. I couldn't believe she was using the baronet's death to blackmail me into staying married to her.

"I never meant it to go on past that first day," she said more gently. "You said you only wanted to speak to me once. I told you we shouldn't meet again. You insisted. And then over the months I fell in love with you. I gave someone up for you, you know. But by the time you proposed I couldn't tell you the truth. It had gone too far. I couldn't bear to lose you. Because I love you, Jack. Don't you see, it's more than she ever did?"

"Don't. For God's sake, don't."

"But it's true, isn't it? She didn't love you. She didn't love anyone – didn't know how after the way she'd been brought up. Who do you think killed Mr Allerton at the farmhouse?"

My heart went cold. "Norland was tried and found guilty for that."

"But it was Grace who put the idea in his head that Mr Allerton had a new lover – you. She showed him the photographs she'd found. Really, she wanted to stop Allerton going to the police about Lorna's death. Norland went berserk. He beat Allerton up. Perhaps he'd have died anyway but he was still alive when Grace got to him and smashed his head with a shovel."

"You're saying Allerton was planning to tell the police about Grace killing her mother," I said, trying to keep up. "But how would he know how Lorna died?"

"From Burris who used to work for the Hamdens. She didn't even remember him when she saw him at the farm, he meant so little to her. But he stayed in touch with Alice, and she told him what she saw – Grace pushing Lorna down the ravine. Burris recognised Grace when you went to the farmhouse and told the landlord who she was.

"It was Grace who poured the acid used for developing the photographs onto Mr Allerton's face as he lay injured on the floor. She told me she did it as punishment for spying on her but I think she enjoyed it. She cut herself out of the photographs so the police wouldn't associate her with the crime."

All I could think of to say was: "Why didn't you tell me any of this before?"

"Because I didn't want to lose you. And I couldn't bring myself to confess to that crime, to being that person. Because I could never have done it – that's the difference between her and me. Why do you think Alice is the way she is? Because Grace attacked her, not her father. He at least had the heart to pay for Alice's care after the breakdown and for Iris's school fees."

She paused for a moment, biting her lip and letting me digest it all. "Don't you see, there is no Giselle? There never was. The person you met was Grace. I'm more Giselle than she ever was."

I looked at her and away at the dark sea churning below us. All I could think was I wanted to kill her. One shove was all it would take. A tragic accident, another foreigner unfamiliar with the terrain who couldn't read the danger signs. Nobody knew who she was. No one would connect her with me.

Instead, I slammed my fist down onto the rock and stumbled on down the path. She caught up with me, but I threw her off.

"Where are you going?"

I didn't answer. I had to get away from her. I ran on and on down steps cut out of the rock, past deserted shells of houses until I eventually reached a small bay. I jumped down onto the sand and stood at the water's edge watching the waves, the spray hiding my tears.

Much later I found her in the same spot where she'd shattered all my illusions. She was shivering in the darkness and her eyes were red, but she looked at me with a mixture of fear and defiance. As though she'd read my mind earlier, she shrank back against the rock.

"All right," I said. "You started this. You have to see you can never go back now. If you want to stay with me, you stay Giselle. For ever. There is no Isabella Matthews. Never has been. You will never mention her name or anything to do with your past. This is who you are now."

Chapter Thirty-Seven

1950

"So," I said when I finally reached the end of my story, "is it what you expected?"

The young man had listened without interruption and without taking notes. I'd almost forgotten he was there. It struck me as ironic that here in these legal offices I was going against everything I'd advise my clients – talking without legal representation, giving away information before it was asked for. Admitting my guilt. But what did any of it matter now anyway?

"How did you find me?" I asked.

"Through Evie."

"Ah." So, Evie had worked it out after all. Oddly enough, I felt glad it hadn't been Gilbert who'd reported me. I wanted to believe some people could still be relied upon. Sitting there in my office and realising it was the last time I'd sit in that chair surrounded by those walls looking onto that park, I felt a terrible sadness that I hadn't achieved more in my life. Summing it up for this young detective made it all sound pointless.

I looked again at the photograph he'd placed in front of me when he'd come into the room without knocking. It was one I hadn't seen before, of Grace – or Giselle as I'd known her – sitting on a train looking exactly as she'd done the day she disappeared. Perhaps it had been taken the day she went to London with Lorna and Alice and watched the ballet that gave her the idea for her new name.

The truth, it turned out, was that I'd killed in vain – for a woman who hadn't cared about me and who had been dead by the time I killed the baronet to avenge her. Sir Hugh had been despicable and perhaps I had done the world a favour by killing him, but I couldn't honestly say I'd done it for any noble reason.

The young man studied me with his intense, dark gaze. What must he think of me? I'd made a mess of my marriage to Janet and murdered a war hero in his own home. I'd continued in a marriage to Bella in order to keep my crime secret and subsumed her identity, calling her by the name of a girl I'd barely known. That wasn't reasonable behaviour. Not the actions of a sane person.

What made it worse was that this was a terrible moment to have to abandon Bella. Despite being tricked into marrying her and despite calling her Giselle, I'd found throughout that first year that I loved her for who she was and had stopped wanting her to be anyone else. And somehow, despite knowing I'd killed a man and although I placed such an unreasonable condition on our marriage, she loved me back.

We'd only recently found out she was expecting our child. I was determined to be a good father to make up for taking the life of a bad one but now I'd have no part in this child's life.

Studying the photograph of Grace, knowing my wife as I did now, I could see the differences between the two women were much more marked than I'd once thought. Nonetheless, something stirred in me when I looked at the picture of Grace. Nostalgia for the young man I'd been when I met her and the innocence I'd lost as a result of that meeting.

He knitted his brows together and smiled that apologetic smile. "I don't think you quite understand."

"Then why…?"

"I believe," he said with some difficulty – and then said the last thing I would have expected to hear, "you're my father."

Everything in the room was the same as it had been a moment before and yet nothing felt familiar. Studying his face it started to make sense.

"Billy?"

He nodded with an uncertain half smile.

"But Evie told me…"

"I was dead – yes, I know. Grace's letter upset me. It's not a nice feeling knowing your mother doesn't want you anymore although I think I'd worked that out a long time before. Evie lied to Grace to protect me, to stop me from going back to her. She knew how I'd end up if I did.

"Then she had to lie to you to stop Grace finding out I was still alive. She doesn't know Grace killed herself as a result of what she told her, and I don't want her to know. Evie might not be my real mother, but I love her as though she was. I'm sure she didn't realise the effect her words would have on her sister. She only told me the truth a few months back after she met you. I've been looking for you ever since."

So, Grace had killed herself believing Billy had killed himself and that she was to blame. What a bloody mess. And yet Billy knew everything now. If he still wanted to know me after everything I'd told him, I'd do whatever I could to make up for the past.

I was ready for him to get up and walk out of my office, and head for the nearest police station. But he broke into a smile that reminded me of Giselle. I put out my hand for him to shake but he brushed it aside and pulled me into a hug.

We'd work something out. If one good thing had come out of meeting Giselle it was this.

THE END

Also by Katharine Johnson

The Silence

The Secret

The Suspects

Acknowledgements

It's always a thrill to see your book take shape. I'm so grateful to everyone at Bloodhound Books for bringing this new version of my first book to publication. Thank you for all you do!

Huge thanks also to Eleanor, Rosie, Jenny and Tessa who read an early draft and gave great advice.

To my amazing author friends and critique partners, Helen Matthews, Jane Risdon and Alex Limia - thanks for all the support, laughs and cake!

And finally but especially to you, the reader - I hope you enjoy this book.

A note from the publisher

Thank you for reading this book. If you enjoyed it please do consider leaving a review on Amazon to help others find it too.

We hate typos. All of our books have been rigorously edited and proofread, but sometimes mistakes do slip through. If you have spotted a typo, please do let us know and we can get it amended within hours.

info@bloodhoundbooks.com

www.ingramcontent.com/pod-product-compliance
Ingram Content Group UK Ltd.
Pitfield, Milton Keynes, MK11 3LW, UK
UKHW040824300925
8140UKWH00026B/161

9 781917 705387